HALF-

TOLD

TRUTHS

HALF-TOLD TRUTHS

AMY O. LEWIS

ARROW ROAD
PRESS

Published by Arrow Road Press, Denver, CO
www.amyolewis.com

Edited and designed by Girl Friday Productions
www.girlfridayproductions.com

Cover design: Emily Weigel
Project management: Katherine Richards
Editorial: Tiffany Taing
Image credits: cover © Unsplash/Charlie Gallant, Shutterstock/komkrit Preechachanwate

ISBN (paperback): 978-1-7372977-2-7
ISBN (ebook): 978-1-7372977-3-4
LCCN: 2022902065

for the skeleton crew—
Alexis, Peggy, Larry, and Jan

PROLOGUE

How silly it had been to worry.

She could admit it now, no longer afraid. Her daughter didn't hate her. Her little girl didn't hate this cabin, built in the shadow of the San Juan Mountains. Her ex-husband had fought this visit to the point where she hadn't been sure he would put their child on the plane that morning. But Jesse was here now, and nothing else mattered.

Late in the afternoon, the girl's chatter mixed with the sunshine spilling in through the cabin's screen door. "Mom, tell me again. How big is the swimming pool at Glenwood Springs? Is it the biggest swimming pool in Colorado?"

"I think so, honey. We'll ask a lifeguard when we're there tomorrow."

The aroma of grilled toast and melted cheese lingered in the air. Only cut-off bread crusts and a few asparagus spears remained on the child's plate. The woman hadn't touched her dinner of vegetables and rice. Her stomach knots had untied since she had picked up her daughter at Durango's airport earlier that day, but not enough for her to feel ready to eat. All she wanted was to gaze in wonder at this beautiful child. Six months was too much of Jesse's life to have slipped by without seeing her. Eight years old now, her little-girl face still showed through leaner, more mature features. The woman ached for the days she had missed, days that had, nearly seamlessly, left their mark on this child. She wanted to spin the wheel of time back and undo choices she had made years earlier. Though what could she have done differently? When their marriage ended, her ex had wielded his father's money and power to yank Jesse away to what he laughably called a "richer, more stable" life in LA.

"Mom, where did you and Dad live when I was little?"

"Paonia. Paonia, Colorado."

"Right. Maybe we could go back there, and Dad could come too."

"Sweetie, your dad's married to Chloe now."

"I know. But Chloe says she's going to be very busy when the baby comes. I think she's going to be too busy for me *and* Dad."

The little girl, with straight blond hair and her mother's unmistakable gray eyes, prattled on, leaping across subjects. She talked about her best friend, Wanda, and the five puppies born to a neighbor's dog. One puppy never stayed on the blanket and was always getting lost. Jesse said she could find it every time. The woman drifted into a dream of Jesse growing up in Colorado, an adventuresome dog at her side. The bucolic image splintered with the piercing ring of the phone.

A chill ran down her spine. She didn't move.

A second jingle followed.

"Aren't you going to get that?" Jesse said.

By the third ring, the woman was on her feet. She collected plates and scraped food scraps into the garbage pail.

"It could be Dad," Jesse said.

"We'll call him later. I don't want to talk to anyone right now."

She turned on the tap and frantically scrubbed plates. She told herself the caller could be anyone, a wrong number, even. But she didn't believe it. By the time she set the pair of dishes in the plastic drain to dry, the ringing had stopped.

"Sometimes Chloe doesn't answer her phone. But she turns it off. It never makes a racket," Jesse said.

The woman wanted to put her head down. She wanted to weep and scream at the same time. She loved this place, but right now, she wanted to be anywhere but here, a thousand miles in any direction with only her daughter at her side. "What do you say we go for a walk?" she said, mustering a cheery voice.

"No," the girl said, suddenly turning stubborn.

"I've told you about the doe and fawn I sometimes see, haven't I?"

"I said I don't want to!" Jesse said with a shout.

The air crackled with heat after the child's words faded away.

"I want to watch TV. How can you possibly not have a TV?" Jesse said.

The woman counted to five while she drew a calming breath. The cabin housed a small library of middle-grade books and several board games. There was ice cream in the freezer for hot fudge sundaes later. She saw her yoga mat rolled up in the corner and the sketch pad she had nearly filled, and understood that, while she had chosen to make this her home, there was no reason on earth why she ought to expect Jesse to make the same choice. She hadn't yet found the words to woo her daughter back to her when she heard the low throttle of a truck engine.

"Sweetie, come with me."

"Mom, what's wrong?"

The woman grabbed the child's hand and hurried her into a back bedroom. She sat her on the bed and looked deeply into her daughter's eyes. "Listen to me. Everything's going to be all right. I have to go out for a little while. I won't be long, I promise."

"But, Mom! I can't stay here by myself."

The mother pressed a finger to Jesse's lips. "Please, do this for me. I'll be right back. Don't say a word. Just don't say a word."

Tears formed in the girl's eyes, but she nodded.

—

She came streaking out of the cabin before he pulled the truck to a stop. There was something wild about the way she looked, something frightened. It told him exactly what he wanted to know. She had heard the phone ringing and ignored it.

"Get in," he said through the lowered window.

She hurried around to the passenger door.

He cast a long look at the cabin and wondered if there was someone inside. It was a violation of their arrangement for her to have visitors. Lucky for her, he was in too much of a hurry to bother searching the place.

He put the truck in reverse and slammed the accelerator.

"So you've stopped taking my calls now?" he said.

"I was outside. I didn't get to the phone in time. Besides, I thought you were leaving for Salt Lake today."

He kept his eyes fixed straight ahead, to where the dirt road began to rise. They were in the middle of nowhere, on ranch land that had been in his family for generations. His land. His rules. "You're a lousy liar. Anyone ever tell you that?"

The truck bounced over ruts. Once they cleared the rise, the big house came into view. He parked at the back. She got out when he did. They went inside through the patio door.

He paused in the den to pour himself a drink. She stood nearby, waiting. Ordinarily, he offered her a glass of wine. Tonight he'd given her goddamned chauffeur service instead.

"Let's go," he said, finishing the Scotch.

He strode down the long hallway. She followed. Once inside the bedroom, he flipped on the overhead light and loosened his belt. She moved toward the bed with an air of resignation that said she only wanted to get this over with.

"Stop!" he said.

She stood a few paces away. Her absent gaze infuriated him. She needed a lesson.

"Stand underneath the light," he said.

"What?"

"You heard me."

Brow furrowed, she moved to the spot.

"Take off your clothes. Do it slowly."

"You want me to strip?"

"Just do as I say," he said, enjoying this new twist.

She stared at him without blinking. He knew he was a good-looking guy and that this arrangement, including the sex, suited her too. He didn't know what the hell her problem was tonight. He was on the verge of becoming seriously annoyed when she reached for the bottom of her shirt. In a single motion, she pulled it over her head. One look at her taut belly and full breasts, and his breath caught. This was some kind of new fun.

She started to undo her jeans. She had the zipper halfway down before she yanked it up again. "This is bullshit. I've done everything you've asked. But not this." She picked up her shirt. Before he could react, she was out the door.

He staggered after her. "You little—"

Bitch, he would have said. By the time he caught up with her, he'd lost interest in saying anything. He grabbed her and tried dragging her back to the bedroom. She wrenched away, stumbling toward the den. He bulldozed past her. Once in front, he seized her by the shoulders and shook her violently, causing her to trip and fall. He dropped on top of her.

"It's just like all the other times," he said as he pinned her arms with his knees. "Just like all the other times."

He didn't know his hands were around her neck until much later, when he moved and she didn't.

CHAPTER 1

The face in the crowd shouldn't have been there.

Kim Jackson wasted time she didn't have riveted to the sight of a man who looked disturbingly familiar. Too late, she caught him looking at her.

His eyes widened. He opened his mouth and shouted at the same time as a train whistle blew. Betraying nothing, Kim turned and walked away. She affected a casual pace along the popular tourist corridor near the Durango & Silverton Narrow Gauge Railroad depot. His name was Anthony Yeager. He was a marketing director for a Chicago-based Fortune 500 company. Seeing him dressed casually in shorts and a T-shirt, lean and towering over the lanky teenage girl alongside him, Kim panicked. Father and daughter were surrounded by a sea of disembarking passengers, everyone flocking into town after a train trip into the San Juan Mountains.

Walking faster, she weaved around pedestrians slowing to window-shop at a Rocky Mountain Chocolate Factory and the Western hats store next door. Beyond the shops, a crowd congregated at the curb. She joined the throng and kept moving. Waiting anxiously for the light to change, she glanced back.

Through the mass of bodies, she glimpsed Anthony. He was on a bead for her and closing the distance.

The light changed. She ran.

A voice she once knew called her name. She told herself not to turn and look, but she did anyway. Anthony, at something over six feet, had his arms stretched above his head. He had his phone out and was taking a picture. Of her.

She ran faster. She dodged pedestrians, bicycles chained to trees, and dogs tethered to the ends of leashes. Main Avenue was the heart of Durango's tourist center. On a summer afternoon, the art galleries and shops drew large crowds. Kim raced past a kiosk advertising white-water adventures. Farther on, she passed tents hanging in the window of an outdoor equipment store. She ran as if her life depended on it, because it did, even though Anthony would never dream of harming her.

But Durango was her town, and she knew things about it he didn't. At a brewpub, she veered in from the sidewalk. With a terse apology to the hostess and a claim to be late meeting friends, she cut through the dining room to the garden patio at the rear. From there, she beat a hasty exit to the alley, turned left, and kept running.

At the end of the block, she darted right. She took her chances that he wasn't there, because if he was, there was no hope of evading him now. The commercial district was behind her. A quiet neighborhood lay ahead. In the stillness of the summer day, she strained to hear his voice, the name on his lips, but all she heard was her own ragged breathing. When she reached the next corner, she doubled over, shirt drenched with perspiration in the arid air.

Furious, she gave herself a scant moment to recover. Twenty-nine years old, born and bred in Chicago, she had never done a thing wrong, and here she was, running like a common thief down the street. Her parents were dead. She didn't know why she was thinking of them now, especially since she had cut off all ties with her past, including giving up the name they'd given her. The strategy had been working brilliantly until a few minutes ago. Then a man got off a train ride into the mountains and threatened to destroy the new life she had worked to create.

Kim pulled herself upright. She checked behind her and saw a banged-up Jeep lurching along, hobbled by a damaged suspension. An SUV loaded with kayaks followed it. Otherwise, the street was deserted. She took small consolation in having eluded Yeager. Worse things could still happen. The phrase had become her motto—unfortunately not soon enough. Too many worse things already had happened by the time she'd properly learned the lesson.

She crossed the street and walked to the blue bungalow, second in from the corner. The door hadn't latched behind her when a different door swung wide on the left wall. Lena Fallon wheeled out from her private quarters into what had once been the home's living room. No living to speak of went on there any longer.

"What are you doing here? Can't you remember anything?" Lena snapped. "You're supposed to use the back door."

Kim smiled, relieved on one count. House rules no longer applied. "Hello, Lena. How are you this afternoon?"

"How am I—what?" Lena's voice rose in disbelief. She demanded, and ordinarily received, complete subservience from her staff of one. In the brief time Kim had been in the thirty-nine-year-old paraplegic's employ, this marked the first time she had spoken to her as a peer.

"I thought you were working at the bakery. Did you get fired?" Lena said.

Rather than answer, Kim gave the weirdly constructed living room a final passing glance. The room was nothing more than a thruway now, furnished with a thinly padded couch, never used. Directly behind the couch was a paneled wall that

served to shut out the former dining room and shrank the
resulting floor space to less than half its original area. Behind
the wall lay Lena's private suite.

Kim only meant to walk by. By mistake, her eyes met Lena's.
For one eerie instant, she felt hypnotized by the sight of Lena's
gaunt face, absent of a speck of human kindness. Lena's stony
torso was sculpted beneath a black turtleneck; her legs were
skinny appendages, welded to a chair. She was an unrelenting
dark storm of anger, a broken soul locked in a broken body.

Kim sighed. Lena, a pain-in-the-ass ex-cop, was one of
the worse things that could still happen to her. "I haven't been
fired, Lena. I forgot something. I'm in a hurry, that's why I used
the front door."

She started toward the stairs. Lena shot forward, blocking
her path. The abrupt movement caused the folder on her lap to
fall. White pages scattered fanlike on the wooden floor. Kim
bent over to gather the loose sheets.

"Get the hell away! I'll get them," Lena said.

Kim, quicker, scooped them up. Curious, she began reading to herself: "Sensory impressions of crime victims are noto-
riously unreliable. Studies show . . ."

It sounded like something out of a journal article. The
typed pages looked like they'd come off a printer. "Did you
write this?" she asked.

Lena snatched away the pages. "That's none of your damn
business."

"Right." Kim sidestepped the wheelchair and headed for
the stairs.

"Get back here! I'm not finished with you."

Kim jogged upstairs. Coming off the top step, she grabbed
the newel post and flung herself around the corner. In the bedroom, she fell on the bed, wondering why she had lied about
forgetting something. She had come here with a short list of
things to do: pack and leave. Now, she reveled in the knowledge

that she was in one of the few places in the world where no one could reach her. Only Lena knew where she was, and she couldn't climb the stairs.

Kim inhaled the musty air clinging to the bedspread. Eyes closed, she saw Anthony Yeager where she had in the past: seated in the corner conference room at a high-rise office building in Chicago. Their gang of seven division managers used to meet regularly on Monday mornings. On clear days, Lake Michigan's choppy gray surface rippled, seemingly forever, across the eastern horizon.

Only four months had passed since she had walked out of that job and out of her life. Anthony Yeager wasn't a man she had known well. His field was marketing; hers, accounting. Before the meetings began, he'd joked with his buddies about weekend golf games. Other times, he'd bragged about his daughter's heroics on the high school track squad. Meanwhile, she had sat by quietly, immersed in numbers, waiting for a different man to arrive, her boss and Anthony's, Stephen Bender.

The past seemed to glisten as though she were viewing it through a clear icy prism. It might as well have been someone else's life she was looking at. In a way, it was. Stephen Bender had stolen that life from her when he'd framed her for crimes he'd committed. He'd banked on her slavish devotion in exchange for concealing the evidence he'd manufactured against her. For fraud. And a murder.

Instead, she'd walked away.

Run, to be precise.

Kim rolled over. Bright sunlight filtered in through pale-yellow curtains fluttering at the open window. Her cheek brushed the satin bedspread patterned in swirls of beige, green, and pink meant to resemble something floral. The bedspread bridged the color of the carpet, green, and the single chair in the room, pink. Besides the bed and chair, she had a chest of drawers, a closet, and a tiny bathroom. The accommodations, however sufficient, were a far cry from the modern apartment in Chicago she'd once called home.

Seconds ticked by. "Go," she whispered. Meaning to her car parked in the garage and to another town to start over. Not a tourist town, this time, a place where no one from her past would ever step foot. She tried to imagine it. All she saw were tumbleweeds and boarded-up buildings. A ghost town. A perfect place for a woman who'd become a ghost.

Inertia held her there, and something else, a pang of grief. With the clock still ticking, she realized the grief was for more than what she had lost. It was for what she was about to lose. If she left now, there would be no coming back. She weighed her choices and realized she didn't need to leave Durango immediately. There would be time to make that decision later. Anthony did not know exactly where she was. He wasn't, at this moment, rallying troops to assist in her capture as though he were a bounty hunter and she his elusive prey. She drew the first deep breath she'd taken since laying eyes on her former colleague.

She stood up and changed clothes, exchanging her white shirt for a green blouse. She grabbed a backpack, thrust a cap and sunglasses inside, and bounded down the stairs. "Found what I needed," she said to Lena, who remained parked in the center of the room, emanating silent fury.

"You're lying!"

Yes, she was, Kim thought, escaping into a sunny afternoon through the same off-limits front door.

CHAPTER 2

Kim took side streets through the neighborhood until she reached a century-old brick building on the north end of downtown. Presently home to the Royal Baking Company, a variety of other businesses had occupied the premises over the years, including a mining company office, a newspaper, and a machine shop. Dennis Royal had given Kim a tour of the bread-baking facility when she was hired. All she could recall seeing were long wooden tables, stainless-steel ovens, and stand mixers the size of ancient washtubs.

Inside, she trotted up the wide wooden staircase that led to a row of offices overlooking the street. Her office was next to last at the end of the hall. High-ceilinged, the room had an aura of mustiness about it. The only furnishings were an ancient oak desk; a couple of chairs; a utility table for a printer and paper; and one bookcase crammed with file folders, contents unknown. Mullioned windows overlooked Main Avenue. The walls were plaster, pitted in spots and in need of a fresh coat of paint. The floor was the original hardwood. In her brief tenure working for the bakery, Kim had come to enjoy the building's throwback atmosphere, including its pervasive yeasty aroma.

And though she didn't love the dated computer software running on a server of equal vintage, she had learned to navigate the system.

Or so she had thought, until today.

Now the system was refusing to let her enter the hours on an employee time card. Each time she tried, the machine beeped and overrode her entry with a higher figure. At her wit's end, she gave up. Dennis was due in at any minute. She would leave it to him either to solve the problem or make the decision to call tech support.

Kim swiveled in her chair to face the window. There were few tourist shops on this end of town, and few pedestrians. She wasn't looking for Anthony Yeager on the street below, but she wasn't *not* looking for him either. He was suddenly the problem she hadn't known, until an hour ago, she had.

Now she understood. She could be seen anytime, anywhere, by anyone from her past.

So much for thinking she was safe.

She'd arrived in Durango less than a month ago after leaving Montrose, the first place she'd called home in Colorado. Barely a hundred miles into her drive and intending to go much farther that day, she'd stopped in Durango for coffee. Something kept her in the shop, besides the coffee. She sat unnoticed amid a crowd of outdoor enthusiasts of all stripes, including hikers, backpackers, river rafters, kayakers, and cyclists. Their energy was palpable. The town was lovely. She found a motel room and stayed the night.

The next day over coffee in the same shop, she searched the local paper for jobs and housing. The price of apartments shocked her. The job postings were sparse. Resigned to driving on to a larger city, she chanced on a listing she had missed earlier. "Housekeeper Wanted. Lodging Included." On a whim, she called the number. The social worker who answered offered to meet for lunch to discuss the job. The next day, Kim had moved into the blue bungalow.

A door slammed downstairs. Footsteps thudded hollowly on the stairs.

"Be right there," Dennis called, passing her doorway on the way to his office.

Kim picked up the employee time card that was giving her fits.

"Hey, I have good news for you. Sit down, sit down," Dennis said when he came in and settled in the chair opposite her, pointedly ignoring the proffered time card.

"Dennis, the system is screwed up," she said, refusing to be sidetracked. "It won't let me enter the actual number of hours this woman worked."

"Yeah, I know. I did that on purpose. Do you want to hear my good news?"

"In a minute. You're telling me that you want to pay someone two days' wages when she didn't work?"

"Carrie's kid was sick again. Special situation. Just pay her. Now can I tell you what I want to tell you?"

"Sure."

"I've got a brother-in-law who owns a construction company. He needs a temporary office manager. I know you're looking for more work, so I told him about you. Hope you don't mind, but I set up an appointment for you. Tomorrow." A satisfied smile broke out on the bakery owner's handsome, weathered face.

"Oh, Dennis. Thank you," Kim said, smiling at the man with a handlebar mustache and bowed legs who looked like he ought to be out riding the range rather than shut up in a hothouse baking bread. Dennis had taken a chance on her when she happened by his building and inquired about the "Help Wanted" sign in the window. She had talked her way into the bookkeeping job and subsequently bailed the company owner out of hot water with his employees, who hadn't been paid in two weeks.

"Here's a map," he said, holding out a hand-drawn map that showed two bold lines and a lightly drawn dotted line. An arrow pointed to a box representing Legrand Construction.

"This sounds great," Kim said, not knowing what else to say.

Dennis fished something out of his pocket. "My brother-in-law needs somebody regular hours. I figure for the time you're working for him, you can come in here nights." He handed her a building key. "Come and go as you please. Hell, it's the way Linda worked," he said, referring to her predecessor.

"Thank you."

"Well, I'd best get to work." Dennis pushed himself up from the chair and returned to his own office.

It was past four thirty when Kim dropped a stack of paychecks on Dennis's desk. He was on the phone. She quashed her affection for him, along with gratitude for the faith he had put in her, and smiled goodbye. She expected she would see him at least one more time, if only to drop off the key he'd just given her.

CHAPTER 3

The alarm clock buzzer wrenched Kim out of a deep sleep the next morning. A gauzy web of thoughts filled her mind as she lay in bed. One surfaced and became clear. She was scheduled for an interview at ten o'clock.

She hadn't slept well. Awake for hours in the middle of the night, she'd only fallen asleep after deciding *not* to go to the interview. While tossing and turning, she'd worked out a plan that included performing her usual routine with Lena this morning, announcing her resignation, and going to the bank to empty her safe-deposit box. After one final stop at the bakery to drop off the building key, she intended to drive away. Last night, leaving Durango had seemed so simple. And necessary.

Now, pulling up stakes didn't seem either simple or necessary.

The incessant argument ended there. She threw off the bedcovers and got up. This interview represented the best break she'd had in four months. She was going to the interview.

Downstairs, Kim made coffee and sliced fresh fruit for breakfast. She brought in the morning paper. Finished with her immediate tasks, she poured a cup of coffee and started pacing. It was past seven thirty. Normally Lena was up by now.

Kim flopped onto a chair and glanced around a room that reminded her of something out of a 1950s TV show. Those shows had aired decades before she was born; still, she'd seen enough reruns to picture June Cleaver presiding over the smallish space. White metal cabinets hung on the walls. Blue-checked curtains framed the windows. The linoleum was an elaborate geometric print, faded from its original gold color. The refrigerator was new, but the electric stove, with its wobbly coils and badly stained drip pans, was ancient.

The day she first saw the kitchen, she had breathed a little easier. She had assumed anyone who made do with such dated fixtures obviously didn't care a thing about food. She couldn't have been more wrong.

She sensed the vibration of the wheelchair a moment before Lena appeared in the doorway. Nodding "good morning," Kim jumped to her feet; she opened the refrigerator and took out a carton of yogurt to add to the breakfast tray. She turned to go outside, stopping when she realized Lena hadn't followed. Lena stared at the breakfast tray, prepared exactly as she had specified it every morning, save one, since Kim had moved into the house. "Oh," she said.

Kim's heart fell.

"This morning, I thought I'd have eggs. I don't think anything there will go to waste. Would you mind scrambling two eggs? One slice of toast will be fine."

Kim knew Lena hadn't awakened with a sudden craving for scrambled eggs. She knew the request wasn't a pop culinary quiz. She had no idea what kind of game her employer was playing, but that it was a game she had no doubt. "No scrambled eggs, Lena. Not today."

The other woman's eyebrows rose.

"I told you. I have an interview this morning. If we have to revise our arrangement regarding what you can ask and how I'm obligated to respond, fine. We can discuss that another time." Kim nodded at the screen door. "In the meantime, your breakfast is ready." She pressed the automatic door button and walked outside.

"You look like hell," Lena said. "Have trouble sleeping last night?"

"I slept like a baby."

"Yeah, right. Maybe like a baby who had a crackhead for a mother."

Kim set the tray on the table.

Lena wasn't finished. "I thought you told me you were only learning how to be a bookkeeper. Now you've landed, what? One job and an interview for a second in three weeks? Is Durango in the middle of some kind of economic boom no one but you knows about?"

Kim didn't take the bait. "The bakery is only six hours a week. The other job is temporary. I hardly think that counts as a boom."

"Still doesn't explain why anyone would hire you."

Kim didn't bother retorting that she hadn't been hired yet. She went inside and topped off her coffee. Between sips, she loaded the dishwasher and wiped down countertops, all the while thinking that Lena's digs hardly fazed her any longer. Since moving into the blue bungalow, Kim had learned to prepare garden salads, fruit salads, pasta salads, and marinades for grilled chicken and fish. She had scrubbed toilets, sinks, and floors, and polished every splinter of wood in the house at least once. She had become proficient in doing Lena's laundry, folding and putting away clothes, and on the rare occasion, doing a bit of ironing. Twice weekly, she assisted in physical therapy exercises for Lena's damaged left arm. Not one of those tasks, laundry aside, had been part of her repertoire a scant four months ago when her job was accounting division manager for the Materials Management Group at Blackwell Industries. Through it all, she had learned to ignore the incessant stream of abuse Lena hurled at her. And she had learned something else: she could adapt. She expected the knowledge would prove invaluable.

She was slouched in a chair, apparently looking too relaxed, when Lena came inside from the patio.

"The cabinets need to be washed. Think you can manage that?"

"I'll do it tonight."

While Lena continued to inspect the kitchen, Kim surreptitiously studied her. Lena would have been about her own height, she thought, imagining her employer standing upright at approximately five six or five seven. If not for the bitterness etched on her face, she might have been an attractive woman. Lena had short, dark hair that curved in a natural wave. Her features were small and even. Only her eyes stood out, though not for a good reason. They were cold. It was as if something had crawled behind the sockets and died there. Which, in a manner of speaking, wasn't far from the truth.

At nine thirty, dressed for the interview in slacks and a nice blouse, Kim left the house. The rear gate, closed earlier, was open. The garage door was raised and the lawn mower pulled out. Grinning, she greeted the tall kid carrying a gas can. "Good morning, Zeke."

"Hi, Kim. Where are you going? Give me a sec, and I'll move the mower. So you can get your car." He pushed the mower from the alley into the yard. "Are you going shopping?"

"No. I have an interview for a new job."

"But wait. Don't you still work for Lena?"

Zeke's brow wrinkled with the question, causing him to look younger than his twenty-two years. Zeke had suffered a head injury in a skiing accident while in his teens. Physically, he'd recovered. Cognitively, he was damaged, and likely wouldn't improve, at least according to Lena, who had told Kim the story. Zeke did Lena's yard work. He lived in the neighborhood with Jeremy, his older brother. Kim had met Zeke her first morning living at the house and since then had become friends with both brothers.

"Oh yes, I still work here. This new job is like the work I do at the bakery."

"Oh, you make sure people get paid."

"That's right. Hey, I wondered if you wanted to ride Horse Gulch again this weekend. Maybe Jeremy too."

A shadow fell over Zeke's features. "I can't go bike riding with you. We can't go. We're going, umm . . ." He glanced helplessly from her to the fence, then lowered his head.

Kim read the situation in an instant. Jeremy and Zeke had other plans for the weekend. Plans that didn't include her. Stung, she resisted lashing out, almost. "Zeke, really, it's no big deal," she said too casually.

She stepped around him to get to her car. "I'll see you some other time," she said in the same cool voice. She left Zeke standing there looking sad and lost.

On the drive out of town, Kim berated herself for the way she'd spoken to Zeke. Jeremy obviously had given his brother orders not to mention their weekend plans. It was nothing she ought to blame Zeke for. Not that it mattered. She was probably leaving Durango soon anyway.

Following Dennis's directions, she drove five miles, making several turns that led her on a circuitous route to a dirt lane. At its end, she reached her destination. Early for the interview, she left the engine running and air conditioner cranked on high while dust kicked up by her tires gradually settled on the road behind her. Aside from having no résumé in hand, no idea what job she had come to discuss, and no expectation that she would accept it if she got an offer, she was intrigued by the country landscape.

She took a hard look at the property. To her right, a yellow forklift sat idle alongside a pickup truck. Two sedans were parked on her left, directly in front of a stucco building. A couple of air conditioners butted out of windows, one at the front and one along the side. She tilted the rearview mirror for a better look at the cavernous corrugated metal shell behind her. A sign on the side read "Legrand Building Supply."

When it was time to go in, she turned off the car and got out. A broad hillside rose in the distance off to her left, bathed in the glow of the morning sun and eclipsing the horizon. Hearing a horse whinny, she smiled. She felt as if she were a million miles from anywhere, and that was a good thing.

Inside, she spoke to the receptionist. "Good morning. I'm here to see Jeannette Winchester."

The woman looked up from her desk without enthusiasm. "Jeannette!" she said, aiming a shout toward a hallway.

"What is it?" a woman shouted back.

"Someone's here for you."

Clattering sounded from the other room, followed by terse muttering. In the ensuing silence, Kim assessed her surroundings. The entry room was long and narrow. Two chairs and a coffee table were to her right. The receptionist sat to her left, facing the room. The carpet throughout was a dingy blue. A couple of metal filing cabinets occupied the far corner. On one, a single tendril from a drooping plant dangled over the side.

A vacant office lay straight ahead. Through the open doorway, she glimpsed portraits hanging on the wall. The largest, centered behind a desk, showed a family of four on horseback: husband, wife, daughter, and son. The man's hazel eyes bore into the camera lens. Skip Legrand, she assumed.

Heavy footfalls rose above the quiet. A middle-aged woman emerged from the narrow hallway, limping noticeably. "Can I help you?" she said.

Kim gave her name. "I'm scheduled to interview today," she said when the woman gave no sign of recognizing her.

"Good golly, is it ten o'clock already?" Jeannette Winchester said. She glanced at the wall clock, which showed four minutes before the hour. "Well, come on back. I'm not nearly ready to talk to you, but that's just the way it'll have to be." Turning to the receptionist, she said, "Trina, do you think you can possibly handle the phones for the next twenty or thirty minutes?"

"No," Trina answered smartly. "Skip said he wanted me in on the interview, too, since I'll be the one working with—what did you say your name was?"

With mock professionalism, Kim stepped forward and offered her hand. "Kim Jackson. Pleased to meet you."

"Well, let's go, then. Both of you," Jeannette said in a weary voice, as though she were addressing a pair of children.

To Kim's surprise, it didn't turn out to be the interview from hell. When Jeannette shifted to business mode, she spoke articulately about the requirements of the job. Kim answered each question without hesitation. She fudged details of her past, fabricating a job history while at the same time emphasizing her accounting expertise. Jeannette's steady nod told her she was doing fine.

"We're both a contractor and a retailer," Jeannette said. "We run two independent businesses out of this office, something Skip doesn't always understand when he wants somebody to run right over there"—she gestured toward the other building—"and pick up a part or some building material without writing it up on an invoice."

Before Kim knew it, they were discussing a schedule. While Trina returned to the outer office to answer a ringing phone, Jeannette said, "Tomorrow's my last day for six weeks.

At least that's how long the doctor tells me I'll be out. I guess you know that's why we're in such a rush to get this position filled. The gal we had lined up quit before she started. The best thing would be for you to work with me tomorrow; that way, I can show you the better part of what you'll need to do."

"I can't come in early. I do home care for someone," Kim said, blurting out the words.

Jeannette's frown deepened. "Now, which is it, are you a bookkeeper or a home health aide?"

"I'm a bookkeeper," Kim said, face burning bright at the understatement. She was an MBA, a licensed CPA, and accustomed to doing work far more complicated than anything she would ever see in this backwater construction company. She swallowed her pride. "Until I can find enough work to keep me going full time, I have to pick up what I can on the side. I do the other job in exchange for lodging."

"Where do you live?" Trina said, having rejoined them.

"In the neighborhood east of Main Avenue. I work for Lena Fallon."

"Oh my God," Jeannette said.

Trina laughed humorlessly. "You work for Lena Fallon?"

Kim nodded.

"That woman." Jeannette stiffly shuffled loose pages lying on her desktop into a neat stack and inserted the collection into a file folder. "I won't say I don't feel sorry for her, because I do. But she has brought a mountain of trouble down on this town." The office manager tightened her lips.

Kim raced to keep pace with the sudden shift. She had no idea what Jeannette was talking about. She turned to the receptionist, hoping the younger woman might be persuaded to reveal more. "I only moved to Durango a few weeks ago. I'm aware Lena was shot on the job, but that's all I know."

Trina eagerly took up the thread. "Lena Fallon shot and killed a guy in cold blood. Sure, she got shot too, but not by him. Now his family is suing the city for about a billion dollars. If they win, which they will, our taxes will go sky-high and the budget for city services will get slashed to pay for the whole mess."

"What does Detective Fallon have to say for herself about this?" Jeannette said.

"She doesn't talk about it," Kim said.

"Well, doesn't that just figure?" Jeannette leaned over to file the folder in a side drawer, closed it, and turned the conversation back to the job.

CHAPTER 4

On the return trip into town, Kim stopped for lunch at a sand-wich shop in a strip mall. She took a rear table in the dining area, intent on keeping watch over the other patrons. It wasn't the sort of establishment Anthony Yeager was likely to pop into for a bite to eat. Still, she wasn't taking any chances.

She laughed. Of course, she was taking chances. She was taking the biggest one of all by staying in Durango. She'd set-tled that decision immediately after getting hired at Legrand Construction.

She unwrapped her sandwich and took a bite.

It was only a matter of time before Anthony returned to Blackwell Industries with word of who he'd seen in Durango. The sensational report would trickle through the grapevine until it reached Stephen Bender's door. Kim chewed and swallowed her food without tasting it. She could almost see Stephen's face when he heard. Whatever his private thoughts, he'd cloak his reaction behind a sober expression. He might feign indifference. More likely, he'd feign concern. Any ques-tion he asked would be strategic, a bit of information extracted without Anthony noticing what he'd passed along.

Kim exhaled softly, staggered by the truth that Stephen had framed her. It began with corporate fraud. It ended with murder. No one knew about the fraud except Stephen and his partners, whoever they were. And her. The murder had been reported as an act of random urban violence. Stephen was sitting on the evidence he'd fabricated linking her to the crimes. It was his insurance policy, his way of controlling her. He'd expected her to be complicit in her knowledge of his crimes and carry on as though none of it had happened.

Instead, she'd slipped away and started over, using a new name.

Now she wondered what he would do when he heard Anthony Yeager's report that she'd been seen in Durango, Colorado.

It was the only question that mattered.

She had to assume he would come after her. Not himself. He'd send someone. The man in the pale-blue Ford, she thought, recalling the man who had tailed her for weeks in Chicago. And that man would have to find her. It was up to her to see that he didn't.

She finished lunch, crumpled the sandwich wrapper, and tossed it in a trash can on her way out the door.

When she reached town, she drove directly to the library. Since leaving Legrand Construction, she hadn't been able to shake the memory of Jeannette Winchester's reaction to hearing Lena's name. Jeannette's scorn was palpable. Though Kim had no trouble empathizing with the feeling, she realized there was more to Lena's story than she knew. Curiosity piqued, she parked the car and hurried into the building.

"I'm interested in reading back articles in the *Herald*," she said to a woman at the front desk, mentioning the local paper. "It's the story involving the police detective who was shot, Lena Fallon. The problem is, I don't know when that happened."

The librarian's warm smile faded. "Oh, I do. It was March, year before last, the second week, I believe. Those articles are in the archives."

Surprised by her power of recall, Kim said, "You have quite a memory. Do you remember everything so well?"

"No. But that was a terrible tragedy. What range of dates did you want to cover?"

"One week, I suppose. Do you remember how long the story ran?"

The woman rolled her eyes. "Months. Even now, an article occasionally pops up."

Five minutes later, Kim was settled at a computer, peering at black text on the screen. Seeing the bold-faced headline, her pulse quickened: "Policewoman Shot in the Line of Duty."

The text saddened her, as did the picture of Lena, which appeared below the headline. She was in uniform, looking vigorous, healthy, and young.

Kim started reading. The first paragraph was chilling. She read it twice. Lena Fallon, a highly decorated Durango police detective, was shot three times while pursuing a suspect in a traffic violation. One bullet severed her spinal cord. A second bullet hit her shoulder; the third shattered her elbow. She was in critical condition at Durango Medical Center.

Details about the shooting were murky. A second person died at the scene. The deceased was the twenty-three-year-old male driver of the car Lena had pulled over. He, too, had been shot. But no gun was found on or near him.

Kim reread the report. Lena had been shot. Another man was killed. Yet no gun besides Lena's was found at the scene. "Someone else was there," she whispered.

The dead man was identified as Bobby Hill, well known to local police with a string of arrests for burglary dating back a decade. Kim was more interested in reading about Lena. A fifteen-year member of the force, she had twice been decorated for outstanding service. She was a lifelong Durango resident. Her parents still lived in the area, as did her sister. Her brother owned a restaurant in Telluride.

Family. Lena had family here. It came as a surprise. Kim knew nothing of them.

Stories reported over the next several days were riddled with unanswered questions. Only the assessment of Lena's medical condition emerged succinctly within twenty-four hours: she was paralyzed. The doctors gave no hope she would walk again. The evolving story told of Lena pulling into a gas station off of US Route 160 during her evening shift. Before she got out of her car, another car squealed in from the street. Without stopping, it sped back onto the highway, barely avoiding a crash with an oncoming car. The driver demonstrated suspicious behavior. Each witness on the scene confirmed that. Lena promptly engaged in pursuit.

She followed the speeding car out of town. When it made a left turn at Wildcat Canyon, she followed. A mile or so farther, the driver abruptly abandoned the attempt to elude capture and pulled over. With the patrol car's red lights flashing, Lena pulled in behind the other vehicle. She radioed in details of the chase and gave the car's license plate number. She left her vehicle, intent upon issuing at least one ticket.

That was the last anyone knew for certain. Shortly afterward, gunfire erupted on that stretch of deserted road. When officers arrived on the scene, they found Bobby Hill on the ground outside his car, shot dead. Lena was lying next to the open door of the patrol car, shot three times. No one else was there.

Several days passed before Lena was able to give her account of events. In her statement, she repeated the known facts: she pursued a speeding car into Wildcat Canyon. The vehicle pulled over within a mile. She left her vehicle to approach the driver. Bobby Hill exited his vehicle and took several steps toward her. He ignored her order to return to his vehicle. Lena fired once in the air as a warning. When Hill continued to advance, she shot him in the leg. She never saw a weapon in his possession. She fired only after he refused to obey her direct order and continued to behave in a threatening manner.

Bobby Hill fell. Before Lena had a chance to reach him, she was shot twice from behind. In one of the strangest twists of the case, the third shot, the bullet that lodged in her elbow, was fired from close range. She swore she never saw her shooter. She also swore she never fired a second time, but evidence showed otherwise. Bobby Hill was dead by her gun.

Of course, her fingerprints were on the gun—it was hers. No other prints were on it. Beyond a shadow of a doubt, there was a second shooter out there that night. The bullets removed from Lena confirmed it. Ballistics proved they were shot from a weapon other than her service pistol. That gun had never been recovered. Theories abounded as to who this person was, how he happened to be there, and what possible motive he had for shooting Lena. The dark, ugly question, intimated at first, and asked directly later: Had Lena Fallon panicked and gunned down an unarmed man?

"It was a setup," Kim said. Startled, she glanced around, relieved no one had overheard.

She skimmed through subsequent articles, surprised to realize Durango's citizens didn't share her conclusion. Even as Lena lay in the hospital, beginning what would prove to be a lengthy recovery, a public outcry demanded an investigation into police procedure. In the strange array of circumstances, with one of the principals dead, the other accused of causing his death, and the third never identified, the tide of sentiment turned against Lena.

Kim flipped ahead. She wanted to read something hopeful, a report of an arrest or, failing that, leads on a suspect. Instead, she came to an article announcing that Lena's parents had posted a reward for information leading to the arrest and conviction of their daughter's shooter. The couple promised ten thousand dollars. A separate community fund held another five thousand dollars.

Kim sat back and exhaled quietly. Something ugly had played out on that lonely stretch of road on a March night seventeen months earlier. Either Lena had been an unlucky victim of a random crime. Or someone had been waiting for her.

At the front counter, she thanked the librarian who had helped her. "Did you find everything you wanted?" the woman said.

Kim shook her head. "There was too much to read. I'll have to come back."

"Thought you might." The librarian pushed a slip of paper across the counter. "When you do, you might want to read this."

Kim picked up the slip. On it was written "Circle of Enemies," "Rich Larson," and a date.

"Rich Larson is a reporter out of Grand Junction," the librarian said. "He came to town a year ago and did a series on Detective Fallon's shooting. It's a terrific read. He was nominated for an award for the piece. But that honor went to someone in Denver, as usual."

Kim started to reply. The other woman nodded at the slip in her hand. "That's the name of the article and the date it ran. If I'm not here when you come back, someone else will be able to help you find it."

"Thank you."

Outside, Kim turned left when she reached the sidewalk. She headed for Second Avenue, in the opposite direction of her car. She wanted time and space to let her thoughts settle.

But they wouldn't settle. At the next block, she turned left again and was only vaguely surprised to find herself outside the Durango police station. She studied the light-colored brick facade and wondered whether Lena's shooting was still under active investigation by her former colleagues.

It had to be. Lena was one of their own.

She resumed walking with a troubled heart. Someone had wanted Lena badly wounded. But not dead.

Yet Bobby Hill had to die.

Because he knew the shooter. Whatever Bobby had been told, whatever he had been promised for his part in the ambush, it was a lie. Bobby Hill was nothing more than bait.

Lena had been the target.

CHAPTER 5

There was another world out there, darker than the one most people imagined.

Jaye Dewey knew this because she had lived it. She thought she would have known anyway. Even as a child, she had been an exceptionally clear thinker, readily distinguishing between the superficial and what lay beneath. The trait hadn't always made her popular, not at home, and especially not in the Southern California high school she had attended.

Now, inside the Mining Company, an upscale Durango restaurant, she sat alone at a table for two. The restaurant served the best steaks in town, but Jaye wasn't here for the food. Nor was she drawn by the ambiance. The place was old-school Durango, with ancient wooden booths and a frosted glass panel separating the bar from the dining room. The patrons were older heterosexual couples. *Dinosaurs,* Jaye thought.

She saw him the moment he walked in. He entered the dining room with an air of confidence that said he *belonged.* Jaye had been on to him ever since he discovered the new waitress working here. The waitress was tall—five nine, give or take an inch. She had long brown hair and the wholesome look he couldn't resist.

It was easy keeping tabs on him in the evenings. He only ever did one of three things: hook up with his regular girl-friend, go home, or go out for dinner at his favorite watering hole. On the latter nights, he didn't always go home alone.

He was hardly settled at his table when he noticed Jaye. The new waitress approached him, all smiles, only to find him checking out the competition. She moved a step to block his view. With an obvious dismissive gesture, he waved her off. And took another look.

Jaye saw it all.

While he, she was absolutely certain, saw nothing except a young blond woman whose wholesome beauty surpassed the waitress's common looks.

His name was Paul Kennerly. He was in his forties, had a slack face and the beginning of a paunch. Despite his fad-ing looks, women seemed to find him attractive. Maybe they didn't. Maybe it was his money they wanted. He was the great-grandson of a Durango land baron, a developer, and a former city councilman.

Jaye finished her meal and slipped out while Kennerly was still dining. From a window table in the café across the street, she kept watch on the restaurant. Kennerly stayed until clos-ing. When he left, he went to the bar next door. Not long after-ward, the waitress joined him there. Ten minutes later, they emerged together. They walked to the end of the block, turned the corner, and disappeared into the night.

Jaye lingered over her coffee. Once she was in her car, she drove sedately out of town, following the Lake Vallecito road. The pavement dipped and rose as it wound around curves bordering a few farms and fewer homesteads. Kennerly's Ford pickup was nowhere in sight. Jaye didn't need to see his tail-lights to know where he was going. At an unmarked country lane, she turned, drove a mile, and made another turn. As a precaution, she dimmed her headlights.

A lone spotlight shone in front of his house. His truck was parked in the drive. She drove on until she came to a gated road that served as a second entrance to the property. With the car idling, she unlocked the gate, drove in, latched the gate, then parked well out of view of anyone passing by.

The house lay a hundred yards away across an open field. Jaye beat the grass with a stick as she walked, not wanting to startle a rattler out searching for its dinner. Warm air brushed her face. Far to the north, the San Juan Mountains inked a purple-black silhouette across the sky. The world had a profound stillness, carved beneath a milky-white canopy of stars. She understood why he liked this place.

And why her mother had, a long time ago.

She slipped around to the back of the sprawling ranch house and tested the patio door. Finding it unlocked, she went inside. He was down the hall, behind the locked door to his bedroom where the waitress was, even now, likely performing a strip show. Eventually they'd end up in bed, he, no doubt, a more enthusiastic participant than she.

Jaye sat on the leather sofa and stared at the black screen of an oversize TV. Deep inside her pocket, she fingered the key ring that opened all of his locks. Three summers ago, she had come here for the first time, intending to pick the back door lock to get inside, if necessary. Instead, she had found a key hidden, not very well, on the patio. She used it to get in, then took it. The next day, she had a copy made, the original returned to its not-great hiding place. Since then, she had come and gone at will, collecting keys to the bedroom door, the gate blocking the property access road, and the granddaddy of them all, the key to the cabinet where he kept his collection of videotapes.

Which was how she knew what was going on in the bedroom.

She had his keys, but she didn't know all of his secrets. With a certainty that defied reason, she knew he had killed her mother, very likely in this house. She didn't know why her mother had died. More disturbingly, she didn't know why her mother had gone out that night fourteen years ago. Her mother had left her, a child of eight, alone in a cabin on the property with only the whisper of a promise: "I'll be back soon."

CHAPTER 6

Monday night, Kim locked the door to the bakery and stepped into an evening that had grown dusky gray. Strolling along Main Avenue, she passed shops and galleries closed for the night. Restaurants were jammed with a dinner crowd, and bars were only beginning to come alive. At the sound of a shrill whistle, she walked a block to join a small crowd gathering at the railroad tracks. Moments later, a thundering rumble filled the air as a massive black engine pulling its fleet of cars came into view. Kim smiled at the children waving excitedly to passengers and crew. Before the tinny crossing bell lapsed into silence, she walked on.

In the heart of downtown, she stopped outside the Strater Hotel. Built in 1887, the redbrick and white-sandstone Victorian-style building hearkened back to another era, one that saw men in bowler hats and string ties and women wearing hoop skirts pass through its lobby. Honky-tonk music still played nightly in the Diamond Belle Saloon. Since last week, Kim had been keenly aware of the Strater for her own reasons. Until Saturday morning, Anthony Yeager had been a guest there.

She had discovered her former colleague's whereabouts on a cold call to the hotel desk. Second on her list of upscale hotels to try, she had called and asked to be connected to Anthony Yeager's room. When a young woman said, "One moment, please," Kim had disconnected. Each day afterward, she had called again. On Saturday, she had learned no guest by that name was registered.

Her snooping went further. She had found two vehicles in the Strater parking lot bearing Illinois license plates. One was a Toyota minivan, the other a Mercedes SUV. Of the two, her money was on the latter, assuming either car actually belonged to Yeager. Between driving or flying from Chicago, she much preferred the scenario where he drove. It would take him longer to get home.

She walked on.

Down the street from the hotel, she dallied in front of a Native American art gallery. Dream catchers fluttered above shelves decorated with hand-carved animals from a town in Mexico she hadn't learned how to pronounce. Next door, photos of gorgeous mountain homes adorned a realtor's window. She inhaled the atmosphere she loved, remembering the promise she had made to herself—to stay out of Durango's popular downtown for the next few weeks. She didn't know when Yeager would return to work, or how long it would take for word of who he had seen, and where, to reach Stephen Bender. She didn't know what Stephen would do once he heard the news. He had no reason to assume she would still be in Durango, especially given her pattern of bolting. What Stephen did or didn't do was irrelevant. It was up to her to keep herself safe.

She headed for home.

At the corner where she usually turned, she hesitated. Twilight lingered. The soft summer air made for too fine an evening to spend indoors. She had spent the weekend alone. On Friday, Lena had announced she was going away again. For the second consecutive weekend, she had left Kim in charge of the house and left with a friend. Other than knowing that the friend was female and that her name was Damian, Kim knew nothing of her. She wanted to ask Zeke and Jeremy about the woman with the curious name. She wanted to sit on their porch and talk, as they often did in the evenings. She wanted friendship with the brothers to be simple and uncomplicated, but already in her brief acquaintance with the elder brother, it had grown tangled.

She liked Jeremy. She had liked him from the moment she'd met him. They'd gone out together twice, not on dates, exactly. More like good friends toeing open a door to see if anything tempting lay behind it. Their second time out, he'd slammed on the brakes. "The thing is," he'd said, somewhat abashedly, "Zeke has a whopping big crush on you."

The revelation hadn't come as a surprise.

Then he'd confessed, "And I kind of do too."

They both had laughed. Jeremy wasn't laughing when he said Zeke would be devastated if he thought his older brother had something going on with Kim. It was messy. Kim had agreed. That night, they'd said they would be friends, all three of them. She'd thought she and Jeremy had a good rapport. She'd thought they could talk to each other. Then came the sudden secrecy about their weekend plans. Now she didn't know what to think.

She detoured one block. As she came around the corner, she decided to walk past the brothers' house. If neither was sitting outside, she would keep walking.

"Kim, hello," Zeke called from the porch steps when she was still two houses away.

"Hey, Zeke," she said, drawing near. Jeremy, to her relief, was also there. He sat on a chair in the shadows, darker than his brother, leaner and more handsome, a complicated man of twenty-seven, two years her junior. For the moment, Kim ignored him. "What are you up to tonight?"

"Me and Jeremy are waiting for beautiful women to come walking by."

For this answer, Zeke received a soft kick in the shoulder from his brother.

"Oh really. Well, then, I'd better keep moving. I'd hate to stand here and block your view."

"No, no, you dork, we were waiting for you." Zeke stood and motioned her up the steps.

On her way, she nodded to Jeremy, who nodded in return. It wasn't the glowing welcome she had hoped for, but at least he was here. She had no sooner joined Zeke on the top step when he leaned forward and shot off a look down the street. "How was your weekend?" she said, puzzled by his twitchiness.

"Awesome. We went to the mountains. We rebuilt a trail that got trashed by an avalanche. It was totally messed up."

"Just the two of you? That sounds like a lot of work," she said, unfairly baiting him. She doubted they'd gone alone.

"No, no. There were lots of people. We couldn't have—"

For the second time, he leaned forward and peered down the street. Then he turned to his brother for help.

"It was a lot of work," Jeremy said. "The mountains got hammered by a blizzard last April. Three feet of wet snow fell on top of the crusty layer underneath. Avalanches let loose through the San Juans for a week."

Funny thing about that storm, Kim thought. She had driven into Montrose, Colorado, on the eve of it. Closed roads had kept her in the town for two days. By the time roads reopened to the south, she had decided to stay in a place where she believed she couldn't be found.

"What kind of work did you do? And where did you stay at night?" she asked Zeke.

He didn't answer. Instead, he shot off another look down the street. His anxiety was contagious. Kim felt a tremor of jealousy and wondered if he was waiting and watching for another beautiful woman to walk by.

Not any woman. Caitlin, Jeremy's ex-girlfriend.

Supposedly his ex.

"Umm, we moved trees and boulders. Some big ones. It was really hard. Oh, and we camped. Well, Jeremy had the tent. I slept out. The stars—I wish you could have seen them." His voice grew hollow. "The whole sky—" He lunged forward yet again to look down the street.

"Yeah, I wish I could have seen them too," she said, not bothering to conceal her disappointment. She wondered who Jeremy had shared his tent with.

She didn't stay long. Unable to bear Zeke's fidgeting, unwilling to listen to one more tale from the grand weekend in the mountains, she made an excuse and left.

—

"What in the world are you doing?" Lena said the next morning. She entered the kitchen to find Kim standing on a chair searching a pantry shelf.

"I'm looking for the bag of coffee I saw here last week."

"Oh." After a pause, Lena said, "It's not there."

Kim turned and looked at her employer, who, for once, appeared slightly chagrined. "Where is it?"

"We took it with us this weekend. Damian and I took it. I forgot to bring it back."

Kim stepped down.

"Is there any left?" Lena said.

"Enough for a small pot. Two cups. Your usual."

"Can you get some at work?"

"Nobody there drinks it. I'll stop and pick up a cup on my way through town."

To make amends for the coffee, Lena volunteered to expedite her morning routine. Kim was dressed and ready to leave twenty minutes earlier than usual. On her way through the backyard, she met Zeke coming in.

His face lit up when he saw her. She suppressed a flare of irritation, which she recognized was meant for Jeremy. Last night, she had decided to steer clear of both brothers for a while, at least until she got a grip on her feelings for the elder one.

"Weren't you here a few days ago? Lena's grass doesn't grow that fast," she teased.

"Yeah." He stood inside the back gate, shrugging in a gesture reminiscent of his brother. "I'm not here to mow. I'm on my way to the Connors'. They don't want me starting the mower too early."

She smiled at his answer that did nothing to explain his presence. She edged past him to get her bicycle out of the garage.

"Where's your helmet?" Zeke said sharply when she emerged from the garage without it.

"Oh right." She leaned the bicycle against the fence and got her helmet, not wanting to waste time arguing. Her extra few minutes for coffee were slipping away.

"No, you goof," Zeke said, still criticizing. "You want a tight fit. You can't get it with a ball cap on."

"I know," she said grudgingly.

Zeke stood close by, watching her make the adjustment. He seemed uneasy, shifting from one foot to the other, hands shoved into the pockets of his worn jeans. She thought about asking him if anything was wrong, but she didn't have the time to spare.

"Are you coming over tonight?" he said after she mounted the bike.

"Not tonight, Zeke." She pedaled away.

It was an easy cruise to her favorite café on Main Avenue. Inside, she waited in a short line, then bought a sack of ground beans for the house and a cup to enjoy now. Though she had only a few minutes, it seemed an inordinate luxury to sit in the fresh air outside the café, answerable to no one.

She had her head tilted back to catch the morning sun when she heard someone call her name.

"Kim!"

Momentarily disoriented, she didn't immediately see Zeke.

"Kim!" he screamed again.

She stood up.

From the corner café on Main, she had a clear view of the street. Zeke was on his bicycle, pedaling madly toward her from the opposite direction. A stoplight was between them. Zeke was flailing one arm, gesturing wildly at the sidewalk. Kim couldn't take her eyes away from him or the traffic light, blazing red. Horror swelled inside her. She couldn't believe he meant to run the light.

At the last instant, Zeke skidded to a stop.

Only then did she glance where he'd pointed. A man in the next block was moving fast on the sidewalk. Not running. But making a beeline for the curb. He was neither young nor old and wore a beige jacket, unzipped and flapping. His hair was dark. There was something brutish about him, something that set him apart from other Durango men, both the tourists and the outdoorsmen.

He was looking straight at her.

She dropped her cup.

The light was still red.

The man ignored it.

He stepped into the street, intending to dart ahead of an approaching car. A single beam of light veered out from the alley behind him. Kim recognized the shape of a motorcycle without hearing its telltale engine roar.

The man never saw it.

"Stop!" Zeke screamed.

The man didn't stop. The motorcycle, in the throes of acceleration, couldn't stop. At the last instant, it spun, too late to avoid the man. Momentum carried machine, rider, and pedestrian into the path of the oncoming car. The motorcyclist bounced once and rolled clear. The other man was crushed beneath the wheels of an SUV that never had time to slow down.

Brakes squealed as cars swerved away from the accident. There was a deafening crunch of metal against metal. Screams of panic erupted in the small crowd. Kim froze. This was about her. Whatever had happened, it was about her. She couldn't bear to know what it was. Then she remembered Zeke. With blessed relief, she saw him straddling his bicycle at the light.

She grabbed her bag and ran. She weaved between cars, dodging people moving toward the accident. Zeke was off his bike when she reached him. Kim took his hand and led him to the sidewalk, away from the accident and the sight of blood oozing onto the pavement.

Several doors down the block, they sank onto the sidewalk. Kim kept one arm around Zeke, hardly knowing what to say. The piercing wail of sirens filled the air. Seemingly within seconds, police cars and a paramedic unit arrived on the scene.

"He—he was after you," Zeke said, stammering. "That man was after you."

"What?"

"He was at Lena's. I saw him drive away after you left. I had to help you."

A thicker crowd gathered in the wake of the arrival of emergency vehicles. Kim's eyes were drawn to the scene, though she had no clear view. She felt sick to her stomach. "How do you know he was following me, Zeke?" she said, not doubting him for an instant.

"I saw him last night. He was around our house. The same man. The same car."

"What car?"

"Black." Zeke pointed down the street. "It's down there. He parked and came this way looking for you."

The revelation that a man had been tailing her came as no surprise. There had been a man before, in Chicago. His car was blue. Same man, she guessed. Different car. Because he couldn't have driven halfway across the country and had time to find her. She shook her head, stunned by the implications. Her brain was too fuzzy to sort out the threads.

"And you saw all this?"

Zeke nodded. "I rode my bike down. When I saw him follow you in his car, I followed him. It didn't seem right."

Kim pulled Zeke close and kissed his forehead. "Thank you, Zeke."

Police officers pushed the crowd back. Unable to see anything from where she sat, Kim stood up and moved close enough for a view of the paramedics working feverishly on the injured men. A second ambulance arrived on the scene. Long minutes passed before one of the medics working on the pedestrian shook his head. The other got a sheet and pulled it over the man, who was, apparently, deceased. After a brief discussion with a police officer, the medics loaded the pedestrian onto a stretcher and wheeled it to the vehicle. With a couple of short, staccato siren clips, the ambulance drove away. By then, the motorcyclist was sitting up; he was speaking to a different police office, gesturing, as he spoke, over his shoulder toward the alley. The conversation ended when two medics assisted the man onto a stretcher and whisked him away in the ambulance.

Immediately, a buzz filled the air as one person after another described what he or she had seen. Kim had to get out of there. It was only a matter of time before someone pointed her out to police and an officer approached with questions she couldn't answer.

"Caitlin told Jeremy about the man," Zeke, who had joined her standing, said.

"What?"

"When we were camping. Caitlin told Jeremy a man showed her a picture of a woman who looked like you."

"Zeke, please tell me. How do you know this?"

"I was there when she told him."

Kim sucked in her fear. "Do you remember exactly what she said?"

"Caitlin said the man came to where she works. He showed her a picture and asked if she knew who it was. She told him it kind of looked like Jeremy's friend. I heard her tell Jeremy. I was there."

"Jeremy never told me," Kim said in a whisper.

"No. He said we shouldn't say anything. It would worry you."

Damn straight it would have worried her. She cursed whatever twisted logic had kept Jeremy from telling her something so vital.

"Come on, Zeke. Let's go home."

Before they left the area, Kim asked Zeke to point out the man's car. He led her a block north on Main to a sedan parked at a meter. It was a midsize black Chevy with a New Mexico license plate.

Walking side by side, they pushed their bicycles to Lena's house. Whatever clarity Kim had felt immediately after the accident, she lost it in the time it took to reach the house. They left their bicycles in the backyard. Zeke made it clear he still had to go to work at the Connors'. Kim was clear on nothing except that she wasn't going to work at Legrand Construction.

She hadn't prepared herself to face Lena.

"What in the world happened to you two?" Lena said, wheeling into the kitchen as they entered through the back door.

Neither spoke. When Kim sensed Zeke was about to answer, she blurted out, "A man was hit by a car on Main. We think he was killed. We saw it happen."

Lena's brow wrinkled in consternation. There was no reason on earth why the two of them should have been together at that hour. Kim was supposed to be at work. Zeke should have been mowing someone's lawn. Unable to bear the tension, Kim rushed upstairs.

Fighting to stay calm, she changed into shorts and a T-shirt. She grabbed her cap and sunglasses and raced back downstairs where she found Lena and Zeke exactly as she had left them.

"I need to make a phone call," she said. She rarely used the landline. Lena begrudged her the use of it. But she went to the phone attached to the wall, punched in the number, and when Trina answered, she told the receptionist she wouldn't be in. She promised to make up the hours. Maybe she would. Maybe she wouldn't. Maybe she would never see the inside of Legrand Construction again. Straining to do one last thing, she forced herself to walk calmly past Lena and Zeke. "I'll see you later," she said, as if nothing the least bit exceptional had happened.

"Kim, get back here! I want to talk to you," Lena called after her.

Kim kept walking.

CHAPTER 7

Kim mounted her bicycle and rode up the street. Numbly, she chose her course, angling toward the edge of town and the only place she could be certain of solitude. Third Street, she remembered. Where Third Street dead-ended, she found the trail to Horse Gulch. She dismounted and pushed the bicycle up the steep trail.

At the top, she resumed riding. Negotiating the deeply rutted ground demanded her concentration, and briefly, she forgot why she was there. But when dry heaves wracked her chest, she started gasping and had to stop. After a moment, she pushed the bike toward a stand of trees flanking the trail, sufficiently dense to shield her from view of anyone passing by.

Not that anyone would be looking for her. The man assigned to that task was dead. Kim lowered her head into her hands. For the first time since leaving Chicago, she sobbed. She knew what had happened. Anthony Yeager *had* spoken to someone at Blackwell Industries last week, probably immediately after spotting her on the street. She would never know the precise sequence of events. What she did know: Stephen had heard the news and wasted no time sending a man to find her. And, presumably, kill her.

She leaned her head against the rough bark of a pine tree. Tears streamed from her eyes. She surrendered to the memory of the life she'd left behind.

—

Michael Leeds was a happy man the afternoon he walked into her office. Puzzled but happy. A half hour earlier, he'd taken a call from a customer desperate to lay hands on a nearly obsolete piece of equipment. It was a compressor for a power plant turbine and carried a price tag of over a million dollars. Such calls weren't unusual in their department. Blackwell Industries was a diversified conglomerate whose business lines included heavy-equipment manufacturing, industrial and commercial construction projects, and a credit operation. It was a running joke at the company that Blackwell built, bought, or brokered the sale of every major type of industrial equipment sold in the United States.

Despite having little hope of finding the unit, Michael performed a routine inventory search. He did a double take when he found the compressor in stock. But when he tried to pull it out of inventory, the screen flashed a perplexing message: "Item unavailable for delivery." Repeated attempts produced the same result. So he'd come to her. As accounting chief in the Materials Management Group, it was her job to oversee the flow of equipment into and out of an inventory consistently valued at over a billion dollars.

"Do you know anything about a warehouse on Fifty-Eighth Street?" Michael asked when he sauntered into her office. He was a big guy, only twenty-five, but looked older. Four years doing desk work for the navy had done that to him, she supposed.

No, she had never heard of a Fifty-Eighth Street warehouse.

He duplicated his previous effort on her computer, display-ing the inventory item and its particulars. She fared no bet-ter when she tried to pull it out of stock. "Item unavailable for delivery," the screen announced, maddeningly unhelpful. And there it was, the mysterious Fifty-Eighth Street warehouse.

"What do you say we take a drive after work?" Michael said, blue eyes twinkling mischievously at the prospect. He prided himself on a thorough knowledge of corporate warehouses and inventory stockpiles. This unknown warehouse offended him nearly as much as the computer system that refused to deliver a pricey compressor into his hot little hands.

In retrospect, it was easy to say they shouldn't have gone. It wasn't part of her job, or his, to visit warehouses to check on inventory. Other people did those jobs. But the combination of this item and this warehouse was so spectacularly wrong, her curiosity was piqued. There might have been something else going on, too, a foreboding, even then, of trouble. That eve-ning, she and Michael drove to an industrial area south of their modern office building. Crawling along at a snail's pace, they checked poorly marked building addresses until they came to a dilapidated structure obviously no longer in use.

"What the hell?" Michael said angrily. "I don't think any million-dollar compressor is sitting in that shack. I wonder what else is supposed to be in there," he said in a dangerous, low voice.

She knew what he was thinking. She was thinking the same. They had stumbled onto evidence of fraud. To her infinite shame afterward, she hadn't been able to face the crisis head-on. "Let's go back," she said, refusing to fuel speculation.

"What are you going to do?" he asked when he stopped in front of her apartment building.

She was the manager of their group. Whatever had happened, it happened on her watch. "I don't know. There must be some mistake. I'll look into it tomorrow."

She thought the mistake was the inventory record. She clung to that belief, holding out against a darker explanation.

She didn't remember how she spent the night. She would have spent it alone, as she always did. In those days, her life had conformed to a simple mantra: get up, go to work, come home. Occasionally she interrupted the routine with a stop at the gym. She almost never socialized. Since her last boyfriend had walked out on her a year earlier, she hadn't had a single date.

By contrast, she remembered the next morning with perfect clarity. Michael came to her office early. He walked in and, unusually for him, didn't say a word. He handed her a sheaf of papers. On top, she found a payment authorization form for the nonexistent compressor. In the lower corner, she read her signature. For one gut-wrenching moment, she stared at the tidy script, unable to speak. It was her signature, and it wasn't. She had never seen that form, let alone signed off on it. It was a forgery, and a good one.

Truly alarmed, she raised her head, eyes bright with denial. Michael pressed one finger to his lips. He took the papers, turned around, and left.

She bought herself a day. The day was followed by a weekend, and before the weekend was over, Michael Leeds was dead. He was shot while sitting in his car outside a popular Chicago sports bar on Saturday night. She didn't hear of his death until Monday morning. She learned the truth from her boss, Stephen Bender.

In a story riddled with betrayal, it was the moment—one of two—when she despised herself most.

Stephen called her to his office early that Monday. He was waiting at the door when she arrived, and closed it immediately after she walked in. For one odd and seemingly endless

moment, he studied her. Then he moved, in a flash grab-
bing her blouse and ripping it open. Buttons popped. Once
her chest was exposed, he cast a cool, appraising look at her
flesh, searching for the wire she wasn't wearing. Certain of its
absence, he laughed.

The bastard had come prepared. He took a new blouse
from a desk drawer, still in its packaging. He handed it to her
and ordered her to change out of the torn one. She only moved
when he came close, threatening to forcibly undress her.

He stashed the ruined blouse in his desk.

In a cavalier voice, he began the tale that ended her life as
she'd known it.

"Your boy found something he shouldn't have," he said,
rocking in his desk chair. "Worse for you, he told you about it.
Oh, here's the best part. I set you up. If anyone finds out about
any of this, it's you who's going down, not me."

He shoved a news clipping across the desk and ordered her
to read it. Buried in the middle of the crime beat section, a
headline announced the city's latest homicide victim had been
identified. Only then did she learn that Michael Leeds was
dead.

She couldn't remember how much Stephen told her that
day and how much she worked out later for herself. The scheme
involved siphoning money out of corporate funds as payment
for false purchases. A payment that appeared to go to one of
their regular vendors instead went somewhere else. No doubt,
it went to an offshore account controlled by Stephen and his
partners, whoever they were. He had to have partners. Stephen
couldn't have pulled off fraud of this magnitude without help.

"I won't bore you with unnecessary details," he'd said that
morning. "What I will tell you is this. There is no evidence linking me to any of these transactions. But there is a great deal of
evidence linking them to you. Lest you worry, rest assured that
within a short period of time, all traces of their existence will

have disappeared from the files. There will be no record left behind of the few items that have come and gone unnoticed."

"You killed Michael," she said hoarsely, struggling to comprehend the unfolding horror.

"Well," he said equivocally. "I didn't actually pull the trigger. That reminds me. Stand up."

She didn't. Not until he came around from behind the desk and again threatened her with force. Standing there, facing each other, she was thrown off by something she saw in his eyes. His expression softened. His smile was wan, and seemingly full of regret. Bizarrely, she thought he meant to apologize. Her mind raced to figure out what she had misunderstood.

"Close your eyes," he said gently.

She didn't.

"Close your eyes," he repeated more firmly, reaching for her hand. Other than an infrequent handshake, he'd never touched her before. Never like this. The intimacy undid her. She closed her eyes, knowing she would, anyway, for the simple reason that she always did as he asked.

A split second later, something hard was thrust into her palm. Her fingers instinctively wrapped around it. Though they released instantly, it was too late. She gasped at the sight of the gun. Stephen took it back using a handkerchief wrapped around the barrel. Once he was seated at his desk, he told her it was the gun used to kill Michael Leeds, now smudged with her fingerprints. It would provide additional evidence against her should the weapon ever find its way to law enforcement.

His phone rang. He spoke to his assistant. The brief conversation cemented her place in a malignant new reality. Life would go on the same for everyone else. Everyone but her and Michael Leeds.

"What do you expect me to do?" she said coldly once all the treacherous pieces had clicked into place. He'd anticipated her beautifully. She'd played straight into his hand.

His eyes widened in feigned surprise. "Why, your job. That's all I've ever expected. But now that you mention it, there is one thing."

Later that morning, she phoned Michael Leeds's customer and said that Michael had been mistaken. Blackwell Industries did not have the compressor they were looking for.

—

She hadn't set out to survive.

In the beginning, she hadn't expected to. She assumed Stephen would have her killed, just as he had with Michael. But as days passed, then weeks, without an assassin's bullet finding her skull, an unexpected desire to live rose in the depths of her frozen soul.

Since her mother's death years earlier, she had made a habit of visiting a woman named Muriel Jackson. Her mother and Muriel had been colleagues and friends in the University of Chicago's Economics Department. Muriel, retired and living alone, welcomed the visits and the chance to reminisce about a woman they both had loved.

One afternoon a few years earlier, she had stopped by to find Muriel frantic over a medical bill for a recent hospital stay. There was nothing to do but help, so she rolled up her shirtsleeves and set to work sorting through prior bills received and medical claims paid. While sifting through files in a drawer, she chanced upon an envelope labeled simply: "Kim." Inside, among school report cards and a child's drawings, she found the birth certificate and social security card for Muriel's teenage daughter, who had died seventeen years earlier in an accident.

The day she found the envelope and its sad contents, she returned it to its place and continued sorting.

Two years later, she recalled the documents with another purpose.

By then, she knew why she was still alive. Stephen couldn't afford to have her killed—not yet. The death of one healthy young adult in his department due to random urban violence was, sadly, par for the course in a city prone to violence. Two deaths might bring a measure of scrutiny down on the group that he could ill afford. Besides, he had nothing to fear. After all, didn't she always do exactly as he asked?

She made a plan. The week before Easter, she phoned Muriel with an offer to take her to church. Muriel accepted. On Easter morning, after walking Muriel to the car, she begged for the house key on the pretext of needing to use the bathroom. Once there, she raced to the file cabinet and searched the folders she had painstakingly sorted through before, desperately hoping the envelope was still there. It was. She removed the birth certificate and social security card, praying Muriel would never notice they were gone.

On an ordinary day in April two weeks later, she walked out of her office and out of her life. From that day forward, she became Kim Jackson.

—

Her tears had dried in the arid air. A familiar sense of numbness filled her, and she knew herself well enough to be glad. The numbness had saved her once before. Maybe it would again.

Another man was dead.

Her cover was blown.

"I didn't do this," she said.

The words hung ominously in the air.

Between what she had done and what she had left undone, her past coiled viperlike, poised and ready to strike. She could sometimes forget the parade of events that had led her here. But the price of forgetting was always too high.

She knew why the stranger had died that morning. She knew his mistake. He saw what he had expected to see: her. But he hadn't expected the motorcycle. He hadn't known to look for it. He had factored in the known pieces of the equation, cars moving with the light through the intersection, and eliminated every other detail, making a split-second decision that had cost him his life.

She sympathized. A little over a year ago, she, too, had seen what she expected to see in a different intersection in a different city. She was driving when she saw red lights flashing and heard sirens. All of it appeared in the distance, far enough away for her to believe she could safely cross the intersection with the flow of traffic. She never saw the other car, the one the police were pursuing. That car struck hers broadside. Her father, sitting in the passenger seat, had died instantly.

She hadn't recovered from his death, or from her guilt for causing it. His death had marked the beginning of the lesson she hadn't yet adequately learned: worse things can still happen.

She felt a chill run down her spine. She knew something worse would almost surely happen.

A light breeze stirred the desert air. It brushed her cheek and reminded her it was time to stand and move.

Where do I go from here? she thought, looking up. She gazed through pine branches, for once not consoled by the vast blue sky.

CHAPTER 8

In her haste to leave the house hours earlier, Kim had left without money, food, or water. And keys, as she discovered when she returned, coming up empty-handed after a frantic search through her pockets. She had no choice but to ring the doorbell. After a brief delay, Lena opened the door.

"I expected to see you here eventually. Your keys," she said, rolling backward and nodding at the couch where the ring lay. "How are you?"

Kim strode past her. "Thirsty." She went to the kitchen, poured a tall glass of water, drank it, and poured another.

"Sit," Lena said. For emphasis, she tugged a chair back.

"I'm exhausted. I'm going upstairs."

"Sit," Lena repeated. "No doubt you're also hungry. Where have you been?"

Kim debated not answering. On reflection, she decided there was no reason not to. "Up the trail."

"Horse Gulch?"

"Yes."

"That's where Zeke thought you might go."

It was as if days or weeks had passed since she had left the house, not a handful of hours. Kim took stock of her physical condition. Her head felt heavy, but her throat was no longer parched. Yes, she was hungry. She knew it as an intellectual concept, not as a raw feeling in her gut. Lena opened a bag of pretzels and pushed it toward her. "These will do for a start," she said.

Too weary to resist, Kim sank onto a chair. She reached for the bag and took a pretzel stick. With the first bite, the salty wheat taste exploded on her tongue. Her defenses shot, she reached for a handful, watching warily as Lena circled around to the refrigerator and removed several packages and a jar. Sliced turkey, Swiss cheese, bread, mayo.

"For God's sake, make a sandwich," Lena said.

Distrust settled in Kim's eyes. She felt like a caged animal, being tended to at one moment, led to slaughter in the next. She opened the package of bread and removed a single slice. Ignoring Lena's fixed gaze, she set about making a sandwich.

"Do you know the name of the man who died in the accident today?" Lena said.

That answered one question. The man had died. "How would I know that?"

"I don't know. I thought maybe he was an old acquaintance of yours."

Kim made a small sound of disdain. She took a bite of the sandwich and stood to refill her water glass.

"In that case, I'll tell you. His name was Byron Jones, at least according to his driver's license. He had registered under the name at one of our shabbier local motels. Curiously, other identification was found in his room. He had a second Illinois driver's license in the name of Henry Straub. Either name mean anything to you?"

Kim's heart jump-started violently. She gave a short shake of her head, rapidly trying to process the information and, more troublingly, the fact that Lena had it.

"Obviously, at least one of the names is fake. The police are running the guy's prints through AFIS to see what turns up."

"AFIS?" Kim's eyes flickered with interest. She tried to affect simple curiosity but failed badly when her glance darted away on first contact with Lena's brown eyes.

"It's the national fingerprint database. All of the bad guys arrested in the last couple of decades in this country are in it. My buddies on the force expect to find your dead guy there."

My dead guy. Kim resented the implication. Ignoring the feeling, her brain fired into gear. She tried to assimilate what Lena had told her with what she already knew. Stephen Bender had hired a private investigator to keep tabs on her back in Chicago; that's what she had assumed. It was no surprise he would have sent the same man to look for her in Durango.

Tentatively, she tried a second time to make eye contact. "I don't understand. Why does anyone think this man has committed crimes?"

"For starters, he was in possession of a fake ID. That always sends up a red flag. The main reason is he matches the description a local woman gave of a man who attacked her over the weekend."

"What?"

"Don't you read the paper?"

"Not every day."

"A woman was attacked on Saturday night. She left friends at a restaurant to walk home. The guy jumped her, dragged her behind a building, and would have raped her had she not scrambled free and screamed for help."

Kim's jaw dropped. "I hadn't heard."

Lena gave her a long look. "Are you ready to start this conversation over?"

Kim pushed away from the table, thinking she meant to stand up and walk away. The chair legs caught on the linoleum. She faltered when she tried to rise and landed heavily on the wooden seat. "I don't want to have any conversation." She saw the turkey sandwich and, against her better judgment, reached for it and took another bite.

Lena cracked a smile. "Christ, I could really get pissed off at you if I weren't enjoying this so much." She drew an audible breath. "After you left this morning, Zeke told me the guy who died at the scene was following you."

Kim took her time chewing while several key pieces of the day's saga fell into place. Naturally, Lena would have turned the screws on Zeke. Zeke would have had no reason not to answer her questions. Kim only wondered why she hadn't foreseen this long before she returned to the house.

"Zeke could be wrong."

"What the hell is wrong with you? I hope you're being extraordinarily stupid because you spent the day getting your brain fried. Zeke may have saved you from a fate you definitely did not want to suffer at the hands of Byron Jones or whoever the hell that guy really was." Lena pulled something out of her back pocket. She unfolded the single sheet and slid it across the table.

Kim shivered the moment she saw it. It was a grainy black-and-white copy of a photograph—of her. It had been taken a year ago at a business meeting. In the original, she had stood in a line of five that included Stephen Bender. The three people to her left and the one on the right had been cut away. Her image had been pasted onto another page and photocopied. The picture showed her as a polished professional, wearing a business suit, hair perfectly trimmed, smiling the smile of accomplishment, easy in this arena with the others—who weren't there.

"That's not me."

"The hell it isn't."

Kim put the dishes in the sink. She returned the packages of food to the refrigerator and headed out of the room. "I'd like to have dinner at six tonight," Lena said. "There's fresh fish to grill and new potatoes. Salad is left from last night. There's enough for us both."

"Thank you. I doubt if I'll be hungry."

In a voice of uncommon gentleness, Lena said, "Get some rest, Kim. I'll see you later."

Upstairs, Kim took a shower. Afterward, she sprawled on the bed, her mind spinning over the day's events. She cringed, recalling the photograph and seeing the ghost of her soul, dressed smartly and off doing the job she was trained to do.

"Think," she whispered harshly.

She had been a fool to stay in Durango. There was no doubt now. Stephen would stop at nothing to find her. As for Lena—Kim laughed. Lena might think she was on to something. She might have resurrected her role as a detective for one afternoon. Kim couldn't worry about what Lena might or might not learn in any feeble inquiry she managed to make. Lena was not now, and never would be, her real enemy. Instead, Kim focused on Byron Jones. The man had been following her when he died. There was some chance he hadn't made a positive identification, and a better chance he hadn't learned the alias she was living under.

She fell asleep worrying about the future. When she awoke an hour later, she couldn't bear to sit still. She went downstairs to begin preparing dinner. Lena didn't join her until the fish was ready to go on the grill. Kim set a single place at the patio table. When Lena saw it, she said, "Set another place. Please. I promise not to ask more questions."

Kim did as she was asked. She could sit there. She didn't have to eat. And she certainly was under no obligation to answer any questions.

But when the food reached the table, she helped herself to a serving. At first, she refused when Lena encouraged her to pour a glass of wine. Then she did. Whether it was the food, the alcohol, or Lena's strange new air of granting space, Kim felt the tense knots in the back of her neck begin to loosen.

The doorbell rang as they were finishing dinner. Unaccustomed to hearing it, Kim jumped. "I'll get it," Lena said.

Kim stacked plates and deposited the load in the kitchen sink. Voices approaching from the other room startled her.

"See, I told you," Jeremy declared as he left the hallway and entered the kitchen. "Hey, Kim," he said. Zeke was behind him. To his brother, Jeremy added, "I told you she would be fine."

Kim went straight to Zeke and pulled him close in a hug. "Hi, Zeke. Sorry I ran out on you earlier today."

"Are you okay?" Zeke said.

"Yes, I'm okay. Are you?"

He nodded.

Lena followed the brothers into the kitchen. "Kim, don't worry about cleaning up. All three of you, go out and sit on the patio."

It was yet another bizarre act of kindness. Kim didn't think she could take much more.

"Uh, we can't stay," Jeremy said. "We just wanted to come by. Zeke needed to see if Kim was okay." He reversed direction as abruptly as he had made his first unexpected appearance. His younger brother followed.

At the front door, Zeke turned to Kim. In a hopeful voice, he said, "Are you coming over tonight?"

"Not tonight, Zeke. I'll come over another night. Soon. I promise."

"Okay. I'll see you when you come over." There was something searching in his parting glance, something Kim couldn't read. With a heavy heart, she watched the door close behind the brothers, knowing the younger had done her a service she could never repay.

When she turned away, she was unprepared to find Lena still there.

"Are you ready to talk now?"

"There's nothing to talk about. Why can't you leave me alone?" Kim said sharply.

"Fine. I'll leave you alone. You know where to find me if you change your mind." Lena spun toward her suite and disappeared inside.

Kim had no doubt about what was going to happen next. She was leaving Durango. She had no choice now but to start over someplace new. It was only a matter of deciding where, and when, to go. She couldn't leave tonight. She couldn't get into her safe-deposit box until morning. Furiously, she considered aborting her escape plan and heading directly for Chicago. Obviously, Stephen considered her a threat. Her best move might be to exploit an advantage while she had one.

Unable to stop thinking, she thoroughly cleaned the kitchen and swept the patio. Upstairs, the mental barrage continued. She sat on the bed clasping and unclasping a set of keys ordinarily kept in a dresser drawer. Two opened safe-deposit boxes; one, a padlock. The fourth was a fob for her real car, the maroon Lexus sedan she'd driven from Chicago. The Lexus was in Montrose, Colorado, locked inside a self-storage unit. Registered in her real name, the car was the sole link to her past, and posed much too great a risk to drive. She laughed. Before leaving Montrose, she'd acquired a different car, a ten-year-old baby-blue Cadillac, not her style at all. The Cadillac had come to her as a gift from a friend, and after all, beggars couldn't be choosers.

Her eyes strayed to the closet where her four business suits hung in dry-cleaning bags. One was the suit she had been wearing in the photo currently in Lena's possession. She should get rid of those clothes. Except, they'd never fit in a safe-deposit box, she thought, laughing a strange, giddy laugh at the image of herself attempting to squeeze the garments into a gunmetal-gray box. All of her life shut in steel boxes. The box in this town. An identical one in the last town. Nor could she forget the constant, the box in Chicago holding papers proving her real identity.

She sat in the padded chair at the window overlooking a quiet western street. She searched for a man in the shadows, a man whose mission was to kill her. And then what? Slice off a hand or an ear to take to Stephen as proof of her demise?

That man was dead. She could sit there for as long as she liked, waiting. He would not be back.

But the question remained: Who would come in his place?

CHAPTER 9

Lena came into the kitchen earlier than usual the next day. "Good morning. Sleep well?" she said.

"Fine," Kim muttered, concentrating on chopping an apple to add to a bowl of berries and sliced banana.

"Have you read the paper yet?"

"No time."

"Read it. I'll get myself a cup of coffee. Oh, there's no coffee, is there?" She glanced at the pot, which was made as usual, then looked up with a question.

"I bought a bag yesterday. Before everything happened."

"Great. I'll reimburse you. Now go read."

Kim picked up the paper and went to sit on the patio. The morning's lead story confirmed what she already knew. The pedestrian who died at the scene was identified as Byron Jones. His death was reported as an accident. Multiple eyewitnesses testified to the fact that he had dashed across the intersection against the light. He would have escaped harm but for the motorcyclist turning out from the alley and flowing with traffic, as he had every legal right to do. The motorcyclist suffered a dislocated shoulder and serious abrasions along one side of his body. The driver of the oncoming car was uninjured.

The article reported that Byron Jones matched the description of a man wanted for questioning in connection with an assault on a local woman recently. The woman's name was not given. More importantly, no other names were mentioned.

Kim knew it was significant that her part in the events had gone unreported. She hadn't consciously considered the detail, but now felt a twinge of hope.

"What do you think?" Lena said.

Kim stood up abruptly. She hadn't heard Lena come outside. "It's what you told me yesterday. What would you like for breakfast?"

"Half a bagel. And the fruit salad."

While the bagel toasted, Kim delivered the fruit salad to the table. "Are you going to work this morning?" Lena said.

"Yes."

Kim ate in the kitchen, as was her custom. Lena finished breakfast quickly. "I'll need help getting dressed this morning," she said when she came inside. "Give me fifteen minutes, then come to my suite."

She didn't wait for an answer. Kim watched her depart. Helping Lena dress had been in the job description when she was hired. This was the first time Lena had requested assistance.

At the appointed time, Kim stood at the partially open door to the suite, unsure whether to knock. She glanced to her right, down the length of dark paneling erected where no wall should be. Ten feet from where she stood, it cornered into an L that ran horizontally behind the couch to the staircase, cutting the living room in half. The wall blocked access to the original dining room. The area behind the wall was Lena's private suite. She had detailed the remodeling specifications from a hospital bed when she knew she wasn't coming home to live alone.

Kim gave up guessing what she was supposed to do. She pushed open the door and went in.

She knew the layout—bedroom, bath, and den—from cleaning the rooms. She found Lena in the bathroom, seated on a bench, wearing only underwear and a bra, still fumbling with the latter's front clasp.

"There's a reason I don't wear the damn things. Would you mind?" she said.

Kim overcame her aversion to touching both Lena and the garment. She leaned over and finished the job.

"The shirt I want is hanging in my closet. It's pushed away from the others. There's a pair of black jeans on the bed."

Kim got the clothes and returned. Moving robotically, she helped Lena with the shirt, then buttoned each button. Lena could have accomplished the task, with a mighty effort and after exhausting a great deal of time. The problem was her left arm. Her elbow had been badly damaged by a gunshot that left her arm muscles weak and her hand unable to grip. The injury prevented her from doing countless simple things, such as clipping her own fingernails. Or gripping the waistband of a stiff pair of denim jeans and pulling them on. It was why she ordinarily wore loose-banded sweatpants or shorts. Her shattered elbow explained why she needed in-home help.

Kim retrieved a pair of sandals from the closet and was dismissed without a word of explanation or complaint.

She went upstairs to get ready for work. The doorbell rang while she was there. She came downstairs to the sound of voices and the presence of a female police officer dressed in uniform and a man wearing plain clothes. Lena's insistence on her choice of attire this morning suddenly made a world of sense.

"Kim, do you have a minute?" Lena said.

Kim descended the last step and approached the trio.

"Mark, Sheila, I'd like you to meet Kim Jackson. Kim, this is Detective Mark Stankowicz and Officer Sheila Moss."

Kim walked forward and shook each officer's hand.

"Sorry to hear you were on Main yesterday morning," Stankowicz said. "That was a lousy thing to see."

Kim nodded. She quickly noted the neutral expression on the man's good-looking face. He had dark curly hair, and easily stood at six feet. His age seemed approximately the same as Lena's, late thirties.

Sheila Moss, younger, was nearly as tall as her partner. She had dark-blond hair, tied back, and a "don't mess with me" edge etched into her otherwise attractive features. Kim wondered if the look masked insecurity.

Lena broke the silence. "It's not her," she said curtly. "Look at the picture."

"Shit, Lena," Stankowicz said. "Leave this to us." In a more controlled voice, he said, "Miss Jackson, I need to ask you a few questions." He pulled a photo from his shirt pocket. "Do you recognize this man?"

Kim took a quick glance. The man in the picture appeared to be in his forties. He hadn't shaved in several days. He didn't look like the face of evil; rather, he looked like a guy who was chronically down on his luck. "I've never seen him before."

"This is a photo of the man who died in the accident yesterday."

"Did you find out his name?" Lena said.

The senior officer shot her a warning look. "Yeah, we found out his name." To Kim, he said, "He was calling himself Byron Jones. His real name is Fred Hansen. He served time in Florida on a conviction for aggravated rape. Does that name mean anything to you?"

"No."

Sheila spoke. "We found a photo of a woman who resembles you in Hansen's vehicle. Obviously, he's not going to be a problem for anyone ever again. But we're curious why he was looking for you, or for someone who looks like you."

Lena pulled the photo from her back pocket. "It's not her," she said, opening up the folded page. "Look at the damn picture. Turn sideways, Kim. Not to the right, to the left. Forehead's different. And the chin."

Kim sensed more than saw the police officers squinting to make sense of Lena's comments. To her, they made no sense. It was clearly a picture of her, albeit a grainy reproduction. Beyond that, she couldn't imagine why Lena was rushing to her defense.

"Well, it doesn't matter," Stankowicz said. "If the guy was stalking you, you're out of danger now."

Kim kept her expression even. The officers thought he'd been a stalker. The explanation was simple, and perfect.

"What else have you found out about him?" Lena said.

"By all indications, the guy was in town alone," Sheila Moss said. "He checked into the motel last Thursday. Paid cash. Spent his afternoons drinking with some locals down at the Star. He seemed to fit in real well with some of our good redneck buddies in town."

"His car. His motel room," Lena prodded. "Did he have a cell phone? Any names or addresses on him?"

Stankowicz's features tightened. "No cell phone. Nothing. The addresses on his IDs are false. A woman who was attacked off of Junction last week picked his picture out of a photo lineup. We're expecting his DNA to match blood found beneath her fingernails."

"Miss Jackson, how long have you been in Durango?" Sheila Moss said.

"A month."

"Where were you living before that?"

"In Montrose, Colorado."

"How long were you there?"

"Three months."

"And before that, where did you live?"

Kim took a chance. A chance that whatever she said wouldn't matter. "Minneapolis. I lived there until I moved to Colorado this past spring." The lie slid easily from her lips.

Sheila leveled a long look on her. Then her mouth twisted in a frown and she looked at Lena. "Doesn't matter," she said flatly. "You're right about that."

Kim made the leap. It didn't matter whether she had any previous connection to Byron Jones or Fred Hansen or whatever other name the man had used.

The police officers had no more questions. They thanked Kim for her time. She left through the back door to go to work. She told herself the visit was nothing more than standard police procedure. The officers were simply trying to wrap up any loose ends in a pedestrian fatality.

She repeated the explanation while pedaling the five miles between home and work. No matter how many times she said the words, she couldn't quite make herself believe them.

CHAPTER 10

Trina greeted Kim with a peevish glare when she arrived at work. Just as happy to skip pleasantries, Kim scooted through the entryway, noting in passing that Skip Legrand wasn't in. She had no sooner turned the corner into the hallway when Trina jumped up and followed her, puppy-dog-like, to the back office, all the while demanding to know why she hadn't come in yesterday. At the same time, she informed her that Skip thought she was a flake and wanted to fire her.

"I'd have to be half dead to miss work on my second day at a new job," she ended shrilly.

Kim sank onto the creaky chair. She flipped the switch to turn on the computer. Her eyes strayed to the inbox. A handwritten note from Skip lay on top of a disorganized pile of papers. She reached for it. He wanted to see a construction scheduling report. It didn't say anything about wanting to fire her.

She was muddling through ideas about how to create the report, Trina already forgotten, when the phone rang. "Don't you have to get that?" she said. Trina stood there glowering, dressed in a dress too short and tight. Long strands of hair dangled in front of an overly made-up face.

In a stroke of defiance, she reached for the phone on Kim's desk. Her voice turned sappy sweet as she spoke.

Kim didn't notice when she left.

She settled in to work and spent the next several hours learning her way around the system's reporting program. Unsure exactly how detailed a report Skip wanted, she produced two versions and satisfied herself knowing that if he wanted something else, she could create it. Unless he really did consider her a flake and was intent on firing her at his earliest convenience.

The thought didn't worry her as much as it might have. If Skip fired her, it would save her the trouble of quitting. Which she would likely be doing soon anyway.

Trina left for lunch at noon. A few minutes later, Kim heard the click of the front door and assumed her coworker had returned. When she went to check on who was there, she found Skip in his office.

"Oh, hi," she said to the man whom she had met only once. On first impression, Skip wasn't as easygoing as his brother-in-law, Dennis Royal. Skip was a ruddy-complexioned man who spent as little time as possible at his desk. She didn't think he was shy, certainly not around women, but he had an air of impatience for his office staff and their questions. "I have the report you wanted."

"Great."

She hesitated, waiting to be chewed out for yesterday's absence. Skip didn't say a word. Kim realized he was waiting for the report, still on her desk. She went to get it, and only after handing it over did she berate herself for having believed a word Trina said.

She spent the rest of the day catching up on two days' worth of work. Jeannette Winchester had been explicit during training: Kim was expected to keep the computer system current with invoices and purchase orders, employee time cards and company expenses. She would need to run payroll and produce reports on request. Some bills would need to be paid. Skip would direct her on that. Anything that came across her desk that didn't fall into one of those categories should be ignored. Jeannette was only going to be absent for six weeks. She would deal with the exceptions when she returned.

Throughout the day, Kim focused on work, periodically managing to forget the dark cloud hanging over her. By the time she left late in the afternoon, she had come to one clear decision. There was a woman in town she needed to talk to.

—

She found Caitlin, Jeremy's ex-girlfriend, at the downtown bar where she worked. "Hey," she said, coming up behind the woman with long braided hair and cool green eyes. Caitlin was chatting with a coworker at the back of the dimly lit room. Happy hour wasn't in full swing yet, and the crowd was light.

Warmth drained from Caitlin's expression.

"I wanted to ask you something," Kim said, pointedly interrupting the girl talk. The other woman took the hint and left. "I heard some guy was around last week, flashing a picture of someone who looked like me."

Caitlin started to turn away. "That's right. At first, I thought I saw a resemblance. Then I wasn't sure." She glanced around the bar as if looking for something urgent she needed to do.

Kim took a step closer. "What did you tell him?"

A startled look flashed in Caitlin's eyes. Kim almost smiled. Though she had virtually no history with the woman, she didn't like her. It wasn't just because Caitlin was Jeremy's ex. She was part of a group of Jeremy's friends that included three grungy-looking guys and two other attractive, insolent women. Kim and Jeremy had met up with the group a couple of times for beers. For her part, it hadn't been a dazzling social success. It likely explained why she hadn't been invited along on the weekend camping trip.

Speaking in a rush, Caitlin said, "I guess I must have nodded or something 'cause the guy said even if I wasn't sure, he'd appreciate any help I could give him. He said he was a private investigator working for your brother. He said there was some kind of family emergency and he really needed to find you."

Kim stared, incredulous that Caitlin had bought the story.

"I probably shouldn't have said anything," Caitlin blurted out. "But I'd just come in for my shift and was talking to Ellie up front. Otherwise, I'd never have seen the guy. It didn't seem like a big deal."

Kim's expression hardened. She almost said it. *Would you have wanted me to give information about you to any stranger, let alone to a seedy-looking asshole who only had a fragment of a photo in his possession?* She pressed her advantage. "Do you remember exactly what you told him?"

"Look, don't get so worked up. I told the guy to talk to Jeremy. I told him Jeremy worked at Wilderness Outfitters. That's all I said. I figured Jeremy would know if it was you."

Kim took a chance. She doubted it would matter but hoped Caitlin would never dwell on the oddity of the next question. "Did you mention my name?"

Caitlin flushed. A deep red spread from her neck into her face. "Yes, except I screwed up. I told him your name was Cam. I'm not good with names," she said, ending in embarrassment.

Kim nearly smiled. "Thanks, Caitlin."

—

Lena was sitting on the patio when Kim came through the back gate a short while later. There was a bottle of beer on the table. "Care to join me?" she said, pointing at the bottle.

"Thanks. No."

"How was your day?"

Kim appraised the woman in the wheelchair. Lena had changed out of her dress-up clothes from this morning into her usual yoga-style wear—cotton slacks and a shirt. Her hair was carefully combed. Her brown eyes were clear. Kim couldn't get a read on her mood.

"Fine."

"I suppose almost anything would have been an improvement over yesterday."

"I'm going upstairs. I'll be down later to start dinner."

"Who's after you, Kim?" Lena called to her back. "It wasn't a man who called himself Byron Jones, that's for damn sure. So who is it?"

Kim whirled around. "Shut up with your questions! There's no one."

"Liar. Who is it?" Lena's expression was stone-cold sober. It was as though in the space of a heartbeat she had become a different woman.

"I'm quitting! Consider this your notice. Find someone else to put up with your bullshit."

Lena didn't react. In a voice colder and more dangerous, she said, "You're afraid of someone. It's written all over you. So who is it? What does he want from you?"

Kim felt the blood drain from her face. Enraged, she shouted back, "Who shot you, Lena? Who set up the ambush? You want the hard questions? Deal with your own and leave me out of it!"

Lena snickered. Given the enormity of what Kim had hurled at her, she found Lena's minimal response especially chilling.

Their eyes locked in a deadly embrace. Neither broke contact. Neither spoke. As the moment lengthened and the sparks of tension shot like flint off Lena's eyes, Kim grew strangely calm. She took a perverse sense of pleasure in the connection.

Lena blinked first. "What do you know about it?" she said derisively.

"Only what I read in the papers."

"There's nothing in the papers."

"There was."

Another beat passed. Longer than a heartbeat, it might have been the beat of a distant drum, heralding invaders.

"I believe I will have that beer," Kim said. She went to the refrigerator and removed a bottle, twisted off the cap, and tossed it into the corner trash can. Outside, she joined Lena at the table. She took a pull from the bottle, then swept dangling strands of hair away from her eyes. "What do I know about it? This is what I know. Whoever's responsible for shooting you is no one who has yet been investigated. Or even named as a suspect. All solid leads were exhausted early. Since then, it's been the same old, same old, dusted off and paraded out every so often only to restate the original conclusion: no leads into the shooting of a decorated Durango police officer. I can't imagine how frustrated you must feel about that."

Lena slammed her hand on the table. "You can't imagine a damn thing!"

"You're right. I can't. But I sincerely doubt whether Douglas Parks or Rodney Mayhew is responsible. Now, Gary Dunkirk, I don't know about him. Apparently no one does. He hasn't been seen in a while."

Lena stared long and hard. "How do you know those names?"

"I told you. I read about it."

Kim didn't bother to explain that she had spent several hours in the library scrolling through digital archives. She didn't confess to having taken pages of notes. Last weekend, with plenty of time on her hands, she had returned to the library to read the Larson article, "Circle of Enemies." The piece was a gold mine of information about the men who had been investigated in the wake of Lena's shooting. It had left her hungry to know more. The librarian on duty during Kim's second trip had proffered another interesting tidbit: Rich Larson had wanted to do an in-depth profile on Lena. Lena had refused to meet with him.

"Why are you so sure about Parks and Mayhew?" Lena said.

"They aren't smart enough. They would have made mistakes. I'm sure more is known in the department about your case than was reported in the press, but it's clear no obvious mistakes were made by whoever orchestrated this. Too much time has passed. He would have been found by now."

"I've never ruled out Parks or Mayhew."

"Maybe not, but you must have a longer list of suspects."

"What the hell is this to you? Who are you?"

Kim ignored the second question. "I don't know what it is to me. Nothing, really. I didn't think about it at first. Then, when I read about it, it felt wrong. Like something was missed."

Her remark set off a maelstrom of emotion in the other woman. "Nothing was missed, you bitch! Every lead was followed. Every rock was turned over, and guess what? Nothing crawled out. The investigation was not flawed! Don't you dare think my guys on the force didn't break their butts trying to find out who did this to me 'cause, guess what? Every one of them knows they take the same risk every damn time they get behind the wheel of a patrol car, every damn time they pull somebody over and get out to see what idiot is driving the other car."

Kim finished her beer. She had swallowed it quickly and felt buzzed. "I never meant to suggest the investigation was flawed. On the contrary, I'm suggesting your enemy is formidable. And he is someone you know." She took a chance and looked over. "It was either for something you had already done, or to stop you from something you were about to do. Do you have any idea which it was?"

"Screw you." Lena pulled back from the table and turned away.

"When is your hearing?" Kim said. "Middle of October? A final report will be drawn up then, which will either exonerate your actions that night, or not. Either way, it affects the basis of your termination. And your settlement."

"There can't be a final report until all of the facts are in."

"All of the facts may never be in. How many open cases does the department have on file, going back how many years?"

"There's no reason to think the final report will come out of that hearing. As I said, all the facts aren't in."

"So, what, that gives you two months to lasso in at least a few of these alleged facts? What are you going to do about it?"

"What the hell do you think I can do about it?" Lena threw her hands in the air. "Get out in the trenches and run the assholes to the ground? Well, sorry. There was a time when I could do that, but I have to depend on someone else to do the work for me now."

"And how does that make you feel?"

"How do I feel?" Lena clenched her fists so hard, her knuckles turned white. She spat out the words, "You insane bitch! How do you think I feel? Get out of here! Get out of my house!"

Kim stood up. "I said I was leaving anyway."

Lena followed her into the living room. When Kim took the first step toward the second floor, Lena yelled, "You're not going anywhere. Get back here!"

Kim turned around. She was taken aback by the violence of color in Lena's face. Apoplectic, her face was beet red and taut with tension. "Who the hell are you?" Lena shouted.

"I'm no one," Kim repeated. She turned and trudged heavily up the stairs, where she fell into the chair at the window in her bedroom and sat looking out, unaware of time passing.

CHAPTER 11

"I don't want you to quit."

Lena made the quiet statement midway through breakfast on the patio the next morning. Standing behind her holding a coffeepot, Kim waited to hear more. When nothing followed, she gave up and took the pot inside.

She rinsed plates in the sink and loaded the dishwasher, puzzling over Lena's pronouncement. She debated pressing for an explanation, doubting she would get one. Besides, she thought she knew part of the answer. Lena had gone through five live-in aides in two months before Kim moved in. Each of her predecessors had quit. The social worker handling Lena's staffing needs told Kim that Lena had exhausted the ranks of available help in town. It was why she had been hired so easily.

She topped off her coffee cup and went outside. "Then I suppose we need to negotiate."

"I can't pay you more money."

"I'm not interested in more money."

Lena, who once would have reacted with pure scorn, quietly said, "Then what do you want?"

In no hurry, Kim admired Zeke's handiwork in the yard. The lawn was neatly trimmed; the twin flower beds on either side of the walkway were picked free of weeds. Tall blossoms of purple and orange intermingled behind the ground cover of pink petunias well past the height of their color.

Kim drew a long breath. She allowed her gaze to drift beyond the neatly kept yard to the wooden fence at the perimeter, all the while poignantly aware of the utter improbability of this conversation.

"What do I want? Now that's an interesting question."

They might have been two poker players sitting at a card table, hands seemingly resting carelessly across their mouths, concealing any untoward twitch. Neither her hand nor Lena's was anywhere in sight, but Kim felt the enormity of their mutual bluff.

"All right, I'll tell you what I want," she said. "I want you to teach me a few things about doing investigative work. Besides that, I want access to your contacts at the police department."

"You what?" Lena's voice pitched sharply.

Kim checked her faint smile, warmed by the return of familiarity. She would have hated for things between them to change much. "You heard what I said."

Birds twittered in the branches high above the yard. A plane droned in the distance. Otherwise, the morning was still.

"I heard what you said. I don't have a clue what you're asking. Or why."

Kim drank her coffee. She credited Lena with greater skills of perception than she had demonstrated thus far in their brief arbitration. She waited for her to put it together.

It was Lena's turn to sigh quietly. When she spoke next, her voice was tinged with an accent that Kim had never heard. It was without artifice, without inflection. It was the voice of a woman who had suffered the catastrophic destruction of the core of who she was yet reached beyond that into a reservoir of strength.

"For nearly a year and a half, I've done everything in my power to put my life on the force behind me. In all that time, I never believed I had any other choice. Two days ago, when you and Zeke burst into this house, seventeen months of discipline went down the toilet. I can't pretend. I won't pretend. I want my life back, however I can get it. It starts with solving my own case. You made that perfectly clear last night." She paused. "Only, I'm not sure how I'll be able to do that."

Kim leapt to the opening. "Then let's start there. Walk me through it. Tell me what you would do. Maybe I'll be able to do some part of it for you. Maybe not. But at least—"

Lena, incredulous, interrupted her. "You idiot! You don't have a clue what you're talking about. This is my life we're talking about, not some textbook case file. I refuse to let what happened to me be simplified or degraded by you or anyone else. Get out of here. Get the hell out of this house. Leave me alone."

Kim sat there placidly. She felt duly chastened but was not willing to turn her back on the opportunity. "I was about to say that maybe by talking about what happened, you'll see it differently. Fit the pieces together differently. Who knows, maybe the evidence itself has changed." She started toward the kitchen, pausing before passing through the screen door. "Whatever it was you were on to, or about to uncover, maybe it's happened by now."

She left Lena sitting on the patio in silence.

—

At work, Kim gave scarcely half her attention to the stack of problem documents she had set aside for the day. She resolved two by dint of poking through computer records to fill in missing information. Next, she picked up an invoice for a load of concrete that had been delivered to a customer named Patterson. The single page had all the earmarks of a legitimate bill. Yet twenty minutes spent searching failed to turn up any such customer. She'd be damned if she'd go crawling to Trina for help this early in the morning.

She gazed around the cluttered room. The brown paneled walls were scarred and stained in spots. Two cheap posters— one showing the glitter of Las Vegas, the other, a Hawaiian beach—failed to brighten the drab atmosphere. Jeannette had visited the former, according to Trina. A vacation on the latter was her dream.

The carpet and walls felt grungy with ground-in dirt. One small window looked out on the rear lot. A floor fan stood idle.

This wasn't what she'd had in mind when she fled Chicago, she told herself, recognizing the lie as soon as it was out. More to the point, this was exactly what she had expected her professional life would be: dull, empty, undemanding. Except she had expected to claw her way into a lowly job in Los Angeles or San Diego. She had pictured herself living in a run-down apartment in an urban nightmare, known to no one.

Durango was a world away from that.

She tossed a pen on the pile of disordered papers and gave up the pretense of working. Swiveling away from the open doorway, she sank into the chair, indifferent to whether Trina found her idling away company time. The faint pressure building behind her forehead increased to a persistent ache. She massaged her temples, trying to relieve it.

A man was dead. Her cover might be blown. Meanwhile, she was sitting in a lousy office pushing papers.

What do you want? she asked herself, repeating Lena's question from earlier that morning.

For one slender moment, the vicious whirlwind of indecision stopped. Without expecting it, she knew the answer. She wanted to go back to Chicago. She wanted to bring Stephen Bender to justice. She wanted to clear her name. In order to do that, several things had to happen. For starters, she had to stay alive.

She settled into a view of the new playing field. She thought back to every detail she could recall about the man who had once been her boss. The first insight brought a surprising flicker of hope. Stephen was not a micromanager. He hired competent people and expected each to do his or her job. He wanted results, not routine updates about a work-in-progress.

He would not have wanted Byron Jones, a convicted criminal, to contact him with anything less than solid information.

No cell phone had been found in Jones's possession. He hadn't had any names or phone numbers on him. He hadn't made any phone calls from his motel room.

For the first time, Kim allowed herself to consider the possibility that Stephen hadn't learned that Jones had found her. She sat with the thought a moment, sorting out the implications. Then, since it was nothing she could be certain of, she chased it away and returned to studying the next set of moves he might make.

Eventually, Stephen would learn of Jones's death. He might tire of waiting for Jones to call with news either that he had found her or not. When that phone call didn't come, Stephen might take to reading the online version of the *Durango Herald* for references to Jones. Or to her. He might be reading it anyway out of simple curiosity for the place where he now believed he would find her. Either way, he would learn that Jones had died on the street, but he wouldn't learn, at least not from any news article, that Jones had been less than thirty feet from her when he was struck and killed.

Kim wished she could see the heat rise in Stephen when he learned that his hired man had played loose in Durango and attacked a woman. She didn't believe he would risk associating himself with the criminal Byron Jones. He wouldn't come calling, seeking clarification from police or witnesses as to what had gone down the day Jones died. And if he couldn't establish the link from Jones to her—she was safe. Until he sent someone else.

A smile spread across her face. She warned herself not to lower her guard. But the smile remained, nonetheless.

There was more to think about. One slip of an opening remained through which Stephen might yet learn of her existence. The police report. The police had her photo, though as far as she knew, no one had officially pinned her name to the picture. That didn't mean her name and address wouldn't be jotted down in the file as a person of possible interest to Byron Jones when he died.

Which brought her back to Lena.

With a bitter sense of remorse, Kim realized the police never would have known about her had Lena not contacted them. It was a bad break, but it might not prove devastating. The fact remained that her name might not make it into the police file. It would mean everything to know that, and also to know if, or when, an out-of-town stranger were to contact the department requesting information about the accident in which Jones died.

Lena would be able to get that information.

Profound heaviness settled over Kim as she gauged the risks of playing this dangerous game with her ex-cop landlady. The negatives piled up on both sides of the argument. If she left Durango, she would never know whether her cover had been blown. If she stayed—

Lena could turn on her.

She didn't like her odds either way.

The longer she thought about it, she knew she didn't have a choice. Staying in Durango was a chance she had to take.

CHAPTER 12

"Is she there?" he said into the phone.

Listening, he smiled. After putting up with more details than he wanted to hear—where she was sitting, what she was wearing—he ended the call with a short, "See you in a few."

It took him five minutes to drive from his office to the restaurant. He walked in, greeted the maître d' with a handshake, and brushed off the offer of a table. He went straight to the bar. Tonight, all he wanted was Scotch and eye candy.

From his perch on the barstool, he could see her reflection in the mirror. She sat at a table behind him, facing into the room, eating her dinner. Looked like a petite filet and baked potato. She was cutting small bites and eating slowly. *Good,* he thought.

The bartender, who'd given him the info on the girl, gave her an approving nod. Ignoring the dolt, he took a swallow of Scotch and felt the slow burn erase everything except his pleasure in the moment.

It was too early to start another game. Usually he waited a couple of months to pick out his next toy. Problem was, he'd spotted this one *before* he'd played out the last round. And it was summer. He hadn't seen this girl until a few weeks ago. She might not stay around long. Not if she was a college kid.

He sat up straighter and turned in both directions, looking for the waitress. It was less than a week since their interlude, as he liked to call it. He smiled, remembering the fun they'd had. Well, he'd had fun. She'd had fun, too, ultimately. He didn't see her and figured she must not be working tonight. Just as well.

He checked out the new girl in the mirror. She was young, blond, and drop-dead gorgeous. She looked like she *belonged*, which was odd, because this restaurant didn't seem like her kind of place. It had been in Durango forever. It was a guy's place, a gentlemen's club, practically. He wondered if she was a James Bond kind of woman: cool and sophisticated, at home in a man's world.

Judging by her age, she was probably a college kid. Or maybe a trust-fund kid.

The latter thought stopped him. He didn't want to get messed up with someone who had money or a rich daddy who did. Of course, he wouldn't know that until he got to know her better.

She raised her head. By chance, she was looking straight at his back. He could see her perfectly. She was too far away to catch his eye in the glass. His pulse quickened. She was even better looking than he'd realized. Long blond hair, great cheekbones, and—

Something about her eyes. *Jesus Christ*, he thought. He felt a jolt in his gut. She was the one he'd been waiting for.

She glanced away and reached for her purse. Without thinking, he swiveled off the barstool and walked toward her. Halfway there, he came to his senses and walked by without giving her a look. He passed the table and went to the restroom.

When he came back, she was gone.

He dropped a couple of bills on the bar, reached for his glass, and killed the Scotch in one swallow. He burst through the door and nearly crashed into her. She was standing under the canopy, fooling with a pack of cigarettes. She had one out, not lit. She rolled it between her fingers and tapped the end against the pack's cellophane wrapping.

"Evening," he greeted, catching his breath.

She gave a curt nod. "Damn things," she said, shaking her head at the cigarette. With a rough move, she jabbed it back inside the pack.

"I quit some years ago," he said. "Nasty habit."

She swung her head back. Her long hair followed, exposing her classy profile. She had smoky-gray eyes and an oval face. Her lips were full, her chin was soft. She was a dream.

"I'm still trying to quit," she said, frowning. "Worst time for me is right after a nice meal."

"Would you care to have a drink?" he said. "Might help take your mind off the urge."

For a fraction of a second, she searched his face in the twilight. He guessed she was too young to recognize him, or to know of his sterling reputation in town. She didn't waste time making up her mind. "Why not?" She tossed the cigarette pack in her purse.

They went to a bar around the corner. He led her to a pair of open seats and pulled a chair out. "What's your pleasure?" he said.

"Jack and Coke."

He smiled. He liked this girl's style. He ordered her drink and a Scotch for himself.

"By the way, I'm Paul Kennerly," he said.

"Nice to meet you, Paul. My name's Jaye Dewey."

CHAPTER 13

"Douglas Parks," Lena stated without preamble. "What do you know about him?"

Kim looked up from a cooking magazine, open to a recipe for a roasted vegetable casserole. A pad with a grocery list lay alongside it. She hadn't heard Lena come into the kitchen. Without missing a beat, she said, "You set Parks up in a gun-selling sting. He was selling stolen guns. He had some idea of creating his own mini-militia. The problem was he stole the guns in the first place, then sold them to idiots who didn't know any better. Denny DeAngelo was your informant. He wore a wire for the deal. You and about six other cops broke in on the transaction, nailing Parks with enough stolen weapons to send him away for ten years."

Lena made a sound of contempt. "We never got him on the robberies. Still pisses me off."

Kim exhaled softly, wondering whether she had passed a first test.

Lena got a glass of water from the tap on the refrigerator. "Parks went away, but DeAngelo's mother's place burned down. We never could prove that connection. It wasn't right."

"But it indicated a man intent on revenge," Kim said. "Which is why Parks received so much attention by Durango investigators and the Colorado Bureau of Investigation after you were shot."

Lena cringed at the bald reference to the event. Whatever she felt, she moved past it. "Douglas Parks was a stringy-haired loudmouth at the center of a nasty group of local boys. They were apt to complain a lot. About tourists and the assholes running the state in Denver who don't know shit about what goes on out here. But mostly, they complained about the flood of new people moving in, jacking up land prices. As if they could have bought land themselves. Not a one of them ever held a steady job. If they had beer money for the night, they counted themselves wealthy men. Those were the guys Parks brought into his circle."

The silence weighed heavily when she stopped talking. Kim allowed it to settle before she said, "Did you ever think Douglas Parks had anything to do with your assault?"

"I never ruled him out. He was angry enough to do it. I can't take full responsibility for the success of the sting, but I did get most of the credit. He would have blamed me."

Loath to break the spell, Kim stood up anyway. She passed Lena, who silently watched her, and walked into the living room. She found her backpack on the steps, and the notebook she was looking for inside. In the kitchen, she opened it and scanned her notes. The trial that had netted a conviction for Douglas Parks happened a year before Lena's shooting. Denny DeAngelo's mother's house burned less than two months after the trial. Mulling over the timing, she said, "I don't see Parks waiting a full year to take his revenge, if that was his intent. Also, I don't see why he wouldn't have had you killed outright."

"Thank you very much," Lena said sarcastically, faintly amused. Kim glanced over, conscious of the fact that it might have been the first time Lena had spoken to her on anything resembling equal footing.

"Sorry. I didn't mean anything by it." She returned to her notes, hiding her smile. "I need to make a list. I'd like to have the names of every single person who had any connection to Parks. His bad boys, and any bad girls, if he kept them around."

Lena didn't reply. Her face was drawn as tight as a mask when Kim looked up.

"What the hell do you have in that notebook? What do you think you're doing?" she said.

Kim flushed. The Larson article, "Circle of Enemies," had provided a wealth of detail. In it, the Grand Junction reporter had painted a vivid picture of rural Colorado life, along with the unique problems faced by local law enforcement. When Kim realized she could never keep all the names and dates straight, she compiled her own record. "I take notes when I read. Is that a crime?"

"Because you want to be a private investigator when you grow up, is that it? And lucky me, you've decided to start with my case?"

Kim gave her a withering look. "All I'm asking for is names. Who did Parks hang out with?"

"Forget it. I do not want you poking your nose into the lives of those lowlifes."

"Okay, I won't. But I still want their names."

"No."

Kim frowned. "Fine. I'll get what I need from the paper. That'll work for a start."

She had moved on in her thoughts and was ready to ask another question about Parks's prison sentence. Glancing over, she was unprepared to find Lena looking at her angrily. "What?" she said.

"What the hell do you think you're doing?"

Kim sighed. "It's an exercise, Lena. For crying out loud, I am not going to go after these people, in any sense of the word. I'm only trying to see the whole picture. The picture is the personalities involved. Knowing a couple of pages' worth of information about this creep doesn't tell me squat about the people who were drawn to him. If there is one unassailable fact in your case, it is that Douglas Parks was not your shooter. He was in prison. Seems to me it's worth knowing whether there was even one person close to him who possessed the skills necessary to carry out the attack, assuming Parks could have orchestrated it." She stared at her notes, puzzling over another thought. "The problem is, Parks would have needed a large bargaining chip to persuade someone else to do it. Hard to figure what that might have been. He was flat broke when he went to prison." She looked up to see Lena still looking at her. "What now?" she said wearily.

"Unassailable. Interesting word. Not one you hear every day."

Lena sat perfectly rigid. From her jawline to the collar of her navy polo shirt to the bend of her arm as it rested on the table, she was utterly still. Kim didn't know whether she was resurrecting a former interrogation technique or whether this was a new behavior, pretending to be a statue.

She shrugged off the unspoken accusation: that she was better educated than she had admitted. "I read. A lot."

Lena wasn't persuaded. Whatever else she thought, she answered the first question. "The guy you're looking for is Frank Deseines. He was closest to Parks at the time all this shit was going on. From what I heard afterward, he cleaned up his act and got hired on with a construction crew. I can find out whether he's been arrested for anything lately. Parks's woman was a gal named Sherri Klerk. My guess is she's still around, probably living with some other guy by now. She had a kid. I don't think the kid was Parks's, and even if it was, my guess is he doesn't care about him. Look, all of the assholes in that crowd were fully investigated over a year ago. I'm telling you, not one of them was sophisticated enough to pull this thing off and get away with it for longer than a minute."

Kim held her breath, waiting. She wanted to hear every-thing Lena had to say about the shooting. No one cared about it as much as Lena did. No one had thought about it longer, harder, or had suffered the consequences of the deadly act more than she had. Kim ached to see the full picture, exactly as Lena saw it.

With effort, she restrained herself and remained focused. "Then the sole question remaining about Parks is whether he was able to set you up from prison. Through another contact he formed there. No one who was ever in the Durango picture."

"Right. I've thought about that. But that goes to what you said a minute ago. What did he have to offer anyone?" Lena pulled her chair back and started to wheel away. She stopped and spoke shortly. "No one goes around shooting cops for kicks. Kill one, and you get an express ticket to death row. Parks was pissed, but the hell of it is, ten years in prison isn't the end of the world to a guy like him. He can be out in seven if he plays the game right. The guy sees daylight. It wasn't Parks," she said.

Lena's need to talk about the case was evident. With each word, her voice grew stronger, less hostile, than before.

With her back still turned, she spoke with authority. "Let me tell you something. The world is divided into far more than two types of people, but for the purposes of abject simplicity, I'll divide it that way for now. There are people presumably like you. People who go through life with the basic intention of abiding by the rules and figuring out how to get what they want within the tenets of the law."

She wheeled around as she spoke. "Presumably?" Kim said, smiling.

"Presumably. I don't know you, and I don't know who is looking for you or why, but you're no criminal. Not unless my radar's gotten totally scrambled in the past year. It could have happened. Leaving that aside, and to finish my opening remarks to Criminology 101, there are other people living in this world whose motivations are entirely otherwise. People to whom the law is nothing but a minor impediment. They see the world as wide open, to take and do with as they please, with no thought to the damage or pain they cause along the way. For these people, the law is only something to circumvent, nothing to respect. In my experience, it is next to impossible for law-abiding types to comprehend the other type of person. It just doesn't compute. You don't see it, you don't get it, you always assume that somewhere down deep, we're all playing by the same rules, and that is simply a crock of shit."

Kim smiled. Lena's words struck a chord. They made her think of Stephen Bender.

"What?"

"Nothing. Go on."

"Go on, my ass. Screw you." She pressed her lips shut. Whatever else she meant to say seemed about to be lost. But then she did speak. "Point two. Every person walking this planet, bar none, has a secret. Maybe one secret, maybe more. Whatever the secret, he or she does not want it found out. People will resort to all manner of unpredictable behavior to protect their secret. Pushed far enough, every single person has the capacity to become both dangerous and criminal, however calm and law abiding they seem to be otherwise. Never under-estimate the length a person will go to protect her secret."

Lena said the last bit with a strong knowing look, which Kim didn't doubt was intended for her. However potent those words, they defused something for her. She understood now that Lena would have assumed the presence of a secret in her life even lacking evidence of its existence.

"That's a pretty dark view of humanity."

"You can't be a cop and believe in lightness and grace." Lena started to roll away. Midway across the kitchen, she stopped. "Let's be perfectly clear about something. You and I both know the photo Byron Jones had on him when he died was of you. You and I also know that Jones was an errand boy who screwed up by getting himself killed. He screwed up, so someone else is going to be coming along. That's why you want access to my contacts in the police department. You want to know when that someone else comes to town, inquiring about the untimely demise of Mr. Jones—a certain someone who will ask a few other seemingly innocent questions about Byron Jones's time in Durango, and oh, by the way, did he happen to locate a certain woman?"

Kim struggled to maintain her composure.

In the same even tone, Lena continued. "I don't know exactly what manner of trouble you're possibly bringing to my doorstep, but this much I can guarantee. Whatever it is, I am more than a match for it, even stuck in this piece of shit." She slapped the wheelchair's arms. "I can also tell you this. Long before that trouble arrives, I will know your secret. When I know it, then I will gauge what ought to be done, for your benefit and for my own protection, if it comes to that." Once again, she seemed to be finished talking. On her way to the doorway, she stopped and called back. "Craig Lowell. You want a homework assignment? His name is Craig Lowell. I'll give you a hint. He lives in town. Don't try to talk to me about any of this other shit until you can tell me something worth knowing about Craig Lowell."

CHAPTER 14

On Friday morning, Kim said goodbye to Lena, who was going away for the weekend with Damian. They were going to a cabin Lena owned. Beyond that, Kim had learned only that Damian lived in Albuquerque, a three-hour drive away. When Lena spoke of her plans, she seemed to soften. She asked point-blank: Would Kim be all right by herself? Kim brushed off her concern. On reflection, she was glad to anticipate having time alone.

She had work to do.

She left the house early enough to stop in town for coffee and to skim headlines in the paper. Byron Jones's name had disappeared from the Durango press. For two days, the paper had carried articles about his death. That was the extent of his legacy. No hint of Kim's existence had ever found its way into print. Jones's violent past had overshadowed the secondary theme running through the story, namely that of the unhappy marriage between cars, motorcycles, bicycles, and pedestrians on city streets. It was a moot point in Jones's death. The motor-cyclist who struck him had been well within his rights crossing that intersection.

Skip was in his office when Kim arrived at work. He called to her when she came through the door.

"Morning. Any chance you could pull a couple of reports for me today?"

"Sure. What do you need?"

"Hold on a sec. I'll write it down."

She waited while Skip scribbled something on a notepad. "I don't know if the computer can even tell me what I want to know," he said as he handed over the torn-off page. "Jeannette never had time to look into this."

One glance at the request, and Kim grasped the problem. "Oh, you're looking for a historical analysis of standard costs as a percentage of construction expenses."

Skip looked at her as if she had grown horns. "If you say so. All I know is I think I'm paying too much for certain things, but I don't have the numbers to back it up. That's what I want you to tell me."

She nodded. "I'll get right on it."

She had the report finished by noon. By day's end, she had learned a great deal about the workings of Legrand Construction, both operational and financial. Jeannette Winchester apparently did her job by rote, exactly as she had been doing it for ten years. She hadn't bothered to learn how to use the new reporting tools that came standard on small office business systems. Kim wondered whether Jeannette even understood the financial concepts behind the sort of reports Skip wanted.

No matter. What did matter was that Kim had another five weeks at Legrand. She intended to learn the business thoroughly, and to set Skip up with a suite of tailored reports he could run at will. She didn't want Jeannette's job. But she did want to leave the temporary position with a glowing recommendation from the company owner.

The temperature had soared into the low nineties that day. Undeterred by the heat, Kim made a beeline for the county courthouse when she left work. She had made little headway into Lena's assignment—to tell her something worth knowing about Craig Lowell. She had the man's address and phone number, courtesy of the phone book. Her first thought was to start by doing basic background research. Lena, she suspected, already had that information. So there had to be something else her employer wanted to know.

The La Plata County courthouse was located on East Second Avenue amid a throng of city government buildings. Earlier in the day, Kim had jotted down a list of broad columns beneath which she hoped to fill in some blanks: birth date, date of death, marital status. What else counted as public information? Civil lawsuits and criminal indictments? That would be fertile hunting ground if it was accessible.

The building posted a directory at the entrance. Kim read the list of offices and immediately realized she was in over her head. The property tax office was there, along with offices selling fishing and hunting licenses. She decided to start with the most innocuous subject: marriage license applications. A woman who looked old enough to be retired met her inquiry with a smile. "All of those records are online now," she said.

"Really," Kim said, wondering why this possibility hadn't occurred to her.

"I don't know what else you might be looking for, but you'll be surprised by how much you can find when you start searching the internet. Start with the State of Colorado home page. Pick your way through it from there. When you can't find what you want to know"—she paused to wink—"then come back and see me."

Kim took the bait. "What might you have that I won't be able to find online?"

"Oh, there's no telling. Details of barroom brawls back before the turn of the century. The century before last," she added with emphasis. "Claim disputes, rustling, territorial infractions."

"What?" Kim asked, thoroughly enjoying the woman's whimsy.

"Property issues." She nodded at something behind the wall. "Got a whole vault of big red books listing every case heard in the courts for the last hundred twenty-five years."

Feigning disappointment, Kim said, "I think I'll be able to find what I need online. But I'll come back if I don't."

"I'll be here," the woman said.

In no hurry to go home, Kim's impulse was to head for the library. On second thought, she opted for a different plan. She had Craig Lowell's address. She decided to ride by the place and see if the house itself felt inclined to give up Lena's gold. Back on her bicycle, she fell in line with the flow of Durango rush-hour traffic. Pedaling north, she reached Junction Street and found West Thirty-Second Street several blocks away from the bustle on Main.

Craig Lowell lived in a small wood-frame house situated beneath two towering maple trees. Noticing that the house next door was for sale, she set her bike aside and walked up to the box holding leaflets. From the outside, both houses appeared to have identical floor plans. The neighboring house boasted two bedrooms and one bath, wood floors, a fireplace, and an updated kitchen. Her jaw dropped when she saw the asking price. Then she looked again from one house to the other, seizing the opportunity to observe.

There was an old Chevy truck parked in Lowell's driveway. The window curtains were parted, but she was too far back on the street to get a view inside. The yard looked more tattered than Lena's did, but after a quick glance up, down, and across the street, she decided Craig Lowell's yard wasn't much different from his neighbors' yards.

Not wanting to draw attention to herself, she mounted the bike and pedaled slowly along the quiet lane. Where the street dead-ended a few blocks farther, she turned around. Approaching Lowell's house, she cursed her bad timing. Another car, a dated blue Toyota Corolla, had driven up and was parked behind the truck in the driveway. Had she stayed three minutes longer, she would have seen the person arriving. She hastily made a note of the license plate number of the car and truck, then continued riding down the street, admiring the larger, more modern, obviously more expensive homes interspersed with the vast majority of cottage houses that looked exactly like Craig Lowell's.

Weary from the day, she went home.

She was at the library when it opened on Saturday and was first to claim one of the internet computers. In less than an hour, she learned that Craig Lowell had paid $258,000 for his home on West Thirty-Second Street ten years earlier. More interestingly, she discovered that he had recently divorced Janet Ivans Lowell after five years of marriage. Try as she might, she could not discover any website that would give her vehicle owner information on the Toyota parked in Lowell's driveway. Apparently that information was available, but to obtain it, she was required to submit a written request to the Colorado DMV along with a nominal fee.

On a hunch, she searched the *Durango Herald* for any reference to Lowell. Nothing was returned going back six months. With her allotment of computer time running out, Kim abandoned her research into Lena's mystery man.

More restless than hungry, she walked down Main in search of a light breakfast. She bought a coffee and muffin and sat outside. Tourists were out early. She sensed the buoyancy in their steps as they walked by without seeing her. The magic of this place wasn't lost on them. As it seemed to be for her, she realized. The past week had taken its toll. At a loss as to how to make herself feel better, she started a slow trudge toward home.

She didn't make it more than a block before she doubled back in the direction of the library. Midway down the street, she stood outside the unremarkable beige brick exterior of the Durango police station. She wondered what contrary impulse had led her here. She waited, and watched, and finally decided to go inside.

"Can I help you?" a blue-uniformed sergeant said from behind a counter.

Kim glanced past the older man to a much younger woman who shared the space. Not in uniform, she appeared to be in her early twenties. She was fair skinned with blond hair. Her round eyeglasses magnified the sharp look she presently held on Kim. There was something odd about her. When Kim couldn't peg it, she lost interest. "I was wondering if Detective Stankowicz is in," she said.

"He's here. And your name?"

"Kim Jackson. I work for Lena Fallon."

Kim had expected the mere mention of Lena's name would bring her a dose of goodwill. It did. The man spoke briefly into the phone. A minute later, Stankowicz emerged through the windowless double doors that led to the station's interior.

"Kim, nice to see you again. What can I do for you?"

She had forgotten how tall the detective was. He loomed over her, standing far too close. "I have a few questions I'd like to ask you."

"Sure. Come on back."

He escorted her into the next room, where she sat down at a small wooden chair adjacent to his desk. Stankowicz finished making an entry at his computer. "So what can I do for you?" he repeated in a hearty bravado.

She smiled through her discomfort. "I hate to bother you. Besides, I'm sure this is none of my business."

"But," he prompted.

Her glance flickered away. They weren't alone in the room. Several other officers sat at desks around them. Though there was nothing overtly threatening in her surroundings, Kim felt unnerved. "If this is a bad time, or if I'm out of line even being here, please say so," she said. When Stankowicz made no reply, she forced herself to go on. "I've been working for Lena for about a month now. I wondered whether you'd be willing to tell me something about what she was like—before the shooting."

He laughed softly. "Didn't expect that one. But I can see why you'd ask."

The detective took a moment to consider his reply. In her lingering discomfort and residual curiosity, Kim glanced around again. The young woman whom she'd noticed at the front counter had come into the room and was sitting nearby, talking and laughing with a male officer. By all appearances, she was flirting with the guy. After catching several sharp looks shot her way, Kim had the distinct impression the blond woman was watching her.

She blinked and shifted her attention to Stankowicz. "I'm sorry if I've asked something I shouldn't have. I'm not even sure why I came here. I wanted to see where Lena worked. I wanted to try and get a feel for the kind of person she used to be. Not that I think it will make any difference."

"Now don't be running away," the detective said. "I was just trying to think what I could tell you, and all I could come up with is that you should talk to Sheila. Sheila Moss. She was with me the other day. She's around here somewhere. First, let me throw out my two cents. Lena had been working a couple years when I joined the department. She was damn good at her job, that much I can tell you. She never took any shortcuts, but she could cut through a pile of shit, usually verbal horseshit, quicker than anyone. She could read a situation better than any cop I ever knew, which is why—"

The detective stopped. Behind his silence, Kim heard the unspoken. "Except maybe for that last time," she said quietly. "Lena may have underestimated something."

Stankowicz scowled. "Yeah." He whirled around in his chair. "Sheila, you got a minute?"

Until that moment, Kim had been unaware of Sheila Moss's presence. When she saw her, she nodded a greeting, then couldn't help sparing a sideways glance, looking for the young woman. She was gone.

"You remember Kim Jackson," Mark Stankowicz said to Sheila.

"Right. How are you doing?"

The detective skipped the pleasantries. "Kim has some questions she wants to ask about Lena. I've said my piece, but I thought you might have more to add."

"I'm not sure what you're looking for, but come on over."

Kim thanked the man for his time and followed the female officer to her desk. Sheila was in her early thirties, give or take a year. She was solidly built through her shoulders, suggesting hours spent working out in a gym. Her blue eyes were guarded. Sheila looked hard. Hard in the way Lena still looked, Kim thought, wondering if it was something that went with the territory.

"How can I help you?"

Kim repeated the question she had asked Mark Stankowicz. Before she finished, Sheila Moss cut her off. "It's the shooting. Lena was always tough. But she wasn't angry or bitter. That's all new."

"Did you know her well?"

"No. We weren't bosom buddies or anything. Lena had nine years on me. A few times, early in my career, she was something like a mentor. With her reputation and all, I was surprised she bothered giving me the time of day. And if you're thinking it was some kind of female bonding thing, it wasn't. She occasionally did the same for rookie guys. With Lena, you either proved you were up to the job or you didn't. No middle ground with her. What?" she said, noticing Kim's smile.

"Nothing. I was just thinking she ran me through the same gauntlet when I started working for her. She tried to break me, and it almost worked."

"Yeah. That's Lena. But you're stronger, more competent in your job ever since, right?"

"Most days, yes."

"So what do you want to know?"

"I'm not sure. I'm just trying to picture Lena walking around on two strong legs, doing her job, rounding up the bad boys. And the bad girls."

"Mostly boys."

"I'm trying to fathom what she lost."

"She lost everything." A flicker of emotion crossed Sheila's eyes. She glanced away. "She lost her whole damn life. Lena lived to be a cop. Ask anyone around here, they'll tell you the same." Sheila picked up a pen, held it a moment, then tossed it back on her desk. With a grudging intake of breath, she reestablished eye contact. "Lena was the kind of person you always wanted to have on your side. At least that's how I felt about her. I was lucky to have her behind me most of the time. On any freakin' bad day, I could walk into this station, and just seeing her around, working some stupid-ass case, I could find a way to suck it up and do my job."

Kim felt moved by the other woman's depth of feeling. Strangely, it was what she had wanted to hear. "Did you ever visit her? Afterward—I mean."

"I tried to. I wanted to. The only thing I want now is to solve the damn case. You know about it, right?"

"I've read about it. I wasn't living here at the time. Lena never talks about it."

"No. She wouldn't." Sheila frowned at her desktop, troubled by some thought. Looking up, she said, "You've seen where it happened, haven't you?"

Taken aback, and guessing that the other woman was referring to the site of the shooting, Kim said, "No."

"Do you want to see it?"

"I'd love to."

As soon as she accepted the invitation, Kim was startled to realize that—bizarrely, incongruously—it had never occurred to her that the physical site where Lena had been shot still existed. In her mind, it had been washed away along with the time when it happened, leaving only the terrible aftereffects. Dread and curiosity commingled as she left the station. Stronger than both was the disturbing feeling that it had been easier to admit Lena's tragedy as a given, a fact, rather than as a horrific reality that had unfolded in a series of moments in a place that still bore silent witness to the event.

Sheila led her to a patrol car. Kim got in.

"I've been thinking it was time to go back and check out the place anyway," Sheila said as she fired up the engine.

Kim buckled her seat belt and furtively studied the host of knobs and gadgets built into the dashboard. Sheila made the turn at the corner and headed toward the center of town. Wary of the growing silence, and not wanting Sheila to ask something she might not want to answer, Kim spoke first.

"Back at the station, I noticed a young woman at the front counter. She had blond hair and wore glasses. She wasn't in uniform but she seemed to be working."

"Right. That's Jaye Dewey. She's an intern. The department runs a program, lets people in the community volunteer. Most folks only do it once. This is Jaye's third summer working for us."

"Really? She looks young."

"She graduated from college in June. Majored in criminology. We'd love to hire her, but she's planning on going to law school."

"Fort Lewis has a criminology program?" Kim asked, naming the one college in town.

"No. Jaye went to school in Arizona. She's a great kid. Next time you come by the station, I'll introduce you."

Sheila drove through town to the intersection with US 160. When the light changed, she turned right. A half mile farther, she pointed out a gas station. "That's where everything started. Lena usually stopped in there when she worked the evening shift. She'd grab a coffee and say hello to a friend who worked there. The store had a string of robberies a couple of years ago. Lena liked to keep tabs on things. Anyway, she had just pulled in when the other car tears in from the street, sees her, and peels out. She hadn't left her car yet. So she took off after it."

Kim could easily picture the chain of events. "It was already dark when everything started, wasn't it?"

"Yes. Happened about seven thirty." Less than a quarter of a mile beyond the gas station, Sheila steered the car into the left turning lane. "Wildcat Canyon," she stated flatly, announcing their route. "The other car turned here, and Lena followed. She radioed in she was in pursuit of a speeder. Nothing unusual in that."

They drove less than a mile. In the bright light of day, Kim studied the landscape. A hill rose on both sides, higher on the right than the left. Trees thick with leaves overhung the road; brush covered the ground. There wasn't a house to be seen. Most startling was how quickly they seemed to have exchanged a quasi-urban setting for the heart of the country. She commented on it.

"Yeah, it seems that way. Don't be fooled. Lots of people live out here. You can't see the houses." Sheila started to slow down. She signaled right, turned, and parked in a pullout.

"This is the first place where a car could easily pull off, isn't it?" Kim said.

"Yes. When you're in pursuit, trying to get a driver to pull over, generally you give 'em a chance to find a safe spot to leave the road. Again, nothing unusual in either Lena's behavior or that of the guy she was chasing."

When Sheila left the car, Kim did the same. Two cars had already passed them, one going in each direction. Kim made a mental note of the fact but remained quiet, intent on absorbing her first impression. Lena's car here, the other car in the clearing less than twenty feet ahead. "Lena radioed in the license plate number before approaching the driver, didn't she?"

"Yes. She knew it was Bobby Hill's car. Fair assumption it was him driving. He wasn't someone she would have been afraid of."

"But when she left the patrol car, he got out of his car?"

"Yes. That's when things turned dicey. She yelled at him to return to his vehicle. He didn't."

Kim strained to picture every slowly passing second of that night. "So Lena drew her gun."

"Her firearm. That's right."

By now, Kim was on the driver's side, picturing the movements Lena had made. She continued to describe a hypothetical scene. "He refuses her order to return to his car. He continues to advance. She warns him she'll shoot. Then she does so, firing once into the air. When he keeps approaching, she shoots him in the leg."

"Yes."

Kim whirled around. "Immediately, other shots are fired from behind. Do you know where they came from?"

If Sheila thought the question odd, she didn't say. "Shots came from across the road, back that way. Probably from that area of brush," she said, waving at an expanse of shrubs more than twenty yards distant. "The bullets were .22-caliber. We figure it was a long gun, a rifle of some make. No shell casings were found."

"Two shots," Kim said.

"Yes."

"Fired seconds apart. Maybe less." When she sensed Sheila looking at her, she explained, "I'm trying to get a feel for how quickly this happened."

"It happened very fast. No doubt about that."

Kim drew a long breath. At that moment, it was over for Lena—and not over. The worst had happened—and the worst was still to come. "Then the shooter walked over and shot her elbow."

"That's right."

It was the piece that didn't fit. She didn't have time to dwell on it. Kim said, "You believe Lena, don't you? About only shooting Bobby Hill in the leg?"

"Damn straight, I do."

"So Lena's shooter took her gun and killed Hill. Lena never saw him."

"That's right."

A question flashed through Kim's mind. About why Lena hadn't seen the guy. She looked around. There were no streetlights on this stretch of road. That time of night, it would have been pitch black, except for Lena's headlights, which ought to have thrown some light. She had been shot three times. Still, the man had to have been within a step of her when he reached down and took her gun.

Something in Sheila's tone kept Kim from pressing the issue.

"Can I ask your opinion about something?" she said instead.

The other woman shrugged.

"I've read about Douglas Parks. I know he was looked at hard for this. But there was another guy, Gary Dunkirk, who was looked at even harder. Do you think Dunkirk was in Hill's car that night?"

According to Rich Larson, author of the article "Circle of Enemies," Dunkirk was considered the prime suspect in Lena's shooting. He currently ranked as Durango's most-wanted man. He was a career criminal who had served time for armed robbery and assault with a deadly weapon. Known to be in Durango at the time of the shooting, he disappeared from the area shortly afterward.

Sheila scowled. "I don't know."

"What does your gut say?"

The policewoman's scowl hardened. "That he wasn't. This is all off the record, by the way."

"I don't see it," Kim said.

"You don't see what?"

"I don't see Lena failing to notice a second person leaving the car, sneaking behind both cars, and establishing a position behind her. It was dark," she repeated for her own benefit, and playing devil's advocate. She had to grant the possibility that Lena could have missed the other man's movements and that he did succeed in slipping far enough behind to shoot her. "Lena's attention was on Hill, who was behaving provocatively."

"Yeah, I've been through that too. We need to find Dunkirk. I can't believe that scumbag hasn't turned up yet. Christ, I hope he's not dead."

Since the shooting, Bobby Hill's family had filed a wrongful death suit against Lena, the Durango police department, and the city. Their contention was that Lena had shot and killed an unarmed man whose only "crime" had been trying to talk to her. No one disputed the presence of another shooter at the scene. The large question hanging unanswered was whether Lena had panicked and shot Hill when she realized she was being fired upon. An answer to that question was expected in the final report of the incident, due out in two months.

In a musing voice, Kim said, "Whoever did this hated Lena." Her thought spilled out, half formed.

"Tell me why you say that." Sheila looked at her with new interest.

"She was left disabled and discredited, that's why. This feels very personal."

"I can see that. Trouble is, the argument works just as well going the other way. Dunkirk was in parole violation and in who knows what other kind of trouble. Hill was the weak link. Hill could have put the shooter at the scene. If it was Dunkirk, he didn't want Hill identifying him and he sure didn't want Lena able to come running after him. So yeah, there's a way all this makes sense if Dunkirk was here."

Speaking slowly, Kim said, "I know. I still get the feeling everything went according to some script. Including Lena being left paralyzed."

"That's a helluva theory." Sheila followed the words with a weighty pause. "You're talking about some kind of sharp-shooter, if you're right. What is this to you? You enjoy playing detective?"

"No. It's nothing like that." Kim closed her eyes, avoiding the question. "Lena's a pain to work for and live with, don't get me wrong. She and I are not and never will be friends. It's only that—"

"She kind of grows on you, is that what you were about to say?" A faint smile eased Sheila's tough look.

Kim nodded, and knew the other woman didn't need a better answer. "Can I ask one more question?"

"Ask away."

"If this was an ambush, if the shooter was waiting here, doesn't it strike you as a huge risk to have chosen this spot? We've seen, what? A dozen cars pass by in less than five minutes?"

"The flow of traffic on this road is irregular. On a winter night, cars go by maybe once every couple of minutes. Sometimes more often, in a string. Cars fly by here. Even if someone had passed by, which they didn't, chances are the driver wouldn't have seen anything except a patrol car with its lights flashing and another car pulled over. The driver wouldn't have stopped. Back to your point. All of the shots were probably fired in under a minute. Let's run with your theory and assume Bobby Hill was going to die that night. Ideally, from bullets in Lena's gun, just as it happened. My guess is that lacking opportunity to get Lena's gun, the shooter would have shot him with his rifle. How did he get away? Two possibilities. Either he walked out through that ditch over there, picking his way a mile back to a car parked on the main highway. That would have been risky. Or he had a car parked somewhere close by, probably right around this bend. There's another pull-out ahead; road crews sometimes leave heavy equipment back there. Plenty of room for a car to pull in, back in deep enough to avoid being seen, especially if it's only there five or ten minutes. The shooter does his job, he slips alongside Hill's car, sneaks around the bend, and he's in his car and out of here in maybe less than two minutes from when the first shot was fired."

Kim squinted in confusion. She hadn't thought this far forward. Obviously Sheila Moss had constructed her theory long before today. "March," she said. "I assume there wasn't any snow on the ground."

"No. That would have made it too easy. No snow, the ground was frozen. No tracks. No shell casings. No trace evidence from the shooter. It was pretty damn clean."

They spent another few minutes pacing the scene. If Sheila was searching for something specific, she didn't say.

Back in the car, they drove out of Wildcat Canyon. "I'm really not trying to play detective, but I do have another question," Kim said as they made the turn onto Route 160. "It's about something different."

"What is it?"

The cautionary tone in the other woman's voice signaled a warning. Kim remembered too late how much she had to hide, and how exposed she potentially was by keeping company with a cop. But there was nothing to do but ask the question. "I was at the library this morning poking around on the internet. Based on a license plate tag, I was trying to find a car's owner. From what I read, I think I have to submit a request in writing to find out who a car is registered to. I was wondering if you know any other way I can get that information."

Sheila smiled. "You mean like if I radioed in a tag number and you happened to overhear the name that came back?"

"No. Not like that."

"Good, because that would be an abuse of privilege. What car?"

"Excuse me?"

"What car are you trying to find out about? And why?"

"Oh. It's a blue Toyota Corolla, older model. It's something—"

To Kim's surprise, the other woman burst out laughing. "Did Lena ask you to check up on her?" Sheila said.

"Check up on who?"

"Her kid sister. Stephanie. Where'd you find her car?"

"Parked outside Craig Lowell's house last night."

Sheila laughed again. She brushed one hand across her forehead, pushing away loose strands of hair, perhaps trying also to brush away the unaffected smile Kim saw flash on her face. "It's nice to know some things never change," Sheila said.

She waited for the green light, then moved with traffic onto Route 550. "Stephanie and Craig have been having an affair for years. It started practically from the day Craig married Janet. Makes Lena crazy."

"Why?"

"Besides the obvious, that he's cheating on his wife, she thinks Craig's a loser."

"How old is Stephanie?"

"Early thirties. So, give. Was Lena having you check on Steph?"

"In a manner of speaking. She kind of sent me on a wild-goose chase."

"Yeah, she did that to me a few times," Sheila said as she pulled to a stop at the station.

Before Kim got out, she said, "I didn't know Lena was close to anyone in her family. I've never once seen her parents or sister come around to the house."

"No. She pushed them away just like she pushed away everyone else."

CHAPTER 15

"Where were you last night?" Lena said on Monday afternoon.

Just home from work, Kim was making a salad for dinner. Lettuce lined the bottom of the bowl. A layer of cucumbers followed. "I went to a movie."

"By yourself?"

"Yes."

"Must have been a double feature. I never heard you come in."

Kim occupied herself chopping bell pepper and slicing a tomato. She didn't want to talk about yesterday.

Jeremy had stopped by. He had arrived alone in the afternoon bearing a six-pack of beer. Zeke was out riding with friends, he'd said. Sitting outside, Kim had told him about her drive to Mesa Verde that morning. The national park was jammed with people. She hadn't been able to see any of the most famous sites. It was beastly hot. She held up her bottle and told him the cold beer tasted great.

He said he hadn't been to the park since high school but it was crowded back then too. He finished his beer. Changing tone, he'd asked, a little too nonchalantly, about the guy who had died in the accident. "You didn't know that man, did you?" he said.

She said she didn't. He persisted with questions long enough for the pleasant conversation to begin to feel like an inquisition. "Zeke and I really don't know you all that well," he said, as if that gave him the right. She could have pointed out that she knew as little about him as he did about her. She said nothing and went inside for two fresh bottles of beer.

He followed her. He was standing at the sink when she turned away from the refrigerator, bottles in hand. His look was gentle in a way his questions hadn't been a moment ago. She forgot she was mad at him. She might have laughed. She was on the verge of saying something wistful, something like, *Wouldn't it be nice if—*

He didn't give her the chance. He took the bottles and set them aside. In the same fluid motion, he moved in closer until their lips touched. The slow kiss took her places she wanted to go but couldn't. "We can't. We said we wouldn't," she said, reluctantly breaking away. She grasped for a way to explain.

"I know. I get it," he said, and he left.

She wondered what he got. Because she didn't have a clue what had happened. Only that he was gone and she wasn't sure things between them would ever be the same.

Crushed, she had walked for hours through town and along the Animas River. In the evening, she was passing the movie theater near the train station when she saw people arriving for the show and joined the line.

"Where is this cabin you and Damian are always going off to?" she said brightly, changing the subject.

It was Lena's turn to stall. "Outside of Cortez."

Kim smiled as she put the dirty utensils in the sink. She chuckled when she took the salad out to the patio table. Her only regret was wishing she had asked a better question about the mysterious Damian.

"There's salmon," Lena said.

"I know. I found it. It's in a marinade."

"Will you join me?"

"Thanks. I will."

Lena went outside. Fifteen minutes later, dinner was ready. Kim spooned sour cream into a small dish and took it and the salt and pepper to the table.

"How much longer is your assignment at the construction company?" Lena said after they both took servings from the various platters.

"Another month."

"And you're still working at the bakery?"

"Yes. I have to go in tonight."

"Do you expect to get other bookkeeping jobs when you finish at Legrand?"

"I hope so."

"Are all of the jobs part-time?"

Kim took a swallow of water. The rapid-fire questions seemed harmless enough. If a trap was being set, she didn't see it. "The jobs aren't usually part-time. Most companies typically want someone full time. I'm only interested in part-time work for now."

"Why?"

Kim shot her an exasperated look. "Because I couldn't bear not to live here and work for you." After a minute, she said, "The truth is I'm better off financially staying here and making extra money from the temp jobs. Even with a full-time job, I'm not sure I could make ends meet if I had to pay rent on my own place."

Lena's string of questions stopped there. The meal drew to an end with no sign of what, if anything, she had wanted to discuss. Before Kim started clearing plates, she broached a topic of her own. "I have a preliminary report on Craig Lowell.

I believe I know the secret you wanted me to discover. Maybe I don't. If not, I'll have to dig deeper."

"And what might his secret be?" Lena asked too quickly.

Kim fingered the rim of her water glass. "It's one he shares with another person, though it's not much of a secret. Everyone in town seems to know Mr. Lowell has been having an affair for several years, practically since the day he got married. The other woman is Stephanie Fallon."

Lena closed her eyes and drew a short breath. She gave up any pretense of surprise. "So it's still going on between them?"

"Yes."

Kim leapt to the conclusion that Lena knew nothing of Craig Lowell's recent divorce. She doled out the rest of her information, which she had procured trolling internet sites, along with a few juicy tidbits contributed by Sheila Moss. "Craig Lowell is a well-known Durango man, generally well-liked. His good looks and charm may have won him the affection of at least two women, but they haven't won him the day in his business ventures. In the past fifteen years, he's owned three companies. The first was a white water rafting company, which he sold to invest in a discount sporting goods store. He was forced to declare bankruptcy a few years later. His most recent venture was in a fireplace business. Curiously, he took that store to the brink of bankruptcy before selling out to a competitor who turned it into a success. My sense is his ideas are good but he lacks something when it comes to implementation. The trait does not bode well for his future success."

"Do you know what he's doing now?"

"He's working as a bartender at the Italian Grill."

Lena swore softly. "Stephanie's still seeing him? How do you know?"

"Her car was parked at his house Friday night." Stringing out her coup de grace, Kim spoke slowly. "There is one other item of information you may be interested to know. Craig and Janet Lowell divorced in June."

Lena closed her eyes and swore again, not as softly.

"Lena, why don't you call your sister and talk to her about what's going on in her life? I have her phone number right here in case you've forgotten it."

"Screw you. Mind your own goddamned business."

"That's not exactly what you asked me to do."

Irritated by the ensuing silence, Kim stood up and started to clear plates.

"I wouldn't mind a refill," Lena said, holding out her wine-glass. "Please."

Kim went inside and returned with the wine bottle. She took a second load of dishes to the kitchen. There was nothing left on the table that needed to be dealt with immediately. She sat down.

In a tone bordering on accusation, Lena said, "Why don't you ever call your family? I've never heard you on the phone. There haven't been any charges on my bill. Do you have a cell phone I don't know about?"

Kim laughed. "I wish I could call my mother and father. They're both dead. Thanks for asking, though."

Lena registered the information without a show of sympathy. "Do you have siblings?"

"One brother. He's twelve years older than I am. We were never close."

"Where does he live?"

"Minneapolis."

Kim fired off the lie without a sliver of conscience. It was the place she had named when questioned by the police. Repeating it seemed simplest.

The tension had escalated. Kim felt her blood pressure rising.

"Does he have a name?"

By now, Kim clearly sensed a trap developing. She heard it in the quiet way Lena had taken control.

"Not one I ever use."

Lena reached for her wine. "Then I gather your statement of not being close to him is rather an understatement. What happened? Did he get too cozy one night under the guise of babysitting his little sister?"

Kim's blood boiled at the insinuation. She stared at the other woman, staggered by the depth of her cruelty. It seemed impossible that she could have forgotten so soon. "He never touched me. Not once in my life. But there are other ways by which one person can damage another. By destroying her spirit. Is there a story there? Yes. Will I ever tell it to you? I will not."

Lena laughed. "You're a woman of many secrets."

As if everything up until now had been but an inconsequential prelude, Lena laughed again. "Last week, you made a bizarre proposition to me. Maybe, all things considered, it stands as the most outrageous proposition anyone has ever made to me. At any rate, without specifically intending to accept your terms, I gave you an assignment. To my surprise, you've fulfilled it. I feel I have no choice but to uphold my end of our bargain."

Kim struggled to keep pace with the shifting winds.

"I shall start your education into the dark world of criminal investigation by offering a few words of wisdom. Listen carefully. In any investigation, begin with a detailed study of what's changed."

"What's changed," Kim repeated.

"That's right. What's changed? Ordinary people are not generally capable of criminal behavior. Something almost always gives them away. Here in Durango, we don't go in much for the career criminal type. There's no one who operates on a large scale and gets away with it for long. So I can't comment on what police work is like in big cities where, for any given violent crime, investigators start off with a nearly boundless array of potential suspects." She finished her wine and pushed the glass away. "Let's take you, for example."

Kim started to object. Lena shut her down. "First clue regarding Kim Jackson: She wants to change her appearance. She is trying to grow her hair out in what will no doubt become a style far less attractive than the cut she's accustomed to. A cut, I will add, that is evidenced perfectly in a certain photo I have in my possession."

Kim choked back a denial.

"So, Ms. Jackson wants to grow her hair out. As that is a time-consuming project, in the meantime, she puts on a cap and sunglasses every blessed time she steps outside this house. Does her disguise ultimately work? No. She is found." Lena held up her index finger, forestalling interruption. "No. She was found by a man who tracked her through casual acquaintances."

"If you're so sure of this pet theory of yours," Kim burst out angrily, "why did you insist to your good buddies on the police force that the photo wasn't me?"

"Good point. Because by then, I had figured out you didn't have a thing to do with our dead man, Byron Jones. You were not, to say the least, partners in any crime. But he scared you. I wanted to find out why. Fortunately, Mark Stankowicz has better things to do than add loose ends to an already closed case."

They were both silent.

"Would you like to know what gave you away?"

Kim didn't answer.

"In that case, I'll tell you. You showed no surprise on learning a man was in town looking for you, and you showed absolutely no relief on learning that man was dead. To the contrary, your degree of paranoia shot through the roof afterward. It soared so high, you were instantly willing to pull up stakes and leave. What does that tell me? It tells me there's someone out there who you fear far more than you do our dead Mr. Jones. Now, why don't you cut through this shit and tell me about him?"

Kim didn't utter a word.

Lena continued. "All right, then. Here's the clincher. You make a perfectly absurd proposition to me. You want to learn to be an investigator and you want access to my contacts at the police department. There can be only one reason you would make such a request. What you really want to know is if, or more likely when, the next bad boy comes looking for you. How's he going to find you? He can take the same course as our dead friend Jones did, beating the pavement and waiting for a face-to-face with you or with someone who knows you. Or he can try an end run and pick up where Jones left off. The only way he'll be able to do that is to show himself to the police and ask for whatever information is in the case file. He may think there's a clue there. Now there's a hitch with that. Jones was a nasty piece of work. If your friend shares Jones's proclivities, he won't go to the police because I'm here to tell you the first thing they'll do is run a check on him to see if he's wanted anywhere in the country."

Kim held Lena's steady gaze. Like it or not, this was exactly the information she wanted.

"What do you think?" Lena said. "Think your guy will go to the police?"

It was a charged question. Kim took the low road in answering. "There could be an inquiry."

"Ah. So you know who your pursuer is, and you also know he doesn't have a criminal record. Very good. That's helpful." In a swiftly changing tack, Lena said, "Kim, talk to me. You're afraid of someone. For the life of me, I honestly can't imagine what kind of trouble you're in. What I do know is there's no reason for you to live in fear. Let me help you."

Kim knew it had been far longer than seventeen months since Lena had uttered those words to anyone. It might have been the single stroke to break her. But her resolve held. She managed to mumble, "It's something I'm working on."

"Good. Then keep working on it. In the meantime, I'll give you your next assignment."

Kim looked up in astonishment. Lena said, "In case you've forgotten, we've entered a binding agreement. I'm going to give you one name, and I want you to ask this woman one question. Whatever she tells you, that's it. You stop there. Her name is Gina Hidalgo. She works for a local doctor, guy by the name of Wilson. That's where you should contact her. Mention you have a question from me. Back when, she knew a gal who was running with Dunkirk. Sleeping with him, at least." Lena's eyes grew hard. "I assume that name means something to you."

Kim nodded.

"All I want to know is, has Gina heard one word about Gary Dunkirk. Not what she's heard. Only *if* she's heard."

Kim nodded again.

"Swear to me you'll do exactly this and no more."

"Lena, I understand."

"The hell you do. You don't understand squat. Swear to me you'll do as I say. If there's anywhere else to go next, I'll handle it."

Kim gave her solemn word.

CHAPTER 16

"How is Lena doing?" Gina Hidalgo said after Kim introduced herself at the doctor's office late the next afternoon.

Kim maintained easy eye contact with the attractive woman behind the counter. Gina Hidalgo had brown eyes and dark wavy hair. Her voice was low and strong and resonated with compassion. Whatever her connection to Lena, Kim sensed it was something more than a passing acquaintance.

"I'm not sure I'm the best one to answer that. I've only known Lena for a month. She doesn't go out. As far as I know, she doesn't see anyone except a friend who lives in Albuquerque. She spends most of her time reading, watching television, or surfing the internet."

"It doesn't sound like much has changed."

"I don't think it has."

This late in the afternoon, the lobby was empty. The phone had rung twice during the brief time Kim was there.

"What can I do for Lena?" Gina asked after ending the second call. "I hope she knows I'd do anything."

Assured of privacy for the moment, Kim lowered her voice and spoke rapidly. "Lena asked me to come here to ask you one question. If you're not comfortable with this, tell me and I'll leave."

"Like I said, I'd do anything for her."

"Have you heard anything—one single word—about Gary Dunkirk?"

She assumed Gina would understand the question's importance. She guessed the dark-eyed woman would react when she heard the name. Gina did. She blanched. Discomfort rippled through her attractive features. "No. Shit, no, I haven't heard anything about that bastard. And I don't want to."

Some of the strain eased from her expression when she realized Kim had no intention of pushing the subject. When the phone rang again and she started to reach for it, she said, "That guy's either dead or living clean somewhere far away from here. My money's on the first." Her expression was rigid with something that looked like fear. Kim nodded her thanks and left.

If Lena had asked, Kim would have given her report from Gina Hidalgo that night. But she didn't ask. She appeared in the kitchen briefly to say she had eaten an early dinner and to deliver a shopping list. Afterward, she returned to her suite.

Kim made a light meal of soup and leftover salad. Knowing the grocery store would be jammed at this hour, she postponed going until later in the evening. She cleaned the kitchen and swept the patio. With nothing left to do inside or outside the house, she went for a walk.

A front-page article in the *Durango Herald* gave her the perfect excuse to drop by Jeremy and Zeke's place. The owner of the outdoors store where Jeremy worked had suffered a serious mountain bike accident over the weekend. The article described the man's injuries and a daring helicopter rescue in a thrill-a-minute tone that the paper's reporters never seemed to muster for national or global crises.

To her disappointment, Zeke wasn't sitting on the porch steps at the house. Through the tattered screen door, she saw the back door ajar. Impulsively, she went to it and tapped lightly. Jeremy appeared a moment later.

Her stomach flip-flopped. A thousand regrets for having come here sprang to life. "Hey," she said. "I dropped by to say hello. Is this a bad time?"

His smile said it wasn't. "Of course not. Zeke," he yelled over his shoulder. "Kim's here."

She figured they might have approximately one millisecond to decide how to handle this. He pushed the door open and came outside. "Are we good?" she said, searching his eyes.

"We're good if we say we are."

She nodded, and he did too.

Zeke bounded to the door from somewhere deep in the house. A broader smile than his brother's lit his face. "Jeremy said you'd probably be working every night," he said.

"I do have to go grocery shopping later," she said, assuming Jeremy had made excuses, in case she stayed away. "But I had time for a walk."

The three settled into their usual seats on the porch, Jeremy in his chair, Zeke on the top step. Kim joined him there, leaning against the opposite post. From where she sat, she couldn't see Jeremy. But she could feel him. "Are you still busy doing landscaping?" she asked the younger brother.

"Umm, yeah. So far. In another week or two, things change. People don't want their grass cut so often."

"What will you do for work once the weather changes?"

"I'll shovel sidewalks when it snows."

"Zeke has his application in for a job with the county maintenance crew," Jeremy said. "We've got our fingers crossed he'll get it. Big responsibility, though, right, Zeke?"

"Big money," Zeke said. "If it happens."

"Speaking of jobs, I read about your boss today," Kim said, turning toward Jeremy. She caught him watching her. She flushed and spoke quickly. "Sounds like he had a terrible accident."

Jeremy made a small sound of disgust. "Yeah. From what we heard, Brad was lucky to come out of that one alive."

"All the newspaper said was that he had a broken arm and cracked ribs."

"What it didn't say was that he nearly rolled off a fifty-foot drop. He was inches from the edge when some guys found him. The idiot."

"The paper said this was his third serious accident in the last year. What's he become, some sort of backcountry daredevil?"

"If he has, he'll kill himself yet," Jeremy said.

"The dude lost his mojo," Zeke said. "Happened at Worlds. He cracked."

"What? What do you mean 'he cracked'?"

"In New Zealand last year. He had the competition sewed up to win the Ultra Endurance World Championships. 'Cept he cracked. Didn't even place. Came home without a penny." Zeke shook his head mournfully.

The article Kim had read said that Brad had begun his career as an Olympic athlete. She assumed that once he became a business owner, his competitions were purely rec-reational events. She turned to Jeremy. "So what's Brad been like as a boss, between jetting off to competitions and getting injured when he's home?"

"Well, there you have it. He's been a complete ass. If it hadn't been for Lydia, the store would be in a lot worse shape. But she's gone now, and I, for one, don't blame her for wanting out of the yo-yo life." A devilish gleam flashed in Jeremy's eyes. "We may need to hire you to clean up the books if Brad doesn't get his act together soon."

Kim laughed. "With a broken arm, he'll likely be out of action for a while. Maybe he'll settle back into his job."

"Who knows? Be a shame if the store went under, though. A shame for me."

"Hey, I wanted to ask you guys," Kim said. "I've been itchy to get out and ride again. Any chance I can talk either of you into another ride at Horse Gulch?"

"Are you kidding?" Zeke practically cried. "Yes. When do you want to go?"

Kim looked at Jeremy. "Why not this weekend?"

CHAPTER 17

The black Ford pickup left the asphalt and bounced over ruts, cruising to a stop at the bottom of the long drive. The man, dressed in boots, jeans, a button-down shirt, and a brown jacket, went to the mailbox. His step was jaunty. It had been a good day. That afternoon, a Houston couple signed a contract to purchase their Colorado dream home. They never balked at the asking price. Because they didn't, they agreed to pay thirty thousand dollars more than the sellers happily would have taken. The man whistled as he flipped open the mailbox. He had netted a healthy chunk of change for his part in the deal. Or he would in three weeks, at closing.

A stack of white envelopes lay on top of a weekly circular. He meant to fold the flimsy bottom newspaper layer over the wad of letters and toss the lot on the passenger seat. Something made him lift the corner of each envelope and flick it forward.

The electric bill was on top. A bank statement followed. His expression tightened when he saw the third envelope. It had a typed label plastered on the front, no return address. Furious at the sight of it, he got back in the truck and threw it into gear. The tires spun madly. The vehicle kicked up a cloud of dust until it skidded to a stop at the top of the driveway.

Inside the house, he used a knife to slice open the envelope. He didn't give a rat's ass about leaving fingerprints anywhere. No cops were going to process this. His jaw hardened as he unfolded the single page and read ten familiar words: "I know who you are. I know what you did."

The next four words were new. "I can prove it."

"Shit!" he yelled.

Against his better judgment, he crumpled the paper into a ball and threw it across the room.

He strode to the liquor cabinet, poured a shot of Jack Daniel's, and knocked back the whiskey in one swallow. The letter wasn't a surprise. He'd been expecting it. This afternoon, when, for once, he'd been in a good mood, he'd forgotten about it.

The first letter had shown up in his mailbox three years ago. Its message was brief: "I know who you are. I know what you did."

Disturbing, hell yeah, it had disturbed him. But he hadn't known exactly what it was about, not until the next letter arrived a year later. It started the same way. There was more: "I know who you are. I know what you did. She died by your hands on August fifteenth."

He'd about come unglued when he read that. More than a decade had passed. Long enough for him to know he'd dodged a bullet. He'd barely gotten a grip on himself when another letter showed up a few days later. Same first ten words. Then the part about the cop: "Fallon knows the truth. She was there that morning. She's gonna be a superstar when she brings you down."

He hadn't been able to breathe. Later, after he'd read it dozens of times, he still didn't know if the letter writer was taunting him, or if the message was a warning. He couldn't figure out the guy's angle, especially with no mention of a payoff. His best guess was there must be a hush-hush investigation going on, something to do with cold cases, and the guy, whoever he was, *was* warning him. And probably looking for a reward somewhere down the road.

Things had played ugly for a while. He'd gotten close enough to Fallon to know she didn't know anything. Whoever wrote the letter was wrong.

He glanced across the floor at the crumpled page. This was the first letter that threatened proof.

He scoffed and poured another whiskey. Proof? That was bullshit. He drained the glass. There wasn't any proof.

If there were proof, he would have had another kind of letter long before now. One demanding money in exchange for silence. But that letter hadn't come. Because there wasn't any goddamned proof.

His head felt fuzzy. He regretted the second drink.

He reached for his keys. Walking out of the house, he punched buttons on his cell phone. When the woman answered, he said, "Hey, I know I said I was busy tonight, but I got some good news. The Tamarron property sold. I'm on my way back into town. Do you want to grab a steak at the Mining Company?"

He listened while she whined about being taken for granted. She complained about the short notice. Then she said yes, as he had known she would.

Twenty minutes later, he flung back the heavy oak door at the restaurant and let her walk in ahead of him. On the way to the table, he shot a glance around the room, looking for his gorgeous new toy. She wasn't there. He told himself it was just as well. He needed to lay low for a while. The words rattled around emptily as he listened to his girlfriend's chatter while his eyes strayed to the table where his new friend Jaye wasn't dining.

—

But she was nearby. She was across the street, watching, when he and his doormat girlfriend entered the restaurant.

CHAPTER 18

One day later, Lena continued resisting being drawn into the only conversation Kim wanted to have with her.

"What I'm trying to say is that it makes no sense to approach this from any other angle than the weakest link. And the weakest link is Bobby Hill," Kim said in a measured tone.

Lena studied her. One cheek tugged sideways scornfully. "Wonderful. Do you flatter yourself with the opinion that no one else thought of that? You think we've all been waiting for you to show up to enlighten us?"

Slightly abashed, Kim lowered her eyes. "No. That's not what I think. This just hit me today."

She proceeded to rehash her conversation with Gina Hidalgo from two days earlier. Lena was unsurprised by the report.

"What was Gary Dunkirk in prison for?" Kim said.

"Oh, so there is something about this case you don't know?" Kim didn't bite.

"Armed robbery and assault. He was convicted on charges of breaking into a home; tying up the couple who lived there; and making off with cash, jewelry, and guns. It's always guns around here. He served most of his sentence, then got out on parole. Scary thing with Dunkirk? His pattern of violence kept escalating. We all figured he was going to kill someone eventually."

"But as far as you know, he hasn't killed anyone?"

"He was questioned about a homicide in Dolores County. No charges were filed. I know investigators there were looking hard at him."

"Did he have anything against you?" Kim said.

"He had something against cops in general and against every single Durango cop in particular. Did he have it out for me personally?" Lena weighed the question. "Not for any reason I know." She snapped to another tone. "Forget about Dunkirk. Bobby Hill. Your weak link. Let's talk about him."

They were sitting in the kitchen, having moved there from the patio when the wind kicked up, dropping the evening temperature into the low sixties. With the back door and windows open, the steady rush of air through the trees was a constant backdrop of sound.

"So who was Bobby Hill to you?" Kim asked when the silence grew long.

"Ah, there's the rub. He was no one to me."

"Did he have a record?"

"Petty stuff. He'd been hauled in along with a bunch of other goons for starting brawls on Main. From time to time, some of our local hotheads decide they want to pick on the flashy out-of-towners, guys who come here to tackle the great outdoors. Not sure why, but the skiers always get it the worst. Hill was a hanger-on, never a ringleader."

Kim noted Lena's curious air of detachment. "That doesn't sound like a heap of trouble. Anything else?"

"As a juvenile, he was arrested for breaking into homes in his neighborhood. Unlike his older brother, he never seemed to have the heart and soul of a true criminal. I know a couple of the guys on the force tried to keep tabs on him, keep him out of worse trouble. Funny family, the Hills."

"How so?"

"Three boys in that family, the father left a long time ago. The mother's worked at the General Palmer Hotel for years. The oldest boy, Andy, was always in trouble. You could see the writing on the wall with him from a long way off. He and a buddy robbed a convenience store, and guess what? They got caught. They're both doing time in Cañon City."

"Did you have much to do with Andy?"

"Everyone in the department had something to do with Andy at one time or another. But no, I didn't have a thing to do with his arrest or trial. Bobby was the second son. He's two years younger, and damned if he didn't look up to his big brother."

Kim considered what she had heard. Before she could comment, Lena continued. "Bobby couldn't have been caught between two greater extremes. His mother always kept a decent home. Miracle in itself how she did that. The youngest boy is a good, smart kid, total opposite of his brothers. But that Andy was one charismatic son of a bitch. He could sweet-talk his way out of most anything. And he did, for years. It was easy to see how Bobby worshipped him. But once Andy was out of the picture, the hope was that Bobby would hitch his wagon to a different star and clean up his life."

"Did he hold a steady job?"

"Best job he ever had was driving a delivery truck. He lost it when he got his third or fourth speeding ticket."

Kim laughed softly. "So when you saw him peel in and out of the gas station that night, you thought nothing of it. Only Bobby Hill being a jerk behind the wheel. Again."

Lena looked at her with no trace of amusement. Reading her expression, Kim sobered quickly. Terrible consequences had resulted from a completely ordinary moment. That night,

Lena had stopped to grab a cup of coffee and say hello to a friend. Then Bobby Hill showed up, out of control behind the wheel of a car. Someone had known both Lena's pattern and Hill's. Kim swallowed the enormity of the conclusion. Someone had known exactly how to set up an apparently non-threatening, all-too-ordinary confrontation.

"You believe you were set up that night, don't you?" she said.

"You bet I do."

Fleetingly, Kim feared losing Lena's trust. Frightened of where they were going, she plunged on, reciting the bare-bones facts. "You went after Hill. He pulled over within two miles after you initiated pursuit. Hill had been pulled over enough times to know the drill. He was expected to remain in his car until you approached. He should have done nothing except obey your clear and concise orders."

"Yes."

"But he left his car." Kim stared at the tabletop. She saw the spot in Wildcat Canyon. She imagined the black night, illuminated only by the patrol car's piercing headlights. The shooter, waiting somewhere behind, had to have been wearing night-vision goggles. Without them, he couldn't have taken Lena down with pinpoint accuracy. Kim spoke slowly. "Bobby Hill couldn't have known he was going to get shot that night. But he'd been promised something. He had to have known he would get in trouble for speeding and disobeying your orders. What could someone have offered to make those risks worthwhile?"

"Money."

It was the likely answer. Money may have been promised, but it was never delivered. Not to him or to any family member. That trail had been scrutinized thoroughly. Something prompted Kim to ask, "Is there anything Bobby Hill would have wanted more than money?"

Lena laughed. "To have his brother released from prison. But there's no way that was going to happen, and Bobby knew it. Or should have known it."

"Someone could have lied to him. If it was someone powerful enough, Bobby might have believed him." Kim's thoughts leapt to someone in law enforcement, and she felt sick. That the person who had set Lena up might be someone on the police force.

Instead, she thought of a lawyer. A lawyer might have been able to persuade Bobby to believe almost anything. A lawyer might have had it in for Lena.

She offered a half smile, hoping to soften the impact of her question. "Were you on the outs with any particular lawyer in town?"

"What is this to you?" Lena demanded. "You propose a theory, then force the facts to fit it? That's a hell of a way to work a case." Gradually some of the tension ebbed from her expression. "Look, here's the thing. The vast majority of four-year-olds and all of the Bobby Hills in this world can be tricked into doing what you want them to do for the promise of something they want. Somebody offered Hill the right price, I'll grant you that. It was probably money. Nobody could have promised him his brother's release from prison. I can't believe Hill would have been so stupid to believe anyone who told him he could deliver that."

Lena had tired of the conversation. Kim saw the signs coming before she made a move to leave. "Forget it," Lena said as she wheeled away. "Just forget it."

—

On Saturday morning, Kim was in her room when Zeke and Jeremy arrived for their bike ride. She grabbed what she needed and ran downstairs.

"Where were you, in the shower?" Zeke said. "I was calling for like an hour. And how stupid would that be, taking a shower before you go riding?"

She smiled at the blond-headed kid's exasperation and held up her empty water bottles. "Give me a sec to fill these, and I'll be ready to go."

Jeremy had wheeled her bike from the garage into the yard and was inspecting it when she joined him. "Good morning. Is everything okay?" she said.

"Good morning. Tires are a little low. Otherwise it looks fine."

They started their ride with an easy amble through town. After zigzagging through the neighborhood, they reached a dead-end street where dusty asphalt gave way to hard-packed dirt. From there, the lane narrowed to a trailhead.

"Holy crap," Kim exclaimed when she saw the steep ascent lying ahead.

"Aw, come on," Jeremy said. "You can do it."

Zeke didn't stick around for the discussion. He flew up the hill. "You go next," Kim said.

Jeremy obliged. She watched him power up the incline with discouraging ease.

Momentum, she knew, was key. With a glance over her shoulder to ensure no other cyclist was closing in, she steered toward the center of the trail. Her front tire bounced over a rut. She kept her weight back and low on the seat and pedaled hard. Twice before, she had attempted this climb. Both times, she'd had to jump off the bike and walk. Today she expected to fare no better, but her legs surprised her. They churned against the increasing resistance. She kept her head lowered, eyes focused on rocks and ruts carved into the ground. She broke into a rare sweat in the arid desert climate and was completely startled when she heard Jeremy whistle and begin clapping.

The terrain abruptly evened out. She shot past him.

"Hey, wait," he said with an injured yelp.

Less than a minute later, he caught up with her. "Great climb," he said.

"Thanks."

They rode side by side until a cyclist coming on forced Jeremy to drop behind. He rejoined Kim briefly. But there were pedestrians walking in both directions, and other cyclists passing every few minutes, requiring them to ride single file. Finally, Kim pleaded for a break. They pulled off the trail.

"I like this," she said, meaning the cycling, the day, and, especially, the scenery. Orange and yellow wildflowers gave a splash of color amid the tan grasses and muted green juniper and piñon trees. From where she stood, her view was to the southeast. Higher hills rose in the near distance. She turned to the right and saw the outline of a piney ridge due west. Then, like the magnet of a compass coming around to its true course, she spun another ninety degrees. Her breath caught at the sight of the snow-capped peaks dominating the northern horizon.

The mountains boxed in Silverton on one side and Ouray on the other. One paved road connected the towns, crossing over Red Mountain Pass. She had driven it once, and now felt a longing to return. "Those mountains," she said weakly. "They kind of blow me away."

She regretted the words the moment they were out. She waited to hear a soft explosion of laughter, and Jeremy's teasing response. When he didn't reply, she looked at him.

"It'll be a sorry day when they don't," he said, equally humbled by the landscape.

The soulfulness in his voice nearly undid her. It made her feel like blurting out everything she wanted to tell him. About how sorry she was for sending him away on that Sunday afternoon when he showed up at her door with a six-pack of beer. About how long it had been since she had wanted to lie in bed next to someone and forget to count the hours. About how sorry she was for the lies she had been forced to tell him and every other person she had met since moving to Durango.

"Shall we keep going?" she said. "There's no telling how far ahead Zeke is by now."

"Lead on."

They put another fifteen minutes of hard riding behind them. Kim finally caught sight of Zeke waiting at the top of a short, steep climb. Jeremy went ahead. On the approach, she tried to mimic his form. She stood on the pedals, keeping her center of gravity low. Her leg muscles burned. She plowed on, through one hard-fought rotation after another. At the top, she skidded to a stop, barely getting a foot down before she toppled over.

"Bravo!" Jeremy cried.

She dropped her bike alongside his and Zeke's. She took off her helmet. She grabbed her water bottle and walked back to look at the last section. A giddy sense of euphoria swept over her when she saw the trail.

She spun in all directions, savoring the mountain views, then joined the brothers sitting on a narrow ledge. "I need to get out more," she said.

"What are you talking about?" Zeke said. He handed her a cookie.

"To see this." Her hand swept the air, primarily indicating north. "I need to come up here more often."

"No, you don't. You can see all this stuff from the college."

It was her turn to be puzzled. Jeremy started to explain. Zeke interrupted. "Don't tell me you haven't been up to the college yet. Where have you been doing your training rides?"

Kim had noticed signs for Fort Lewis College ever since she had arrived in Durango. Weeks ago, she had planned to go in search of the school. Too much had happened in the mean-time, and her interest had lapsed. "The only training I've been doing is riding to and from work. Where is the college?"

"Practically right outside your door," Zeke said disdainfully.

"Not quite," Jeremy said. "To get there, all you have to do is go straight up College Avenue. We crossed it on our way here. It's a helluva climb to the top. Zeke and I zip up and down a couple of times a day when we're in serious training."

"And there are nice views from there?" she said.

"Excellent views," Zeke said.

Kim wanted to laugh and cry at the same time, hearing Zeke's serious intonation. No doubt it was a mimicry of words he'd heard spoken by someone else, probably Jeremy. She felt a stab of mixed emotions: of gratitude for the kindnesses, large and small, Jeremy bestowed on his brother; and of grief, for the cruel consequences of a single mistake that had led to Zeke's accident and forever changed him.

The bikes lay scattered off the trail. The three sat on a low rock wall advantageously placed to afford the best view. Sandy soil and clumps of dried grass were interspersed with small rocks at their feet. Kim ate her cookie and tried not to think about her aching muscles.

"Are you bleeding?" she said when she caught sight of a line of blood trickling down Zeke's knee.

"No. I mean yes. But not from today."

On closer inspection, she saw a large bruise surrounding a cluster of cuts. "What in the world happened?"

"I crashed last Sunday. No biggie," he said, though he leaned over and peered at his banged-up knee.

"Does everybody who rides mountain bikes crash?" she asked, half sarcastically.

To her surprise, both brothers nodded.

She was about to suggest she might need to reconsider her interest in the sport when she thought of something else. "Did Brad come back to work this week?" she asked Jeremy.

"He came in yesterday. He actually managed to focus on the store for about three hours. After that, he was on the phone lining up his next competition."

"How can he do that? I thought he had a broken arm."

"He does. The event isn't until December. He's certain he'll be ready to compete by then."

Kim reached for a blade of grass and began shredding it. "What is he, some kind of overgrown kid who wants to spend his life playing?"

"That's about it. His whole life has been one competition after another. Ask me, I'd say it's nothing but addiction. Ask him, he'll tell you he's trying to strike while the iron is hot."

"You have to explain that."

Jeremy consumed a cookie, then chased it down with a swallow of water. "Brad figures he only has another couple of years to compete at his prime. That's assuming he isn't past it already."

"And so what? Whoever has the tallest stack of ribbons and medals at the end wins? He has a girlfriend and a kid, right? Not to mention a business to run. Do any of these competitions pay well?"

"Some do. He gets some endorsements. It's weird. Brad has a ton of first-place finishes under his belt in some really intense events. But to hear him talk, the greatest thrill of his life was competing in the Olympics. And he didn't even place. It's like he's always trying to get back there. Short of going to the Olympics again, which he'll never qualify for, nothing matches up."

Zeke jumped up and began mimicking the motions of what Kim could only assume was a cross-country skier. He flailed his arms back and forth and pretended to breathe heavily. She didn't know what he was up to and had glanced away when he shouted, "Pow! Pow!"

"What in the world?" she said.

Zeke had stopped his skiing act and now stood stock-still holding an imaginary rifle. "Biathlon," he said. "That's the event Brad competed in. Stupidest event in the Olympics." He was still breathing hard. He had apparently forgotten his own game.

"You dork," Jeremy said, tossing a pebble at him.

Something about the way Zeke pretended to hold a rifle sent a chill through Kim. "What's the biathlon? I thought it was some kind of running event."

"Biathlon's a generic name," Jeremy said. "It means any two events combined. In the Winter Olympics, it's specific. The event combines cross-country skiing with shooting."

"Stupidest event in the Olympics, not counting curling," Zeke said. "The geeks have to cross-country ski carrying rifles on their backs. When they reach the target area, they have to shoot. From different positions. It's really hard to do 'cause they're so out of breath."

The chill hadn't left Kim. "You're telling me a competitor has to ski until he's exhausted, then shoot a bull's-eye?"

"Yeah."

"That's what the good ones do," Jeremy said.

"And Brad was a good one?"

"He had to be much better than good to make the Olympic team."

Zeke started performing his charade again. Jeremy ordered him to cut it out.

"Does Brad shoot now?" Kim said.

"Nah, it's not his thing," Jeremy said. "But we do sell guns at the store. Occasionally a customer comes in and wants to deal with Brad specifically, so he gets involved in a sale."

Kim let the subject go. She didn't care a thing about Brad Chase. But she had glimpsed something unexpected. She had imagined a wraithlike man, either an outdoorsman or a hunter, someone adept at blending into the scenery, hidden in the brush off the side of the road the night Lena was shot. A man who also happened to be a crack shot.

The insight gave her a moment's hope before reality caught up. Needle in a haystack, she thought. Even if she were right about the how of the shooting, she could never hope to discover who might have committed such a cold-blooded act.

They got back on their bikes. Zeke immediately launched into a sprint. Near the end of the loop, Kim and Jeremy came upon him waiting in a shady spot, sucking water from his bottle. "Riding with you two is like watching paint dry," he complained.

"Well, excuse me," Kim said. "If you want better company, go ahead and find him. Or her."

"No, no. I didn't mean anything," he said, scrambling to put things right. "I'm glad you're here. I just wish—"

"That I rode faster? Hey, I'm getting there. Give me another week, and I'll be leaving you in the dust."

"You'll what?" he said incredulously.

"You heard. Just try and catch me!"

She took off fast. Bumping along, she picked up speed as the trail wound downhill. Within seconds, Zeke sped past her, screaming jubilantly before he dropped out of sight around a curve.

CHAPTER 19

On Sunday morning, weary of Lena's mood shifts, Kim left the house to walk into town. Ordinarily she avoided popular Durango venues, well aware they were the locations where she was most likely to be spotted. She had no good reason to believe she was safe, but it was too hard constantly living according to the opposite belief. For one precious hour on a Sunday morning, she let herself relax in a bustling java house.

She read the local paper and skimmed headlines in a copy of the *New York Times* someone had left behind. She kept the paper, intending to read it more thoroughly later. After finishing her latte, she settled in to reread Rich Larson's "Circle of Enemies," which she had printed out on her last trip to the library.

She read slowly. She surfaced from the dark tale, humbled by an impression she had missed previously. According to Larson, Lena Fallon's Durango was a known world. The criminals knew the landscape intimately, every back street and dirt road that dead-ended in national forest land. Law enforcement officers knew their citizenry, their neighbors, their complainants, their wealthy, and their poor. Kim had allowed herself to be deceived by the constant flow of new faces passing through town. She thought herself obscured amid that crowd and knew now she had been wrong. It wasn't that the police dismissed the tourist population. It was rather as though they skimmed off their presence unless called in to investigate a specific matter, usually involving an out-of-towner as a crime victim.

Their sights were set firmly on the men and a few women who were the serial offenders when any crime of note was committed.

Lena Fallon's shooting, Rich Larson affirmed, had happened in a known world and ought to be solvable.

—

"Sheila Moss stopped by while you were out with your boyfriends yesterday," Lena said late that afternoon, startling Kim, who was cleaning the refrigerator.

"That's nice. Was it an official visit or a social call?" Kim said flippantly, standing up and admiring her handiwork.

Lena ignored the question. "I asked Sheila to attach a note to Byron Jones's file. She said she would, no problem. Anyone calls or stops by the department asking about Mr. Jones, I get a call."

Kim recognized the gift. "Thank you," she said, meaning it.

"Hey, it's no skin off my back. Sheila asked what my interest in the file is. She wanted to know if it had something to do with you. I told her it was simple curiosity and likely wouldn't amount to anything. I declined her offer to pursue any additional leads, which, naturally, I don't have. Should anyone come calling with questions about Mr. Jones, our loosely established ground rules on this subject will change."

"Probably won't happen."

Lena maintained an edge in her voice. "I will ask one thing of you. Go on thinking about all of this. Don't hesitate to talk

to me when you're ready. And don't be surprised when you feel
ready. No one wants to carry around this kind of shit. You, in
particular, don't have to."

Lena moved to the table and began inspecting dates on the
bottles and jars blanketing the surface. Kim worked quickly
to finish the cleaning job. Once the interior was spotless, she
began replacing the contents on the shelves. "Do you know
Brad Chase?" she said.

"Of course I know him. Every person in this town has had
Brad Chase in his or her face at one time or another."

"What do you mean?"

"He's one of our local media sensations. What about him?"

That morning, after leaving the coffee shop, and in no
hurry to go home, Kim went to Wilderness Outfitters. Jeremy
wasn't working. Yesterday Jeremy had said he and Zeke were
going riding today on trails, he'd added without apology, that
she wouldn't enjoy. Brad Chase wasn't in the store either, which
didn't matter since she wasn't looking for him. Simple curiosity had led her there. Inside, she spent a long time standing in
front of Chase's glory wall of photos and newspaper and magazine articles. The collection chronicled a dazzling career that
began when Chase was eighteen, a blond youth with a winning
smile who had earned a spot on the US Olympic Nordic squad.

Over the years, Chase's hairstyle had shortened and his
boyish smile had given way to cocky arrogance. By the time he
was in his midtwenties, he was routinely winning triathlons,
including the prestigious Hawaiian Ironman. From there, he
moved with the changing face of endurance events to increas-
ingly grueling multiday, multisport competitions.

Not Brad Chase, she reminded herself, standing in Lena's
kitchen with a condiment bottle in each hand. Brad was a
world-renowned athlete, a successful businessman, a local
hero. He may also be a self-obsessed endorphin junkie, but she
had no reason to target him as a suspect in Lena's shooting.

It was his skill set that intrigued her: a long-distance runner blessed with a sniper's uncanny accuracy.

She replaced the condiments in the refrigerator.

Lena was still waiting for her to say something.

"I've been reading about Chase this week. That latest accident of his. He owns the store where Jeremy works. Apparently he's doing a lousy job managing the business."

The subject held no interest for Lena. Kim knew she should let it go. She ignored her own best advice. "So you never had any run-ins with Brad?"

"No." Lena spared her a look thick with wonder. "As far as I know, Brad Chase is squeaky clean. His store was broken into a few years ago, but I wasn't involved in the investigation. I think they caught the kids who did it. One was an ex-employee. What's this about?"

"Nothing. I just wondered. Seems like life is going south for him, health-wise and business-wise. I wondered if you thought anything about it."

"Not a thing."

Lena's expression tightened in a question she didn't ask.

Kim heeded the warning look and let the subject go.

But she didn't stop thinking about Brad Chase.

—

Monday night, after finishing her work at the bakery, she took advantage of the company's internet to research Chase. He was an easy man to find online. She bypassed recent articles until she came to the story of a kayaking mishap Chase had suffered in April. Heavy spring runoff had made the Animas River more dangerous than usual. As an experienced kayaker, Chase had no reason to expect trouble, but in one disastrous roll, he was ejected from his craft. He hit his head on a rock and lost consciousness, despite wearing a helmet. He owed his life to the quick actions of a commercial rafting crew who pulled him out.

Working back chronologically, she found a story reported in December of the previous year. Chase went cross-country skiing on a day when a major snowstorm was predicted. Two days later, searchers found him lying outside a snow cave he'd built, jacket off, apparently close to death. Two days in the wilderness, even in December, should have been easily survivable for Brad Chase. Yet why, the reporter speculated, had he gone out that day in the first place?

Kim scrolled back to articles written after Brad's last major event: the Ultra Endurance World Championships in New Zealand. To everyone's surprise, he had performed exceptionally well. Going into the final event, a fifty-mile ultramarathon, Brad was the hands-down favorite to win.

He didn't win. Twelve miles from the finish line, he wandered off course. Even though he regained the trail soon afterward, still in the lead, the mistake did something to him. Or perhaps the something happened before he wandered off course. He stumbled along for the next mile, continuing to lose precious minutes. He was passed by a man who was not his closest competitor in the standings. Still, that seemed to be the end of him. He struggled to finish, placing a disappointing twelfth overall. It was his lowest place finish in any event in his professional career. When it was over, the haggard near-champion was quoted as saying, "I just want to go home."

Those were not words Brad Chase had been heard to use before.

There never was a good explanation for what happened. He wasn't dehydrated. He wasn't injured. He had victory in his sights and gave it away. As Zeke had put it so eloquently: he cracked.

—

At work the next day, Kim spent most of the morning assembling a purchase order to submit to Legrand's major lumber supplier. Skip had given her an assortment of barely legible notes concerning specialty items to add to the standing monthly order. Afterward, he left to go to a job site. Between phone calls to him and to the supplier, she figured out what she was supposed to be ordering, finished the paperwork, and faxed it before noon.

She was eating lunch at her desk when Trina stuck her head around the corner of the door. "Skip asked me to pick up some stuff for him in town. Can you handle everything while I'm gone?"

Kim managed not to laugh. It hadn't escaped her notice that Trina frequently found an excuse to leave the office when Skip wasn't around. "I shouldn't have any problem."

Soon afterward, she heard the front door close. She stood up to stretch her legs. In the outer room, she watched a cloud of dust kicked up by Trina's car settle. Assured of privacy, she reached for a phone book and found the number for Wilderness Outfitters. She made the call from Trina's desk, panicking at the last moment when she couldn't remember the name of the manager who had recently left. Linda—no, Lydia, she recalled. She held her breath, hoping not to hear Jeremy's voice on the other end of the line. When a woman answered, Kim spoke brightly. "Hi. I was in the store a few weeks ago and spoke to your manager, a woman named Lydia something. Sorry, I've forgotten her last name. Is she in?"

"She no longer works here. Can I help you with something?"

"Shoot. I don't think so. Lydia—what was her last name? Do you know if she's still in town?" Kim wracked her brain trying to think of a plausible reason for needing to talk only to Lydia. She didn't need to. The woman gave her one.

"Her name is Lydia Brooks. As far as I know, she's still teaching at the city rec center. Are you sure I can't help you?"

"No. Lydia told me about some classes in town. I couldn't remember where she said they were taught. I bet she said to check at the rec center. Thanks for your help."

On her way home that afternoon, Kim detoured off the Animas River trail to stop at the city rec center. She left her bike in a rack outside the main entrance and went in. When she asked for Lydia Brooks, a man working at the front counter made a call. A few minutes later, a woman emerged from somewhere in the building's depths.

Tall, slender, and muscular, Brooks had an air of self-possession Kim had rarely encountered in anyone before. Brooks looked like a model walking off the pages of a glossy magazine. Or a goddess emerging from the mist. Her shoulders and hips were narrow; her sleeveless tank top revealed feminine curves. She had long, dark hair tied in a band, and hazel eyes set in a frank, no-nonsense expression. Far from being cold, they were open and interested.

After rejecting a handful of false claims on which to introduce herself, Kim opted for starting with the truth. From there, she planned to make it up as she went along. "I'm a friend of Jeremy's from Wilderness Outfitters," she said after introducing herself. "He's encouraging me to apply for a job at the store. Right now, I'm working two part-time bookkeeping jobs but would like to have something full time. The problem is Jeremy doesn't have a lot of confidence in Brad. He's hoping someone, not necessarily me, will start working there and pull things together."

"You want my old job," Lydia said bluntly.

"No. I don't know the business well enough to be a manager." Kim blushed faintly at the lie. "I'd like to know something about what Brad Chase is like to work for."

Lydia waved for Kim to follow her. On their way to the administrative wing, they passed a rock wall where a climber was working her way up the face while a young man at the bottom managed the rigging. Just beyond, glass windows opened up on a view of an Olympic-size swimming pool. "This place is beautiful," Kim said.

"Yeah, it is."

Lydia took the chair behind the desk. Kim sat opposite.

"Okay, Brad Chase. You want the lowdown on the man or the boss?"

"The boss. To start with."

Lydia said, "The store's had a rough year, I'm not going to sit here and tell you otherwise. Do I think it will go under? Not a chance. It's been too big a part of this community for too many years. Brad will find a way to keep the business afloat. How painful will it be for everyone working there in the process? I can't answer that question."

"Is that why you left? You didn't want to ride out this soft period?"

"I worked for Brad for five years. We had our share of down times. What I got tired of, plain and simple, was watching Brad take profits out of the store that a staff of fifteen, give or take, busted their collective butt to make. If anyone's telling you there will be profit sharing or bonuses with this job, they're full of shit."

Kim laughed uneasily. "That's good to know." Something nagged at her, even as she struggled with what to say next. "Jeremy didn't mention that."

"Did he tell you to come and talk to me?"

"No. I decided to come on my own."

To Kim's surprise, the other woman laughed. "If you know bookkeeping, I almost wish you could get in and take a look at what's going on. I never figured everything out on the accounting side. I managed the inventory, did the ordering and returns. And, of course, I had to deal with customers and staff. Brad had someone else handling the accounting. I wondered sometimes about the money."

"About how much was there?"

"About how much wasn't. Brad has taken a lot of money out of the store to support his addiction to competition. I know on at least one occasion he took a personal loan using the store as collateral. He sweated that out, swore he'd never do such an idiotic thing again. Damn near lost the business that time. But that's Durango for you. There's always someone around to bail out a superstar like Brad Chase."

Kim's mind was racing. "I never thought about that. About how much it would cost him to enter these competitions."

"A bundle, that's what. In money, but also in time. Days, weeks, when he never once showed up at the store."

"That big event in New Zealand he competed in a year ago, was that expensive?"

"He nearly didn't enter it because he couldn't raise the money. About three months before the event, he lost one of his sponsors. The company was doing some cost cutting and dropped most of their second-tier athletes. Brad came unglued. He was counting on that sponsorship to cover his expenses."

"He found the money somewhere. Do you know where it came from?"

Lydia laughed. It was an ugly laugh, empty of mirth. "Yeah, I know. It came from a fund—the kind people start when a family loses their house in a fire or a kid gets diagnosed with a hideous disease."

"Oh, like a GoFundMe account," Kim said.

"Same idea. Different era. Brad had an account from a couple of decades ago when he was trying to make the US Olympic team. He used the same one this time around. It was at one of the local banks. Charity," Lydia said in disgust. "The great Bradley Chase had to go begging for money."

"And he found it."

Lydia Brooks merely raised her eyebrows.

CHAPTER 20

The image of Lydia Brooks leaning back in her chair, arms crossed and eyebrows arched knowingly, stuck with Kim long after she left the rec center. At home, she made a salad and warmed a vegetable casserole for Lena's dinner. She set one place at the patio table and claimed to have eaten a late lunch when Lena asked why she wasn't joining her. She had too much on her mind to sit and pretend to make small talk.

After Lena finished eating, Kim cleaned the kitchen, then went to work at the bakery. She only had an hour or two of work to do and could easily have put off going in until later in the week. Tonight she wanted to keep moving.

She followed her usual route through the neighborhood. Main Avenue was quiet this late in the day. The shadows were growing longer. The air seemed to hold a different quality, a hint of a changing season. Walking, Kim replayed her conversation with Lydia Brooks. Brooks had said Brad Chase had money problems. So what? Lots of people did. But Chase wasn't just anyone. He was Durango's favorite son, the fabled prince of the San Juan wilderness, the local boy who had ventured into the world and returned a conquering hero.

Not Chase, she repeated.

She kicked a stone, frustrated. Someone in Durango had a secret worth keeping; of that she felt certain. The question was who, and where could she or anyone else start tugging to discover the reason why that person had taken such extraordinary measures to ruin Lena?

By the next morning, Kim had the rudiments of a plan. The first part was obvious: find the fund Chase's friends had donated to and see whether he had received any suspicious gifts. She had no idea whether that information was public. In any case, trolling for it would have to wait until after nine, when banks opened. In the meantime, she had another idea. She left the house earlier than usual, taking her car.

Durango boasted two indoor shooting ranges. Little as she knew about guns, Kim knew that no ordinary marksman had shot Lena in Wildcat Canyon. Whoever he was, he was not only good, he had practiced. She took the back way out of town. She passed the turnoff at Third Street that led to Horse Gulch and drove along the east side of the river. She was dressed in blue jeans and hard-soled shoes. She would have preferred boots but didn't own any. She tucked a long-sleeved shirt in behind a belt. No cowgirl in appearance, she at least managed a slightly tougher look. She hoped it would help her cause.

A long display case occupied the front room inside the Durango Sportsman's Club. Kim walked in to the sight of dozens of pistols lining two shelves in the case. A man sat behind the counter, middle-aged with a guarded look on his square face. "Help you?" he said.

"I'm not sure," she said, glancing at the wall behind him where rifles of all makes and models hung. She swallowed hard, moving past her unease at being here. "Do you offer firearms training?"

"All our instructors are certified. What are you looking for?"

"Personal protection, I think."

His hard facade eased slightly. "Some asshole causing you trouble?"

"Maybe. Or maybe I think he might. Right now, I'm only looking for information."

The man handed her a brochure. "This page has our rates. You own a gun yet?"

"No."

"We stock a limited selection of pieces you can try out." He pointed at the guns in the case. "You prefer getting training from a woman, we can arrange that too." He gave her a considered look. "My advice is don't wait. Not because I'm looking to drum up new business. Just my opinion."

She nodded. As she started to turn away, she said, "Does a guy by the name of Brad Chase teach here?"

"Brad? No. As far as I know, he's never been a trainer."

"Someone mentioned him to me. I wondered. Does he come in here much?"

"Nah. Only time I see Brad is when he's got a fussy client who wants to try out a bunch of guns before he buys. About twice a year, Brad brings somebody in. Hunters, mainly. Listen, I don't know if you've got something in mind to buy. I promise I can beat hands down any price Brad gives you by at least fifteen percent."

"Thanks for your help."

It was hard not to think of the interview as a bust. As she drove on to work, Kim tried to eke out anything helpful from the conversation. The sole bright spot was realizing she had a legitimate cover for her inquiry by posing as a woman looking to arm herself against a threat. Nor were questions about Brad Chase as a local gun seller likely to arouse suspicion.

Trina was her usual chatty self that day, babbling on about subjects worn to death long ago. For once, Kim hoped the receptionist would announce she had yet another important errand to run for Skip and leave the office. But that never happened. Between entering employee time cards and running a preliminary payroll report, Kim only had enough time to make a partial list of banks to call concerning the location of Brad Chase's fund. The actual phone calls would have to wait for another day.

When she left Legrand late that afternoon, she drove into town, bypassing the road leading home. She turned right at Fifteenth Street and followed it to Florida Avenue. Once there, she found herself on an unassuming road that, according to the map, promised to lead north and east away from Durango. She followed it for several miles through residential neighborhoods. Eventually the landscape gave way to a less developed setting. Broad hillsides flanked the road. The road itself became a gray ribbon, visible only in brief snatches as it wound in serpentine fashion through the rolling terrain.

Five miles farther, she spied a sign for the Vallecito Gun Club. She pulled into the parking lot of a building equally as nondescript as the Durango Sportsman's Club.

Her visit took half as long and yielded worse results. Brad Chase had never been known to step foot in the place, according to the man who worked at the front counter. He was burly and unpleasant, and gave her no opportunity to ask additional questions, even if any had occurred to her. After spending less than two minutes inside, she left.

Irritated, she strode away from the building, head lowered, fuming. She had no idea she wasn't alone in the parking lot until movement caught her eye. She looked up. A woman was approaching. Dressed in black jeans and a white T-shirt, she carried a leather shoulder bag. Kim didn't have to wonder what was inside. She did a double take when she recognized the woman's face but couldn't think how she knew her. The woman was young and pretty. She had shoulder-length blond hair. Kim pegged her to be in her early twenties, though something in her manner suggested she was older. It wasn't until she realized the woman was staring back that Kim placed her.

"Jaye," she said. "Jaye Dewey?"

The other woman stopped. "And you are?"

"My name is Kim Jackson. I saw you when I was at the police station a couple of weeks ago. Sheila Moss told me your name. I work for Lena Fallon," she said, as if that would explain everything.

"Oh right."

Kim expected the mention of Lena's name would buy her at least a flicker of interest from Jaye. If this was Jaye's third summer volunteering with the department, as Sheila had said, Jaye must have known Lena when she was still a cop. Kim rapidly tried to reconcile her impression of the attractive coed she had seen flirting at the station with this aloof woman. "So, you shoot?" she said.

"I'm just learning." Jaye glanced at her watch. "And I'm late for a lesson." She walked away.

Kim wondered if there was something about being around guns that gave people the right to be perfect assholes. First the guy inside the building. Now Jaye.

"I'd love to talk to you sometime about your volunteer work with the police department," she called. "Sheila told me it's a community program. I might be interested in doing something like that myself," she said, stubbornly persisting.

"Then I'd suggest you talk to someone at the department. Anyone there can tell you about it."

Kim waited until Jaye disappeared inside the building. On her way to her car, she passed a gray Honda Civic with an Arizona license plate. The only other vehicle parked on that side of the lot was a beat-up van. She assumed the Honda belonged to Jaye.

That evening, Lena appeared in the kitchen long before the brown rice had finished cooking. She neither contributed to nor directly obstructed the meal preparation. After determining that Kim had not been working at the bakery before coming home, she spoke of nothing of consequence. Still, there was an undercurrent of agitation in her manner.

"You're not going to join me?" she said when she saw the single place setting on the table.

Kim hadn't intended to. On second thought, she was too hungry to resist.

Lena ate sparingly of the grilled chicken, sautéed vegetables, and rice. When only a few vegetables remained on her plate, she laughed awkwardly. "What have you been up to these past few days? You'll have to pardon my saying so, but I have a hard time believing you haven't been doing something."

"Nothing, really. Well, nothing productive."

"Do tell."

Kim stabbed a chunk of zucchini. She thought about her visit to Lydia Brooks and the complete waste of time spent visiting gun clubs. The latter, especially, was nothing she wanted to confess. "I've been doing some basic background research into Brad Chase. Similar to what I did for Craig Lowell."

"Brad? Why?"

"It's just a hunch. I keep coming back to the string of accidents he's had lately. What were your exact words? Look for what's changed? It seems to me a hell of a lot has changed in Brad Chase's life in the last year and a half. You're not the least bit curious why?"

"He's an idiot, that's why. He takes on insane challenges. The bigger question is why he never got hurt before now. I'd say the law of averages caught up with him."

"Maybe. Or maybe it's something else."

Kim stacked Lena's dinner plate on top of hers and carried the load into the kitchen. She took a pitcher of iced tea from the refrigerator and returned to the patio, refilling two glasses.

In a voice fractionally too quiet, Lena said, "So what's your precious theory—that Brad Chase pulled the trigger that night? I've already told you. There's nothing between that man and me. Not one thing."

"I don't think this was between you and Chase. Someone paid him." The words slipped out too quickly. *If it was him,* Kim had meant to add. Her mind jammed around too many things she wanted to say. She choked on the feeling she already had said too much. Not Brad Chase. *Someone like him,* she wanted to explain, exactly as she had been saying it to herself.

Lena didn't give her the chance. In a voice suddenly hard, she said, "Listen to me. You cannot go around accusing ordinary people of crimes and then squeeze them into some criminal profile. You'll include everyone, exclude no one, exhaust yourself in the process, and come up with zilch in the end."

"I'm not accusing everyone. I'm not even accusing Brad Chase. Look, I thought you and I had a deal, but then you went mute on me." She stopped short of saying she understood why. Lena, she suspected, was as stumped as the men and women on the police force charged with officially investigating the shooting. There simply were no leads to follow. "I wanted to do something, so I decided to take a hard look at him. As an exercise. That's all."

"Two minutes. I'll give you two minutes, and after that, I don't want to hear another word about Chase."

Kim knew she had two choices: either put her cards on the table, or retreat and let Lena have the last word. The wiser course, no question, was the latter. But she had gone too far down this road to backtrack now. "Several things stand out for me. The first is that Brad Chase is obviously a good shot. As an Olympic biathlete, he had to have been incredibly well trained in target shooting."

"It's a long way from being a good shot to being a killer."

"I know. Anyway, he also probably had access to night-vision goggles. I'm not sure his store sells them, but he could have ordered a pair for his own use, don't you think?" When Lena didn't reply, Kim said, "Do you think the person who was out there that night wore night-vision goggles?"

"Yes."

The single word resonated with strength. Taking heart from the concession, Kim continued. "There are probably dozens of guys in Durango who are skilled marksmen—"

"Try hundreds. Try thinking of a number you don't even want to know. Haven't you lived here long enough to have figured out these backwoods are crawling with guys who love guns, love to shoot, and detest government authority in whatever shape or form it pops up?"

"Yes. I know. He isn't the only one who could have done this. What sets Brad Chase apart is the way his life seems to have gone to hell corresponding to the time frame after you were shot."

Lena flinched. "So your pet theory has it that a good man can't live with the consequences of a bad act? And his run of bad luck with injuries is a form of self-punishment?"

Kim blushed. Put so bluntly, it sounded like a sack of horseshit. Nevertheless, she was compelled to admit this was more or less what she'd had in mind.

"What was his motive? I've told you, Chase and I have no history. We've been in the same room maybe a dozen times at social events over the years, but that's it."

"His motive would have been money. If it was him. Someone paid him to do it."

"Oh great. Now we get to make up a new character in this story of yours. Hmm, what about the mayor? What about the police chief? Or, I know. You wanted a lawyer to pin this on. Here, hand me the phone book. Let's start going through the directory."

"Stop it," Kim said. "I have one question for you. If this was your case and you had any reason to think Brad Chase might be a suspect, how would you investigate him?"

"I'd find out if there was a money trail. There isn't going to be one, by the way. He's a freakin' endurance athlete, for Christ's sake. I bet he hasn't fired a gun in over a decade!" Lena ended with a shout.

An uneasy silence followed.

Lena broke it. "You're going to have to stop this," she said too quietly.

"I presume you mean I have to stop pursuing any line of inquiry that may or may not have a thing to do with your case."

"Damn straight that's what I mean." Lena's eyes flashed angrily. "A couple of weeks ago, you told me you wanted to learn how to be an investigator. For the moment, I'm willing to set aside the question of why. Now that we're on that subject, I want to know precisely which skills you wish to acquire. Start with a short list."

Kim sensed a new trap developing. If it was, she had invited it. This was exactly what she had asked for. More troublingly, she hadn't thought far enough ahead. She didn't have a clue how to answer.

Lena laughed. "I thought so. For your information, I've made a couple of phone calls concerning you. I started with your references—the good folks up in Montrose who were willing to vouch for you when you applied to work for me. Eventually I ended up talking to a detective by the name of Dan Czernak. That name mean anything to you?"

Kim stared at her.

"Turns out I know it does. And what I found out is that you pulled this same damn shit in Montrose—sticking your nose where it doesn't belong. What the hell is it with you? You think police work is some fascinating goddamned academic game?"

Kim's face reddened. "It's not a game."

"So in Montrose, you decide to do what the police can't, namely solve the case of a murdered teen. Along the way, you waltz into the arms of a dangerous man who nearly kills you."

Lena's neat summary caused Kim to burn deeply. She would never have described events in those terms. But there was no use arguing with the truth.

"Maybe you don't know it," Lena said, "but most folks are lucky enough to go through their whole lives without experiencing so much excitement."

"What's your point?"

"Oh, I've made my point. I've told you point-blank. You will stop doing anything remotely related to my case. You want to play that game, go play it somewhere else. But I'll warn you right now. Innocent people get hurt when idiots like you trample the playing field."

An ugly silence ensued. Kim recognized the dark truth in Lena's words. She was an amateur. She had developed an unaccountable predilection for investigating crimes. And if she had an ounce of integrity or courage, she would take that newfound passion where it belonged: into proving her innocence in the crimes she had been framed for in Chicago.

"Speaking of theories," Lena said speculatively. "Tit for tat, it's only fair. Here's my theory about you. The guy you're running from is an ex-sweetheart, either a husband or boyfriend, I'm not sure which. Now Byron Jones and your ex were good buddies. No great reference there for your lover boy, by the company he kept. Or for you either. Something must have gone very bad in your relationship for you to get the likes of Jones on your tail. How am I doing so far?"

Kim didn't reply.

"Now here's the part I'm not sure about. Is he after you for purely personal reasons, or is it personal plus?"

"Plus what?"

"Plus some other reason you pissed him off. Here's an idea. Maybe you had a family business. Maybe it was legitimate, for the most part, and maybe it wasn't. One angle of my theory has you keeping the books for the business. Suppose you found out something you weren't supposed to know? Now that would be a darn good reason for you to leave home. More likely, your honey has himself one hell of a temper and this is all about jealousy and control. How many times did he hit you before you left?"

Kim said nothing.

"Funny thing about you, Ms. Jackson. Your driver's license and car registration tell me you're a Colorado resident. At least you've been one for a whopping four months. You passed the state driver's test back in April when you got your license. Didn't exchange a valid license from another state the way most people do when they take up residence in a new place. Hard to believe you didn't have one at your age. Now, it could have expired. Or it could be you just love jumping through bureaucratic hoops and didn't mind taking the test. Or it could be you were trying to close down one avenue to your past, namely, providing a former address. All I know about you is that you lived in Montrose, Colorado, from April of this year until July, when you moved here. I know you worked at a grocery store, played softball, and did volunteer work at a nursing home. And I know you got yourself messed up in some nasty business that nearly got you killed."

"Where are you going with this?"

"I'm just sharing what I know." When Lena spoke next, she made a total shift, dropping her sarcasm. "The guy who tried to kill you in Montrose is in prison and will be for a good long time. You mind answering directly if he's the one you're running from?"

"No."

The answer was deliberately ambiguous: No, she didn't mind answering? Or no, he's not the one?

Lena didn't care. Her gaze narrowed, at the same time pulsing in intensity. For the first time, Kim felt herself splayed beneath a veteran cop's microscope.

"What the hell are you doing in my house?" Lena said.

"What?"

Lena shouted, "You heard me! Did someone hire you? Someone from the media or that damned lawyer working for the Hill family? Who?"

Kim released the breath she had been holding. "No one hired me," she said, straining to understand where this was coming from.

"Then answer my question. What are you doing in my house?"

Kim felt the last vestiges of hope for a reconciliation fade away. She wrestled with her tongue and the only words she could think to say. "I don't have much money, Lena. That's the truth. I wanted to live in Durango. Living here with you was the only way I could afford it."

Lena's fixed stare never left her. Kim didn't buckle under it, even though she was certain she was about to be fired. A full minute passed before Lena spoke. "I have one thing to say to you. Either pack your things and leave tonight. Or sign this." She produced a page from the side pocket on her chair.

It was a nondisclosure form. Kim read the key sentences twice. With her signature, she agreed not to discuss Lena or the civil suit pending against her with anyone, ever.

"Do you have a pen?" she said.

Lena gave her one.

Kim signed. As she handed the paper back, she said, "Whatever you paid your lawyer for this, you wasted your money."

Lena folded the page and inserted it in an envelope.

Afterward, she continued to sit at the table unperturbed, or seemingly so. Eventually Kim stood to finish clearing the table. As she moved between the house and patio, observing Lena from behind, she felt as if a tornado had blown through the backyard, lifting everything in its path only to return it to its former place, leaving her with the eerie feeling that everything had changed and everything remained exactly the same.

CHAPTER 21

Kim had every intention of abiding by Lena's demand to quit any activity resembling an investigation. She burned at the insinuation that she was a "crime hag"—someone who fed off the criminal misfortunes of others. She didn't know where she and Lena stood with one another. All she knew was that she had made a promise, and she meant to keep it. As soon as she did one last thing.

She left work late the next afternoon and went directly to Four Corners Bank and Trust. It was the bank, she had learned, that managed Brad Chase's curious fund. She reached the entrance shortly before five. Inside, she was told to speak with the director of customer accounts.

"You have a question about Brad's fund? What can I tell you?" a stout woman, impeccably dressed in a suit, asked.

"Is the fund still open?"

"Yes. The account has existed for over fifteen years, ever since Brad made his Olympic bid."

"I don't know whether you know he's had bad luck with injuries lately. I've been talking with friends about doing something in his honor. I was able to get a partial list of supporters who contributed when he made a run at the Ultra Endurance World Championships last year. I was wondering if I might see the complete list, just to be sure I haven't overlooked anyone."

"No reason not to. It's public information. We provided the list to the paper last year, but I don't believe they ever printed it." She typed a few commands on her keyboard. A moment later, she spun the screen partway around for Kim to read.

Kim's eyes popped wide when she saw the information. It was vastly more detailed than she had expected. Contributors were listed, along with the amount of their gifts. It didn't take half a second to spot the two five-figure entries. Kennerly Properties, a local real estate company, had donated ten thousand dollars to the fund. Kim knew the name. She had come across it while working at Legrand Construction. Skip was currently involved in a Kennerly project, renovation of a four-unit apartment complex. She hadn't met Paul Kennerly but had seen his face on billboards around town.

She pointed at the second five-figure line, which boasted another ten-thousand-dollar gift in memory of Dorothy Fitzsimmons. "I'm not familiar with this name. Do you know who Dorothy Fitzsimmons was?"

"Oh my, yes. She was a wonderful lady. She moved to Arizona a number of years ago when her health began to fail. Before then, she taught school here for more than twenty years. I don't believe it's an exaggeration to say she educated more than half the people in town."

"Who donated the money?"

"Paul did, of course. Paul Kennerly is her grandson." The woman laughed. "Paul's a good man, but I won't say he didn't have ulterior motives, donating as generously as he did to Brad's ambitions. Paul had just purchased the Animas River property and was trying to market it as an upscale resort when Brad was about to go halfway around the world. Brad really has helped put Durango on the map. Savvy a businessman as

Paul is, I'm sure he saw an opportunity to promote his interests through Brad."

While the woman spoke, Kim skimmed the page. Besides the two entries totaling twenty thousand dollars, the next largest single entry was for five hundred dollars. The vast majority of entries were for one hundred dollars or less. "We wanted to send special invitations to those people who contributed most generously. Of course, it will be an open event. I see now that I have the names I need. May I come back and double-check against this list before the invitations go out?"

"Certainly." The woman turned the screen back to face her. "As I said, the information is public. I won't be able to give you addresses, though."

"No. I'm sure we have those."

—

Kim took special pains preparing dinner that night. The entrée was pork tenderloin simmered in a rosemary tomato sauce. She chopped vegetables for a salad. Broccoli was in the steamer. She paused to inspect the kitchen, noting all was under control, then glanced at the patio where the edges of the tablecloth were flapping in the wind. Clouds had been gathering since afternoon; the first drops of rain fell as she watched. Uncertain whether she would be invited to share the meal, she set the kitchen table for two, regardless.

Lena didn't emerge from her suite until minutes before dinner was ready. Kim poured two glasses of water, then waited to hear Lena's choice of beverage. It was a merlot, her current favorite. Through dinner, Kim spoke of nothing extraordinary, only the bits of gossip she had heard that day from Trina.

"The pork was delicious," Lena said when the meal was over. "Old family recipe?"

"No. Something I saw in a magazine last week. It looked like something even I could manage."

"Don't sell yourself short. You've come a long way in the cooking department."

"Thanks." Kim stood up to remove the plates to the sink. "Do you want coffee? Or tea?"

"No, thanks. You go ahead."

After Kim put on water for tea, she sat down again. In the kitchen's tight space, she and Lena were closer than when they sat on the patio. Kim fidgeted. Finally Lena said, "Go ahead and say it. You're acting like the cat that ate the canary. So whatever it is, just tell me."

Kim sighed. "I know you told me to back off from doing anything remotely connected to an investigation. But I did find something new. It's not anything big. It's—I don't know what it is."

Lena didn't seem surprised. "What did you find?"

"First I should tell you what I didn't find. Earlier this week—before we talked—I had already checked out two gun clubs in town. I wanted to find out whether Brad Chase ever goes to shoot at either. The answer is he doesn't. He occasionally takes clients to the Durango Sportsman's Club. He's never stepped foot inside the Vallecito Gun Club, according to the bear of a man who works there."

"Fred Vaughn," Lena said without missing a beat. "Yeah, he's a prize. What else?"

Kim drew a deep breath. "I don't know what to make of this last piece of information. I found a money trail, but it's not much of one. When Brad was making plans to go to New Zealand to compete last year, he was short on money. He had recently lost an endorsement from his major sponsor. By then, he had already taken every penny out of the store he could squeeze. Apparently someone suggested that he resurrect an old fund, one set up years ago when he competed in the

Olympics. He hoped to get contributions from people in the community."

"Is there a point to any of this?"

No, there wasn't a point, Kim thought. Paul Kennerly was almost as much of a Durango icon as Brad Chase. Reputed to be a millionaire several times over, he was one of the town's largest landowners and private developers. He had been a city councilor and was on the board of directors of many corporations. Kim thought she knew his type: He was a good old boy with a touch of the Midas in him. Whatever he did turned to gold.

She spoke reluctantly. "Only one guy was a big contributor. His company donated ten thousand dollars. He ponied up another ten in his grandmother's name. I think it was all a ploy to—"

"Who was the guy?" Lena said, interrupting.

"Paul Kennerly. I know, for a man like him, even twenty grand is a drop in the bucket."

She glanced over skittishly, dreading Lena's wrath.

What she saw shook her worse. Lena's eyes were closed. She sat so still Kim couldn't be sure she was breathing.

The whistle on the teakettle blew. Kim jumped up to remove it from the burner.

Lena wheeled away from the table.

"You know him?" Kim said. Too late, she realized the question was moot. The whole town knew Kennerly.

Lena opened her mouth. No words came out. Then she said, "Swear something to me, Kim."

"Yes, of course. What is it?"

"Don't ask another question of anyone in this town. Not about me. Not about Brad Chase, and certainly not about Paul Kennerly. Damian is coming tomorrow. We're going away for the weekend. Don't talk to anyone until I get back."

Kim knew she had no choice. Whatever promise Lena had exacted from her days ago paled in comparison to the urgency of this one. "I won't."

After Lena disappeared through the doorway, Kim stared at the space she had vacated. She felt haunted by the emptiness. Stinging questions rang in her ears. Paul Kennerly's name meant something to Lena, and not from having seen his image plastered on local billboards for the last two decades.

But what did it mean?

CHAPTER 22

Dark circles rimmed Lena's eyes in the morning. She barely spoke during breakfast. As she was leaving to bathe and dress, she exacted a second promise from Kim not to approach anyone in town with questions on any subject. "You're good at what you do," she said after getting that promise.

"Thanks."

"No, I mean it. You're good at finding things out. You should be a cop. Ever thought about it?" She raised her head, inviting a first meeting of their eyes all morning.

"Not really."

"Well, like I said. You're good at it."

The conversation ended there. Kim left for work without seeing Lena again.

Throughout the morning, she found it impossible to think of anything besides Paul Kennerly. She perused computer records and thumbed through file cabinets, in the process learning that Skip had been doing work on Kennerly projects for more than ten years. She clamped her mouth shut each time she felt tempted to ask Trina what she knew about the man. Considering the link between the two businesses, she thought Trina a likely treasure trove of information. Kim kept her promise and didn't ask.

—

Saturday morning, she was up early. She spent an hour reading the paper. Later, she did laundry. As she surveyed her meager wardrobe, she tried to anticipate what other clothes she might need, come autumn. A flannel shirt and a fleece pullover to start with. Eventually a warm winter jacket.

Shortly past noon, she was sitting outside when the sound of a car pulling into the driveway caused her to jump. She walked over to peek through the slatted fence. A petite blond woman got out of a small sedan. Damian, Kim assumed. Lena was in the passenger seat. Kim returned to the patio to wait.

The back gate opened. Lena led the way across the sidewalk. When she reached the patio, she said, "We need to talk." She went inside without another word.

"Hello, Kim. I'm glad to meet you, finally," the other woman said. "My first name is Jill, but please call me Damian, my last name," she said, extending her hand.

Searching the eyes of the diminutive woman whose relationship to Lena was shrouded in mystery, Kim said, "It's nice to meet you. Is everything okay?"

"No. I'll let Lena tell you about it. Do you have dinner plans?"

"No."

"Plan to join us. Please." Damian followed Lena into the house.

Kim didn't move again until she heard sounds from the kitchen. She went inside.

Lena had the refrigerator door open. Without taking anything out, she roughly closed the door. "You were right," she said flatly.

Dark circles shadowed her eyes again today. More disturbingly, the corners were tinged red. Kim stood inside the screen door, afraid to move.

"About Chase," Lena said. "I found the gun club he used. It's in Cortez."

Kim's heart plummeted. "How did you?" she stumbled, unable to articulate the question.

"I know the manager at the club. I stopped in and asked. Turns out Brad was a regular there for a couple of weeks one winter about a year ago. He stopped coming in as abruptly as he started."

Kim had no alternative but to sink onto the chair she had managed to slide out from the table. "And you think—" she started to say.

"I think what you think."

She glanced at the doorway when Damian joined them. Then she looked at Lena. "Who's Paul Kennerly? I mean, who is he to you?"

"An asshole, that's who."

Lena might have left it there, if not for Damian, who said, "Tell her."

Drawing herself tighter, Lena seemed to suck all the energy from the room. "You must know who Paul Kennerly is. Don't tell me you haven't seen his signs all over town."

"I've seen his signs. I don't know anything about him."

"He's a big shot in the community. He's filthy rich, but a total freakin' cheapskate. He'd never give Brad Chase a dime solely out of the goodness of his heart." With obvious reluctance, she added, "He and I dated a while back."

"What?"

Lena's eyes shot daggers. Kim couldn't have checked the exclamation had she wanted to. Tension laced the moment. New questions begged to be asked, about Lena's past with

Kennerly, about her present with Damian, whatever that was. Kim didn't dare say a word.

By degrees, the story came out. Lena backtracked through her life, telling about a deputy sheriff in Bayfield whom she had dated for several years. They had discussed marriage. Neither was in any hurry to tie the knot.

"I don't know what the hell happened," she said. "One day, Paul showed up in my life. Paul was always showing up, not just at community events but at the police station too. He wasn't married, but he had a longtime girlfriend. He said it was over between them. The first time he asked me out, I thought it was a joke. I knew I wasn't his type. That didn't stop him. Or me." Lena's voice sank. "Ron and I broke up. Paul and I started dating."

Kim's mind raced. She had never dreamed Lena would make this kind of confession. Nor could she assemble all the pieces of the story into a coherent whole. She simply didn't know what to make of the history of the men in Lena's life. Or Damian's place in it now. Damian, presently standing close to Lena, wasn't touching her, but she might as well have been. The sense of intimacy between them was that strong.

"How long were you and Kennerly involved?"

"We weren't," Lena said sharply. "Not the way you think. We dated."

Her words rippled with scorn. They sent another message, one Kim couldn't decipher. "Okay, how long did you date?"

"A few months. Two. It's hard to remember when things started."

"Who ended things, you or him?"

Lena's brow narrowed in rage. "It was mutual."

And that's when Kim knew Lena was lying. She exhaled softly, at a loss as to what to do with the knowledge. "When?"

"Two years ago. Around Thanksgiving."

More tentatively still, Kim said, "And you don't have any idea why he might have—"

"Paid Brad Chase to shoot me? No. I don't have a clue!" Tears sprang to her eyes. She balled her fists to her face, then pulled away from the table.

Damian stopped her. "Don't leave. You have to get through this. You know that."

Kim broke the silence that fell afterward. "What happens next?"

Lena muttered something about wanting a drink. Damian took three glasses from a cabinet shelf and a pitcher from the refrigerator. "This will do for a start," she said.

Lena scowled. But after drinking the iced tea, she seemed to recover. "I'll talk to the captain. Find out who's working my case. Then I find someone who will put the screws to Chase and make the link to Kennerly. That's what happens next."

She drank her tea and left the room. Damian followed. Kim returned to the patio, staggered by the revelations. She tried to fathom a motive. Chase's was clear: he'd needed money. But Kennerly's?

It was something big, she thought.

Unless Kennerly was a madman. Unless he thought himself beyond the reach of the law.

Gazing absently at the back fence, Kim wondered whether there was more to the story of a soured romance than Lena was willing to admit.

CHAPTER 23

"What are you reading?" Damian asked when she came outside.

Startled, Kim exclaimed, "Oh! *Mrs. Dalloway*." She glanced at the closed book in her hands.

"Are you a Virginia Woolf fan?"

"No. This is the first book of hers I've read."

"I'm going to start chopping vegetables. I thought I'd make pasta for dinner. Would you like to help? I'd apologize for interrupting, but it doesn't look like you were doing much reading anyway."

"I'd love to help."

While Kim washed broccoli and cauliflower, Damian peeled an onion and chopped it and a carrot into small pieces. The two fell into an easy rhythm. Damian seemed subdued. For good reason, Kim thought, taking advantage of the close quarters to look at Lena's friend. Damian's features were even and attractive. She seemed pale and insubstantial, which hardly figured in her favor when dealing with someone as forceful as Lena. Kim assumed she was made of sturdier stuff than her slight physique suggested.

"How do you know Lena?" she said.

"I was her nurse. I'm a graduate student in psychology now."

"And you live in Albuquerque?"

"Yes. It was the best choice for school."

Lena came into the kitchen while they were talking. She looked tired and haggard. She poured a glass of wine. Kim refilled her glass as necessary and otherwise played the role of sous-chef, fetching ingredients and watching the pasta dish come to life.

Through dinner, no one mentioned Paul Kennerly.

Afterward, Lena retired to her room. Damian accompanied her. Kim cleaned the kitchen, then went upstairs. She was still trying to rouse interest in her book when she heard the distinct sound of someone climbing the staircase. She leapt from the chair and searched the room for anything she didn't want seen. The closet door was closed. The four business suits hanging there were hidden from view. There was nothing else.

"Hello," Damian called from the top step. "May I come in?"

"Yes. Come in. I don't get many visitors," Kim said cheerily, sweeping away the remnants of her panic. She pointed Damian toward the pink chair.

"No, no. You sit there. I'll take the floor." In one motion, Damian sank onto the carpet.

"Is Lena still in her room?" Kim said.

"Yes. She's sleeping. She took a pill. It's something she rarely does. Tonight—she's very upset."

"I would say I understand, but I'm sure I don't."

Damian didn't reply. She sat there, taking in her surroundings. Kim followed her gaze. There were no framed photos to engage her interest. Other than the library book on the floor and the cap and sunglasses on top of the dresser, the room was absent of clutter.

"This is a nice space," Damian said. She nodded at the chair. "I imagine you spend a lot of time sitting there."

"Yes."

"It's the obvious choice. No TV. No computer. What else to do but read and watch the world go by?"

Any number of pleasantries came to mind. Kim didn't say anything.

"My stomach is in knots," Damian said. "I didn't expect this." She closed her eyes and leaned against the wall. "All this time, nothing. I realize now I've lived in a twin state, both expecting and not expecting that whoever shot Lena would be found. It's easy to think the path is clear. That if an avenue to the truth presents itself, one should march down it without pause. Now I'm not sure."

Kim smiled. "You've lost me."

"I don't know whether knowing the truth about her shooting will enable Lena to live better with it."

The thought had never occurred to Kim. She was still considering it when Damian spoke again. "You've been good for her," she said.

"What?"

"It was only me before. Now she's let you in."

"I don't think so."

"Think what you want."

Her words were equally without warmth or malice. Kim found the conversation odd but not unpleasant. With knees bent and drawn inward, Damian appeared perfectly at ease on the floor. She looked like a disciple, a novitiate folded into herself.

As if somehow aware of the direction of Kim's thoughts, Damian smiled. "Please don't take this the wrong way, but I have a hard time getting a sense of you."

Kim wanted to laugh and say she felt the same.

"I would like to get to know you. I hope I have the chance. Lena would never say it, but I know she's afraid you're going to leave."

Kim's chest constricted. She wanted to lie and say it wasn't true. Then she didn't know which part she wanted to be false: That she might disappear without a word of warning. Or that Lena would give a damn if she did.

"I'm not going anywhere. Not anytime soon."

"I should get back," Damian said as she pushed herself to her feet. "I don't think Lena will wake before morning, but I want to be there if she does."

—

Over the next two days, time blurred between hours passing rapidly and moments ground slowly to a halt. Kim wasn't home when Durango's police captain stopped by for a conversation Lena had waited seventeen months to have. She heard about it after dinner on Monday night.

"The captain was skeptical," Lena said. "Hell, why wouldn't he be? Brad Chase? He's the last man in town anyone would point a finger at. I told him all I wanted was for someone to check out Chase. Stop by for a friendly chat. Find out how he acts under questioning. In a situation like this, you need to let on gradually why you're there."

"Did he agree to have someone do it?"

Lena frowned. In the dimly lit living room, Kim sat on the sofa. Lena was nearby. A soft rain fell, creating a pattering sound on the roof. Between the gray light and the sound of raindrops, the atmosphere between them felt close. Lena said, "I didn't get any guarantees. The captain said he'd talk to Stankowicz and Moss. I gather they'll be looking into whatever gets looked into."

A thought occurred to Kim. She kept it to herself. "Any idea when this might happen?"

"No. The captain knows my time frame. He won't wait. Not unless he thinks I've lost my mind and taken to pulling suspects out of the phone book."

"You didn't mention Kennerly?"

"No! Of course not."

A minute passed. The room's shadows swallowed the cry. Kim thought she understood. Lena couldn't mention Kennerly without losing complete credibility in the eyes of her former commander. And Chase-as-shooter was an empty theory without a bread-crumb money trail leading to someone, in this case, Kennerly.

Kim pondered her other idea. The enormity of the proposal stopped her. Lena had been a virtual recluse for more than a year. In that time, she had dealt with doctors, nurses, physical therapists, and a revolving door of paid live-in aides. She had cut herself off from family and her fellow officers, the men and women who were in the best position to bring her shooter to justice and exonerate her last actions as a police detective.

She spoke cautiously. "Please think about what I'm going to say, Lena. Don't say a word until I've finished. What if you and I were to take a shopping trip to Wilderness Outfitters? What if we arrived at a time when we knew Brad was in the store?"

"What? No!" Color rose in Lena's cheeks.

"Think about it. Chase isn't a career criminal. If he did this, what's it going to be like for him to see you?"

"It won't happen. I'll kill the bastard first."

Kim said nothing.

Lena's expression tightened. "The captain's probably right. I'm way off base. We don't have a lot to go on here," she said, angry again, almost seeming to blame Kim for the deficit. "The truth is, we may have our heads up our asses. Even if Chase had the motive of wanting money to do this, Paul had no motive to harm me. None. We've built an entire conspiracy theory on two flimsy facts: Paul gave Chase money, and Chase visited a shooting club. Neither fact holds an ounce of water. The money may have been a loan. Chase may shoot regularly. Just because we don't know where doesn't mean squat."

"Yet somewhere down deep you believe Kennerly was capable of doing this," Kim said, treading lightly.

Lena spoke with emotion. "Paul thinks he owns the whole effing world! He couldn't own me. But that wasn't why we stopped seeing each other. The better question is why he came on to me in the first place. I wasn't his type. I was never going to be his type. We played a freakin' game with each other for a couple of months, then it stopped. That's it. To answer your question, I don't know what Paul would stop at to get what he wants, but the question is irrelevant. He always gets what he wants simply by lifting his little finger."

For the second time, Kim was struck by the feeling that there was more to Lena's romantic past than she was telling. She took a different tack. "Then there must have been something else Kennerly wanted from you. Something you didn't see."

"Chances are much greater we're both wrong. Deluded by apparent coincidences. And chances are I'm going to be thoroughly humiliated when all of this turns up nothing."

"All the better reason to press Chase's buttons now—assuming they can be pressed. Put him on notice. Make him squirm when someone in uniform stops by."

"I'll think about it."

It was a concession Kim hadn't expected. She was more shocked when Lena came full circle at breakfast the next morning. Out of the blue, Lena said, "I've thought about what you said. It's not the worst idea I've ever heard. I'll do it. I'll go to Chase's store. Just tell me this. How the hell do we guarantee he's there? Because I promise you I will only go once."

"I'll take care of that," Kim assured her.

—

That morning, she drove to work. She told Skip she had a late-afternoon appointment. He told her to take off when she needed to. By three forty-five, she was parked in front of the garage. She had phoned Lena from work to pass on the news that Chase was at the store and was expected to be there until six, according to an employee she had spoken to. It wasn't an ironclad guarantee of finding him there. But it was all they had to go on.

Neither woman spoke while Lena wheeled out to the driveway and managed the cumbersome process of maneuvering into the passenger seat. Kim stood back, sobered by the sight of Lena's struggle to force her damaged left elbow to bear weight. Once she was settled, Kim drove into town. She circled the block twice before finding a parking space. She removed the wheelchair, set it up, then waited while Lena levered herself into it.

The store's front door was propped open. Kim followed Lena inside. She trailed behind while Lena skirted past the camping equipment near the front. "Hey," she called in a friendly voice to the woman working at the checkout counter. "How are you doing?"

"Fine. Is there anything I can help you with?"

"No. I'm just looking." She pushed past the counter to a rack of long-sleeved shirts. Kim kept her expression neutral, staying close while feigning interest in a different rack.

"Do you like this one?" Lena said, holding out a fleece V-neck.

"Yes. How much is it?"

Lena checked the tag. "Seventy-five dollars."

Kim checked the display of socks while Lena moved deeper into the store's interior. *Fifteen dollars,* she noted in disgust, bouncing the pair of wool socks in one hand. Expensive, but probably necessary come winter. So far, she hadn't seen any sign of Brad. Nor of Jeremy.

She tensed when she heard an unfamiliar man's voice followed by a deep laugh. Resisting the urge to whirl around, she kept her head down. This was Lena's show.

"Brad, hey," Lena called, setting it all in motion. "How are you doing?" She wheeled out of the morass of racks to the aisle. "Lena Fallon," she said, approaching the man who was trotting downstairs from the second floor. She offered her hand. "We met a few years ago at a fundraiser for the Open Trail Space."

Chase had little choice but to shake Lena's hand. In the perfect position to observe, Kim didn't miss the sudden evaporation of expression from his face. No hint of joviality remained.

"Right. How are you doing?"

He looked like a giant standing next to the wheelchair. Brad Chase was better looking in person than in his photos. He was at least six feet tall. His arms and face were tanned. Kim's first thought was that Chase had a showman quality about him, evidenced in his broad smile and laughing eyes. He wasn't laughing now.

"Oh, I'm terrific," Lena said. "Lots going on these days. I'm looking forward to ski season. I want to get fitted for one of those butt skis so I can head out to the slopes. Think we're in for a good snowpack this year?"

"I, ah, really don't know."

Chase grew more uncomfortable with each passing second. Coupled with her fury for the man, Kim felt something more—raw admiration for Lena. Riveted, she watched the performance.

"Listen, I have another question for you," she said, wheeling toward Brad the instant he started to back away. "I wanted to look at your selection of Glocks. Do you have a second now?"

The question nearly sent him over the edge. "Actually, I—I don't have time," he stammered. "I only carry a small inventory, and it's upstairs." He pointed weakly toward the second floor. "I'm sorry, we don't have an elevator."

"No problem." Lena shrugged. "I just want to check out a couple of models. Something easy to handle. Maybe you could walk me through a few recommendations."

"The truth is I'm not all that familiar with the guns you're talking about. And just now, I don't have time." He backed up another step.

Lena appeared nonplussed. "Do you suppose we could make an appointment? My schedule's wide open. Hardly a blessed thing to do all day." If her tone became subtly accusing, no one besides Kim, and possibly Brad, knew it.

"Call," Brad said, moving away. "We'll see if we can set something up. Western Guns probably carries more of the models you're interested in. I don't want to give away business, but you might be happier with what you find there."

"I'll check over there too. But I definitely want to see what you carry. Thanks for the help." She resumed her inspection of long-sleeved shirts.

Brad went to the front of the store. "Back in a minute," he said tightly to the woman working there. He bolted from the premises.

"I think I've seen all I need to," Lena said to Kim.

She didn't speak again until they were in the car. She waited until they were driving away from the retail district. "That bastard," she spit through clenched teeth. "Did you see him? He did it."

Kim agreed. But she tempered her reply. "He certainly seemed uncomfortable talking to you."

Lena shifted sideways. With her upper body turned, she looked at whatever lay beyond the side window. They crossed one street, then another. When Kim slowed and signaled to make the turn onto their street, Lena said, "No. Don't turn. Let's drive. Do you mind?"

"Any place in particular you want to go?"

"No. I don't care. Stay on this street. Let's drive up to the college."

Kim crossed the intersection at East Eighth. Once through it, the road wound to the left and began to rise. A cyclist pedaling in the opposite direction reminded her of Zeke's advice about doing her training here. She understood why. After rounding the first curve, the road continued to rise. The grade stayed constant for a mile or so. When they emerged onto the hilltop, she saw houses scattered across the open plain.

"Turn left," Lena said.

They drove through the gates onto the Fort Lewis campus. Lena directed her across the plateau to an overlook. Kim parked. She removed the wheelchair. Once settled in it, Lena wheeled away. Kim walked in the opposite direction, gazing down on the valley floor. She spied the snaky dark line of the Animas River. The peaks looming due north humbled her into deep silence.

And, finally, into deep sadness. If Brad Chase wasn't guilty of shooting Lena, nothing he'd said or done in the last hour argued in favor of his innocence. It was too much to absorb. More so for Lena, Kim thought, glancing over to see the ex-cop staring at the landscape. What she was seeing was anyone's guess. Kim wondered if her inner vision was riddled with the darkness of night, punctuated by a pulsing red strobe and the white glare of headlights.

Later, when they were ready to leave, Lena said, "Damian is certain life still holds promise for me. I've never been sure I believe that."

"I hold with Damian."

Lena made a small, brittle sound. "I guess that doesn't surprise me."

CHAPTER 24

"Paul, what's this about? What's going on?"

Jaye Dewey hit the Pause button, freezing the image of the attractive brunette on the screen. From the woman's drawn brow to her pursed mouth, her fine features contorted in a look of dismay. A moment before, her step had been buoyant; she had laughed. Now she stood stock-still. Though the video hadn't advanced a single frame, Jaye swore she could see terror edging into the woman's eyes.

She pressed the Play button.

"I said take your clothes off."

Though Paul Kennerly was nowhere in sight, his voice was easily recognizable.

"Or what?" The woman tried to laugh. She made the mistake of taking a step forward.

"Don't! Don't do a damn thing except take off your clothes. Over there. Stand under the light."

His first explosive word stopped the woman in her tracks. The rest brought tears to her eyes. *"I don't understand,"* she said in a small voice.

"Oh, I think you do."

There followed a pause. The woman did as instructed. She stood beneath the light and undid her blouse. She stepped out of her jeans. She stood trembling in her bra and panties. In super slow motion, she slid the panties down her legs. Slower still, she reached for the clasp behind her back.

"There, now. That wasn't so hard, was it? Ah, ah, no need to be shy," Kennerly said when she moved to cover herself.

Shuffling sounds ensued. The screen went black. Jaye pressed the Stop button and sat back, thinking. Imagining, rather, Kennerly and the woman in bed. For that, surely, was why they had come to this room. Four times, she had seen him leave the bar with a different woman. Each one had accompanied him as a willing companion, but none, she suspected, had signed up for giving a private strip show as a prelude to sex.

The strip show, she was convinced, was the point. It was his power play, his big turn-on. It was the climax of his protracted seduction. And once he brought a woman to this room, she had no choice but to do his bidding. There was a keyed lock on the inside of the door. Jaye suspected that once a woman was in his lair, Kennerly locked the door.

It was kidnapping. It was coercion. Jaye didn't know how many crimes Kennerly had committed, but she did know that no woman who had ever been in this room had pressed charges against him. Jaye had searched for reports at the police department and found none.

She thought his collection of tapes numbered ten or so, which explained her reluctance to take a second, until last week. Having watched it several times, she still didn't know whether she'd hit the jackpot or chosen a dud. She popped out the first and inserted the new one in the machine. She hit Play.

The screen lit up with the bedroom scene. Lena Fallon came into focus. She was wearing tapered black jeans and boots. Her blouse was low cut, tucked in. Jaye couldn't believe how good she looked. Nothing like a cop. And not anything like the women Kennerly usually brought here. Fallon was older, past thirty-five, for sure. In her own way, she looked really hot.

"I have a certain order I like to do things in," Kennerly said on the tape.

"What kind of order?" Fallon said, laughing.

Jaye tracked the length of Lena Fallon's legs down, then up, startled, as she had been each time, to see her standing.

"If it wouldn't be too much trouble, take your clothes off."

Fallon's face came large into the camera lens. She drew close to him before speaking. *"What?"*

"Over there." A pause. *"Stand over there and take your clothes off."*

"Is this some kind of joke?"

"No. No joke. It's a simple enough request. Take your clothes off. Then we'll roll around on the bed and have some fun."

Jaye pushed the Pause button. She tried to fathom—as she had tried before, each time she reached this moment on the video—to grasp what was in Kennerly's mind that night. The other women he had brought to the room had been singularly lacking in the one thing Lena Fallon had in spades: power. Had they made a deal ahead of time, something on the order of: *Let's do a bit of role-playing. I'll give the orders, you follow them, and see where it goes.*

Jaye thought not.

The sparkle of laughter hadn't faded from Fallon's eyes. Then, as though a curtain fell, it was gone. She said, *"A strip show—is that what you want? You're not getting it from me, pal."*

Jaye grinned. She loved that word: "pal."

"Take me home. Now."

The screen went black.

CHAPTER 25

"Jesus, Lena, you know better than to pull a stunt like that."

Detective Mark Stankowicz stood in the living room, speaking angrily. He pounded his notepad with a fist. "Let us handle Chase. You'd have had my head if I'd ever done anything like that."

It was the day after their visit to Wilderness Outfitters. Lena's carefully composed features betrayed nothing. Kim watched the proceedings unfolding, her attention moving from the senior male officer to Lena, occasionally flickering to Sheila Moss. She hadn't expected to be allowed to sit in on the meeting when the officers arrived unexpectedly at the house. She stayed when no one asked her to leave.

"No law against going shopping," Lena said. "No law against talking."

"Sometimes there is. I'll say it again. Leave Chase to us."

Obviously someone had told the officers about the visit to Chase's store. Kim wondered who.

"What do you have so far?" Lena demanded.

Stankowicz ran down his report. He said they had verified the dates Chase was at the Cortez Gun Club, year before last.

When asked about the visits, Chase answered that he some-times went target shooting to relax. He said he had no particu-lar recollection of what he was doing the night of the shootings in Wildcat Canyon.

Moss spoke for the first time. "We're going easy on him, to start. We don't have much to go on. We need him to give us something." She met Lena's stare head-on. "Before we have probable cause for a warrant to search his house for a gun."

"And his store."

"Right."

Stankowicz asked Lena whether she knew a woman named Maggie White. "She's Chase's girlfriend. Mother of his son. We interviewed her. Seems that in early March a year back, she took the baby and went to visit her family in Arizona. The trip wasn't planned. She said she wasn't too excited about going. The trip was all Brad's idea. She was away the week you went down."

For the first time, Kim noticed the measures Stankowicz took to avoid direct reference to Lena's shooting.

"She can't alibi him."

"That's right."

Lena closed her eyes. Palpable relief flooded through her. "You're getting close," she said.

"That's what we came here to tell you," Stankowicz said. "So don't go screwing up our case by interfering." He penciled something onto the pad, then looked up. "What we're short on is motive. You still swear you've never had any bad dealings with the guy? Nothing's occurred to you?"

"I've had almost exactly zero to do with him. Ever. Look for money."

"Yeah, well. We're looking."

The officers didn't linger for a social call. Kim followed them to the door and watched them get into the patrol car. The headlights came on, sending twin beams into the gray evening. "So what do you think?" she said when she turned around.

Lena's expression was grim. "I think they're blowing smoke up my ass. Maybe they do think Chase had something to do with what happened. They still aren't going to get any warrant. Not without corroborating evidence." She looked down at her fingers, entwined on her lap.

"You're not going to tell them about the money Paul Kennerly gave Brad?"

"No. They have to find it. If I breathe one word about that, Stankowicz will turn dead set against me. Plain stubbornness. No cop ever wants another cop telling him how to run an investigation."

Kim walked over and dropped onto the sofa. It was the singularly most uncomfortable piece of furniture in the house, padded so thinly, her bones sank directly onto the wooden frame. "Tell me more about Kennerly," she said. When she didn't get an answer, she pressed harder. "You've had all week. Don't tell me you haven't been thinking about him."

"I haven't found what I want to know."

"Which is?"

Rather than reply, Lena wheeled to the window. The porch light was off. The nearest light shone from a streetlight on the opposite corner. Each night, its glare penetrated the second-floor window, casting a thin beam across Kim's bedroom.

"I give up something, you give up something," Lena said in a curiously detached voice.

"What?"

"I answer your question. In exchange, you answer one of mine."

"Lena, this isn't a game. We're talking about making the case against the man who all but took your life away."

"He did take my life away! Agree or don't."

Kim frowned. "Okay. Maybe."

Lena remained at the window. "Kennerly wanted some-thing from me. I should have seen it back then. It wasn't romance, though, for a time, I—"

Thought so, Kim added when Lena didn't finish the sentence. "How long did you know him? Before you started dating?"

Lena didn't answer. A minute or more passed before she pivoted away from the window. "I guess you still don't understand life in a small town. Why is that? Oh, that's right. You're a big-city girl, Indianapolis, I believe you said?"

"Minneapolis," Kim said stiffly, knowing perfectly well Lena hadn't forgotten.

Whatever was on Lena's mind, she let it go. Her voice was softer when she spoke next. "Paul was a few years ahead of me in school. To answer your question, there wasn't a time when I didn't know him, or at least know of him. I have no idea when we reconnected as adults. It must have been after I was on the force. He was elected to city council. Unlike most of the men and women who elbow their way onto city council, he made an effort to get to know everyone in the department."

"So you knew him for years before you started dating?"

"Something like that. What's your point?"

"I don't know. Forget it. So two years ago, you started going out."

Grudgingly, Lena resumed her story. "The city threw a party for its employees two years ago. It was an Oktoberfest thing. Ron—the guy I'd been seeing—he'd tell you it started that night. Paul and I danced, no big deal. Afterward, he started coming on to me. It was all very flattering. He was a total charmer, tons of money, good looking. Take all that and put it in a guy who's cocksure, he's tough to resist. I couldn't resist him." Lena's voice grew pensive. "I swallowed his line that he wanted me. He didn't want me. I was an idiot."

"Did you fall in love with him?"

"For about five minutes. Have you ever been in love?"

"Is that your one question?" Kim flashed a smile. When she saw the complete lack of amusement in the other woman's eyes, she sobered quickly. "Yes. Once. For slightly longer than five minutes."

Lena exhaled tiredly. "There's no telling what I missed in Paul. I thought he wanted me. Now I think he wanted something from me. I'm nearly certain he didn't get it."

"Why?"

"Because I never would have given up privileged information!"

"And you think that was what he wanted."

A beseeching look came into Lena's eyes. "It was the only thing I had that he could have wanted. Almost anything else, he could have gotten from someone else. A woman more his type. A woman more susceptible to his influence."

"But you don't know what he wanted."

"Kim, I don't have a clue. I've been wracking my brain all week trying to answer that."

It still startled Kim when the veil dropped, and Lena ceased to be vicious. The transformation wasn't always welcome. When she appeared vulnerable, Lena seemed inordinately more dangerous than she did as a hard-edged cop.

She swiveled the chair a few degrees. She didn't move closer to where Kim sat on the couch. Yet for a fraction of a second, it seemed as if she had. "I keep looking at that picture of you. These past few days, there's only so much thinking about Chase and Kennerly I can take. So I've thought about you. I believe I know the mistake I made. I let myself be blinded by my own damn prejudices. Worst mistake a cop can make, aside from letting herself get shot."

A beat of silence fell.

"You want to know my mistake?" Lena said. "I assumed anyone working here had to be pretty damn desperate for a job."

"Or for a place to live."

"Yes, there's that. I assumed any woman who came to work in this house would be someone who didn't have much going for her. Otherwise she wouldn't be here. She'd be anywhere else."

Kim cracked a smile, deflecting her emotion.

"That picture your buddy Jones had of you has corporate written all over it. In my defense, I'll admit I don't see a whole lot of corporate out this way. Which is why I missed it. Or maybe I'm just missing clues right and left these days. You're not a battered wife running from some redneck asshole."

"Is that what you thought?"

"Yes, that's what I thought. Now, if I knew who was standing in that picture beside you, I'd have something to go on. The asshole you're running from is in that photo, isn't he?"

"How do you know he's an asshole?"

"Because I've been getting to know you."

Unsure she could bear any more, Kim stood up. "Wait," Lena said. "I haven't asked my question."

"Seems to me you have."

"Tell me this. Are you, or were you ever, married to the man you're running from?"

Kim turned the question over one way and another. Finally she told the truth. "No."

"So his interest in you isn't personal."

She struggled not to blurt out, *Of course it feels personal when someone wants to kill you!* Instead, she mumbled, "I'm not sure what you mean."

"Did you have a personal relationship with him?"

"No."

"Okay, not personal. That opens up two possible scenarios. Either you've done something that he knows about. That doesn't feel right to me. Other explanation, he's done something and you know about it."

Kim willed herself to betray nothing. "It's not such big a deal, Lena. It's nothing I can't handle." This time, the words sounded empty, even to her. She waited for the other woman to rail at her.

But Lena only laughed. "There'll be time to figure it out. Obviously you think you have time. You're still here." She shrugged. The gesture seemed at once appallingly casual yet a relief under the strained circumstances. "Lately I've been wondering which I'll be most surprised by when you finally tell me the truth. Will it be the trouble you're running from? Or the place you've fallen from to land here?"

The first question didn't surprise Kim in the least. The second made her think Lena was getting to know her entirely too well.

CHAPTER 26

Twenty-four hours passed without further developments. On Thursday evening, Kim went to work at the bakery. She had payroll to run and a stack of invoices to pay. When she finished a few hours later, she shut down the computer but remained at her desk.

An admissions application for Fort Lewis College lay on the corner. The information required for a non-matriculating student was simple enough: name, address, and date the applicant moved to Colorado. Other questions pertained to previous education, including colleges attended, high school name, and date of graduation—or, alternatively, GED details. The first time she read the application, she had stopped there. Kim Jackson didn't have any of those credentials. Now she realized it didn't matter. She could lie. No one was going to check her high school record. When it came to admitting her as a non-degree student, Fort Lewis would happily take her tuition money.

The form was still blank. She told herself there was no rush to file the application, but there was more to it than that. The future itself seemed to have dropped off the horizon. She could no more imagine August giving way to September than she could see herself driving up the hill two or three times a week to attend accounting classes. Her life was on hold, maybe not as completely as Lena's. They were both waiting for the case to be made against Brad Chase.

News came before either of them expected it. The doorbell rang early on Saturday morning. Lena, home for the weekend, was in the middle of breakfast. She lagged behind as Kim went to answer the sharp, insistent rapping at the front door. Two police officers were there when she opened it. One was Detective Mark Stankowicz. The other was Captain Greg Hodges.

Their faces were grim. "I won't mince words, Lena," the captain said. "Brad Chase is dead. He died last night. Circumstances are being investigated."

Kim gasped.

"How did he die?" Lena said.

"Gunshot wound to the head. It happened on the running trail near the high school. He went into the river."

"A jogger found his body early this morning. It was caught in a tree limb near shore. According to Maggie White, his girlfriend, Brad went out late last night and never returned. He told her he was going for a run. He still had his arm in a sling but had resumed running," Stankowicz said.

"The gun?"

"A Glock. It was in the water near his body. We're tracing it," the detective said.

Kim's mind raced. The Animas River Trail paralleled the river through town. It was heavily used by joggers, walkers, and cyclists. She passed the high school every day on her way to and from work.

"Preliminary determination as to manner of death?" Lena said.

The captain frowned. "Too early to tell. You know that. So far, we can't rule out homicide or suicide."

Suicide. The possibility hadn't occurred to Kim.

"Was there a note?" Lena said.

"Nothing's been found yet," the captain said.

"It wasn't a suicide," she said, answering her own question.

"Do you have any evidence supporting that conclusion?" Captain Hodges said.

"No."

The silence grew thick. Kim watched, and listened, and suffered a foreboding of something terrible in the offing.

"This is purely a formality, Lena," the captain said. "Mind telling me where you were last night?"

Lena shot him an incredulous look. "I was here. I gave up jogging a few years back. Oh right. It was after I lost my legs."

The captain ignored her sarcasm. "And you, Ms. Jackson? Kim, isn't it?"

"I was here, also."

"You two see each other last night, watch a movie together maybe?"

"I was upstairs reading," Kim said.

"All night?"

"Yes."

Lena could not have been a suspect, not without the involvement of someone else. Kim knew her movements were another matter.

"You hear anyone come in or go out last night?" the captain asked Lena.

"I hear every damn thing that goes on in this house. No one came in. No one left. Why the hell are you bothering with this?"

"Procedure. You know how it works."

The officers didn't linger. As they turned to leave, Stankowicz said, "I'll be back later to give you an update, Lena.

We've only been on this a couple of hours. Something will break."

Kim followed the men to the door and closed it behind them.

Lena didn't move. She cursed softly. "I never thought anything like this would happen." She brooded over some private thought.

"And you think—what?" Kim said, unsure how to finish.

"I don't know what I think."

She remained immobile for several minutes. Just when Kim could bear the silence no longer, when she was about to suggest returning to the kitchen to reheat coffee, Lena spoke angrily. "Kennerly probably killed him. Brad, idiot that he was, probably called Kennerly. Told him he was getting some heat. Expected Paul to save him."

She grew quiet again. This time, Kim filled in several large pieces for herself. If Chase felt he was about to go down, what reason would he have not to take Kennerly with him? Brad Chase wouldn't concede defeat easily. Even in his last hours, he likely harbored visions of escaping discovery. It followed that he would lean on his patron for help. If their conspiracy theory was correct, Kim thought, cautioning herself against leaping to conclusions.

"It's the damn crime scene," Lena said. "It's not intact. Chase was shot standing on land and his body ends up in the water. Shit."

Kim didn't ask what she meant. That could wait. For now, she wagered a guess that in the worst case, the scene would prove ambiguous, unreadable as homicide or suicide. "There must be some evidence against Brad," she said, working out a theory as she spoke.

"What kind of evidence?"

"I don't know. A gun, maybe."

"It's bullshit. All Chase had to do was sit tight. The cops weren't going to get a warrant. He must have come unglued."

"And either shot himself," Kim said, puzzling out the possibilities, "or called Kennerly and told him what was going on. Same difference. He's dead either way."

The suicide theory was the simpler of the two, looked at from the point of view of Durango investigators. However dedicated they were to securing justice for their fellow officer, they hadn't yet connected Paul Kennerly to Brad Chase.

"We have to know what Kennerly wanted from you," Kim said.

Lena didn't reply.

The morning dragged on. Lena withdrew behind a mask of stony silence. Kim knew better than to try and penetrate it. Besides, she had nothing to offer, no distraction, no solace, no promise of better days to come. A life had been lost. A woman had lost the man she loved. A child had lost his father. And Lena had perhaps lost the one person who could—or would—tell her the truth about why she had been shot on a cold March night.

After satisfying herself that staying home would serve no purpose, Kim knocked at the closed door to the suite and announced she was going for a walk. She left the house and wandered toward downtown, hardly aware of her surroundings.

Brad's death hadn't been discovered in time to make the paper. Passing his store, Kim saw that someone had received word. A "Closed for Business" sign hung on the door. For the first time, she thought of Jeremy and wondered what Brad's death would mean for him if the store closed permanently.

Beyond the train station, she came to a bagel store. She went inside and got in line. Her interest deepened in the conversation between the two women working at the counter.

"It's so creepy," one said. "The guy goes out for a run and gets shot. I still can't believe it. I run on that trail all the time."

"Of all the people in this town," the other said. "Why him? Why Brad? I'm not saying I wish it was someone else. I just wish it hadn't been him."

"I won't be running on that trail by myself again, I can tell you that much."

Kim's turn came. She ordered her bagel. By the time she returned to the sunlit sidewalk, she had lost her appetite. She ate a few bites before tossing the rest in a trash can. She couldn't shake a terrible sense of doom. The mystery had intensified. Chase's secrets were about to become public. It seemed only a matter of time before his connection to Lena would be revealed. Meanwhile, Kennerly was still out there, lurking in the background.

Mulling over what she knew, Kim didn't think there was a chance in the world the police would prove any link between Brad Chase and Paul Kennerly. Not now. Not with Brad dead.

"Kim."

She glanced up sharply, heart racing. She was standing in front of Jeremy and Zeke's house, oblivious to where she was. Jeremy sat on the steps.

"Hey," she said weakly. "I didn't see you."

"You didn't see anything."

One look at his face and she knew he had heard the morning's shocking news. "I heard about Brad," she said. "I'm sorry, Jeremy."

"Yeah, well. Thanks. Everyone's blown away, including me."

There were countless things she could have told him. Even if the police captain hadn't warned her and Lena not to breathe a word to anyone about the ongoing investigation, Kim knew she wouldn't say anything.

"Do you feel like coming in? I could make coffee," he offered.

She shook her head. "Thanks. I just feel like walking. How's Zeke?" she said as an afterthought.

"He's great. Sleeping in this morning."

She stayed too long. Her glance lingered on Jeremy's brown eyes and tousled dark hair. She wanted to go to him. She wanted to scream and cry and shout—but more than anything, she wanted to feel his arms around her, holding her, just holding her.

"I should get going," she said hollowly.

He nodded.

She walked on.

CHAPTER 27

Officer Sheila Moss stopped by late that afternoon. "Thought I'd come by and give you an update," she said, joining Kim and Lena on the patio. "The techs have finished working the scene. Brad's autopsy won't happen until tomorrow or Monday. We traced the Glock. It was stolen from a local woman about eight months ago. Strange thing is, she bought it at Brad's store. As soon as the autopsy's complete, we hope to match bullets from it to the one we think is still in Brad."

"Any traces of gunshot residue found on the body?" Lena said.

"No."

"What about time of death?"

"The ME puts it between ten and midnight."

Kim wondered what effect six or more hours of cold, rushing water had on gunshot residue on Brad's hand—assuming it was ever there. Any trace found would easily make the case for suicide. The absence of residue didn't necessarily tell the story against it.

"What can you tell me about the entry wound?" Lena said.

Sheila frowned. "Not much. You know it's not our job to make conclusions about that."

"Presumably the wound isn't inconsistent with the appearance of suicide."

Sheila hesitated. "Yeah. You could say that. We'll know for sure after the autopsy."

Before Lena could say anything else, Sheila said, "There's more you should know. Yesterday Stankowicz and I went back to Brad's store. We wanted to press him harder on his alibi for the night you were hit. Right away, he started dancing around, acting all huffy. Finally he said he was at his gym that night. He belongs to the one on Florida Avenue. So after Stankowicz and I left, we took a drive out there. Not surprisingly, no one could tell us if Brad had or hadn't been there that particular night. Here's the thing. That place has all the newest equipment, state-of-the-art machines that include personal program monitors."

Kim smiled. She guessed where this was going. "The kind of machines that use a code," she said. "Brad would punch it in before he started a workout. It would track his stats." The health club she had belonged to in Chicago had the same setup.

"That's right. Members can pull reports anytime showing their performance. Brad was at the gym the night before the shooting and the night after. In fact, he was there every single night that week, working his butt off, according to the report we saw. But he wasn't there that Tuesday night. It wasn't a hell of a lot to go on, but it was enough to send us back to the store for another chat. Course, Brad swears he was at the gym that night and forgot to plug in his code. According to everyone over there, the man's totally anal about tracking his workouts, so that didn't fly."

"Is that it?" Lena said.

"No, that's not it. While we were in the store, we decided to take a look at his firearms inventory. At least what he had on display. We still didn't have enough for a warrant to search the place. Brad might have been pissed off at us on our first visit, but he went white as a sheet when we started poking around those guns. He started sputtering all kinds of bullshit about calling his lawyer."

"And afterward you walked away from him?" Lena said angrily.

"Well, yeah. We'd pushed him far enough, we thought."

"Oh yeah. You pushed him right over the edge. Jesus." Lena glared at the younger officer. "It never occurred to you or Stankowicz to have someone watch Chase?"

The other woman glared back. "Yes, we thought of it. You know perfectly well we don't have those resources." Sheila's voice grew cold. "For your information, we executed a search warrant at Chase's home and store first thing this morning. We didn't find much at his house, only a pair of rifles he'd had since he was a kid and a Colt pistol. Caliber doesn't match on it, and the rifles don't look like they've been fired in a decade. But we're testing them."

"What about his store?"

"We collected eight rifles, all .22s. They're being tested. According to the paperwork, all eight were received at the store within the last year."

Lena started to interrupt. Sheila cut her off. "Listen to me. We found other paperwork in his files. It's a long shot, but last year, Brad sent a couple of rifles back to the manufacturer on damage claims. Three, to be exact. This happened in April a year ago."

Kim held her breath.

"Can you get the guns?" Lena said.

"We can get the guns."

A half smile crossed Sheila's face. "Of the three rifles Chase claimed were damaged, only one was, according to the manufacturer. They still have it. The other two were shipped out to other stores. One was sold in Denver, the other in Reno. I spent the afternoon on the phone, identifying the new owners and working with local law enforcement in both cities to get the rifles. You should know, Lena, we're getting swift cooperation from everyone we've contacted. Everyone wants to make this case."

Something washed over Lena's face, relief and a new wave of tension at once. "One of those guns is going to nail Chase," she said.

"That's what Stankowicz and I think too."

CHAPTER 28

Lena was already in the kitchen when Kim came downstairs on Sunday morning. One look at the dark circles under her eyes, and Kim knew it hadn't been a good night. "I'll get the coffee started," she said. "Are you hungry?"

"No. I don't know. I don't feel like eating."

Kim felt the same. Nevertheless, she sliced an apple and bananas and added late-season berries to the bowl. She opened a carton of yogurt and toasted a bagel. To her surprise, between them, they ate everything she had prepared.

"I've been thinking," Lena said as she picked at a last bite. "I spent all night doing what you've wanted me to do for a week. Think about what Kennerly wanted from me. They're going to get Chase. For the shooting. They'll never convict him, seeing as he's dead. But they're not going to get Kennerly. Even if they find the money he donated to Chase's fund, so what? He didn't break any law. There isn't going to be one goddamned piece of evidence linking him to me! That's what I spent the night thinking about."

The same picture came into focus for Kim, and her hopes sank. More, she heard something dark in Lena's voice. She almost spoke but was glad when she didn't.

"Every time I walk through it, I come back to the same. They can find the money. They won't find anything that stinks of conspiracy. Paul's going to get away clean. And I ask myself, how am I going to feel about that?"

She sat back in her chair, coffee cup raised to her lips, an ease in her posture belied by something foreboding in the air around her. "You ever read anything by a German guy named Nietzsche?"

"Who?"

"Some nutcase of a philosopher. You ever read anything by him?"

Kim shook herself out of a fog. "I think so."

"You read him where? Maybe in some college course you took?"

"What's your point, Lena?"

"Right. My point. The point is about a year ago, Damian gave me a book by the guy. *Beyond Good and Evil*. Silly me, I thought it was going to be some two-bit inspirational crap about turning the other cheek. It's not." She paused. "I don't know what the book's about. But one passage stuck with me. The guy says the big whoop-de-do in life is when you get to the place where you can say: *This is it. Life is what it is right now, at this moment.* And enlightenment, or bliss, or whatever the hell you want to call it, is being able to say to yourself, I take it the way it is. Not only for this one moment. I'd take it this way, again and again. Over and over, every single moment, just the way it happened, again and again."

Kim felt stricken by the sight of tears rolling down Lena's cheeks.

"Well, I can't say that," Lena said in a voice that pitched with emotion. "Can you say it?"

Kim brushed away her own tears. It took her a second to realize Lena was dead serious. "No. I can't say it."

"What's the worst thing that's ever happened to you?" Lena said.

Kim shook her head. It was impossible not to answer. But she had to think. She had legitimate answers in her back pocket. Her mother's early death; the car crash that killed her father. Those paled. Acting against her own best interests, she said, "I think the worst thing hasn't happened yet." She thought of Stephen Bender. She thought of an unknown fate lying in wait somewhere down the road, prison or death.

Lena wheeled away from the table. Whether or not she meant to leave, she didn't. Raw weariness showed on her face. She either hadn't heard Kim or paid no attention to her answer. "In all the years I was a cop, all the years I prided myself on being good at my job, I never knew—I never had a clue—how god-awful hard the waiting is. Waiting for someone else to fix your life. The cops. The justice system." Her shoulders drooped. "As a crime victim, it's what you expect." After a moment, her expression cleared. The defeat written on her face seconds earlier gave way to determination. "I got sidetracked. What I meant to say is that last night I realized you were right. I have to find what Kennerly wanted from me. It's the only way I'm going to get to him. So we need to talk."

They didn't start immediately. Kim cleared the breakfast plates. She loaded the dishwasher and poured two fresh cups of coffee. In the space of a few minutes, the atmosphere between them became infinitely less charged.

"For the sake of starting somewhere," Kim said, "let's begin with what was going on when Kennerly initially came on to you. Besides being attracted to you—"

"I don't know that."

"Let's assume he was. Let's also assume he wanted something in addition to a relationship with you. To keep it simple,

let's say he wanted information. That information had to per-
tain to a crime because that's the kind of information you had.
So the information had to concern a crime he had committed or one he knew someone else had committed, someone he
might have hoped to protect."

Lena's eyes shot up.

"What?" Kim said.

"Nothing. Go on."

Kim frowned, afraid to let on how much she was grasping
at straws. If something was there, Lena would have to recognize it. "I guess it's fair to assume Kennerly's name has never
been linked to any crime."

"No."

"Maybe some of his business deals were shady."

"I wouldn't know. I never heard one word."

Kim imagined it. Kennerly wanting to lay his hands on a
certain property owned by a reluctant seller. How far might
he go to persuade the owner to come to the table? Blackmail?
Extortion?

"Was there anything different about the kinds of cases you
worked compared with your colleagues in the department?"

"No."

"But you were the most senior woman."

"Yes."

It was a small point won, possibly irrelevant. Kim needed
to hear Lena talk at length about something—anything, it
didn't matter what. "I know you received two special commen-
dations. What were those for?"

Lena vented her frustration by speaking gruffly. "You know
about one. It was the Douglas Parks gun-selling sting. I got
more credit than I deserved."

"What was the other?"

"Unrelated to anything. I got lucky." With an angry sigh,
she said, "Twenty some years ago, an old man was killed in his

home by an intruder. I wasn't on the force then. I came across the case my first or second year. I reviewed the file, dumb shit that I was. My gut told me this was one that could get solved." She drew another long breath. Her voice, when she spoke next, sounded less angry. "There was a kid who lived in the neighborhood. Name was Aaron Booth. He was only sixteen or seventeen when the old man died. Complaints had been made against him by the guy, harassment charges, that sort of thing. The kid was looked at but never made a suspect. Main reason was the crime scene was too clean. The old man died a bloody, violent death, beaten with some object, never recovered. No one working the case thought a kid could get in and out of the house, inflict that kind of damage without leaving so much as a fingerprint or shoe print. Plus, the kid had an alibi. Or claimed he did. I was never sure Booth had done it, but I wished someone had looked hard at him.

"To make a long story longer, there was some blood evidence in the house. The old man's, naturally. And someone else's. Fair to assume it belonged to the killer. But that long ago, DNA technology was new. Okay. Fast forward. One night about ten years ago, I arrived at the scene of a traffic accident to find a young man unconscious but still breathing, head bashed in from having plowed into a tree. The guy was Aaron Booth, and lying on the ground was a bloody baseball cap. His. I took it. I pulled evidence from the locker from the Miller case, submitted blood samples to the state crime lab to get DNA profiles. And I submitted Aaron Booth's cap."

Kim smiled. Seeing it, Lena spoke harshly. "Now, the real hero in this case was the officer who preserved evidence. Yes, Aaron Booth's DNA matched what was found at the murder scene. We nailed the bastard. He's in prison."

Kim sipped her coffee. After gauging that enough time had passed, she asked, "Did you work other old cases?"

"We all did. Every year or so, the captain would toss out assignments, get a new pair of eyes on an old crime. With the breakthroughs coming right and left in crime-scene technology, no effort on old cold cases was considered wasted. Even so, usually the only way anything gets solved is with a new lead. And the way that happens is when someone comes forward to talk."

"How many unsolved cases are there in the files?"

"Hundreds. Maybe thousands."

"Any of those stand out for you? Anything you kept going back to?"

"Yeah, there were. I always had my own damn list."

"What was on it?"

"Top of my list? A little girl kidnapped and murdered. Walking home from school one day, she waves goodbye to a friend and was never seen alive again. Lousy, damn case. We found her three weeks later. Never got her killer. Want to know what pissed me off about that case? Same thing happened to a girl down in Farmington, New Mexico. Now the cops there did a fine job of collecting evidence. Within a year, they identified the guy, convicted him for the murder. Meanwhile, our case stays open."

"But you think it was the same guy?"

"Yes. Still, our little girl's mother never got a knock on her door from an officer in a freshly pressed uniform delivering the news that her daughter's killer is locked up good and tight and will never again see the light of day."

Lena clenched the wheels of the chair. Her mouth twisted into a scowl. "I'm missing something."

"Missing what?"

"Don't you think I'd tell you if I knew?" she shouted.

Kim recoiled.

"Give me some time. I'll either get it or I won't. Talking isn't helping." She wheeled away from the table and left the kitchen.

Kim put their coffee cups in the sink. Seated again, she gazed absently at the white metal cabinets. They could stand to be washed, she thought. Her glance flickered to the yellow geometrical print linoleum, scuffed and stained with age. Once a week, she scrubbed it, yet it never looked any different. Was there a point to any of this, she wondered. Everything—even tragedies—ultimately became a relic of a bygone era.

She didn't know where her thoughts went. She didn't know how deeply she had sunk into herself until she heard Lena speak sharply. "Kim, where the hell are you?"

She jolted alert. Lena was back in the kitchen.

"What?"

"There was another case."

"What case?"

"A woman went missing."

For one bleary-eyed moment, Kim thought Lena was talking about her. Then she snapped to attention.

"Kennerly may have had some connection to the woman. He might have been her boss. Maybe he just knew her. I can't remember. Jesus. It's the only thing."

The announcement left Kim momentarily paralyzed. Competing thoughts flooded her brain. "Did you and Kennerly ever talk about the case?"

"No. I haven't thought about it in years."

"Was he considered a suspect?"

"Absolutely not." Lena made a move toward the living room. "That much I would have remembered. I have to read the case file. I don't want to talk about this again until I've read the file."

CHAPTER 29

Kim spent the remainder of the morning waiting for a knock at the door that never came. She spent the afternoon watching for a patrol car to turn the corner and stop in front of the house. Late in the day, she roused herself from her stupor to go to the grocery store where she sprang for a couple of swordfish fillets. Energized by the prospect of a nice dinner, she took her time choosing fresh fruits and vegetables before going home to spend the next hour chopping mango and red and yellow peppers for a salsa.

Lena didn't join her until nearly six. One look at the array of dishes—fish marinating on one plate, the colorful salsa on another, salads prepared, and snap peas ready for the steamer—and she opened her mouth to complain.

"Forget it. Dinner's on me," Kim said. "Can I pour you a glass of wine? There's a chardonnay chilled."

"Thank you."

They didn't talk about Kennerly.

"I didn't hear anyone come to the door this afternoon," Kim said when she could hold back no longer.

"No one did. Why?"

"I thought Sheila or Mark might have brought over the case file. The one you mentioned this morning."

"Oh." Lena raised her wineglass and took a sip. "No. I didn't call them. Someone would have to make a copy. That's a pain in the ass. There are rules against removing original files from the premises. Anyway, I decided to let Stankowicz handle this."

Kim tried to ignore a stinging sense of disappointment. "Have you spoken to Damian today?"

"No. She has tests this week. I'll talk to her tonight, but I'm not sure I'll tell her—well, I don't know what I'll tell her."

By the next morning, Lena had changed her mind. Over breakfast, she asked a favor—a ride to the police station. She wanted to read the case file there. "This shouldn't take long. If you help me get dressed and we leave by eight, we should be home in less than an hour."

She didn't say why she had reversed last night's decision. Kim didn't ask. It was enough trying to absorb the enormity of what they were about to do. After Lena went to her room, Kim went upstairs to dress for the day. When she was ready, she went to Lena's suite to help her dress.

Lena took some pains with her appearance. She chose a pale-blue button-down shirt, cotton vest, and dark pants. Her hair was combed nicely; her eyes were bright. The change went deeper. Whether it was in her straightened shoulders, her chin held high, or the glint of determination in her eyes, she exuded pride.

They went out the back door. Kim opened the gate. She backed out the car, then waited while Lena propelled herself into the passenger seat. Kim folded the metal chair along its hinges and stowed it in the trunk.

This early in the day, there were plenty of vacant parking spots near the station. Lena pointed one out. Kim nosed the car in, put it in park, and had the wheelchair out of the trunk and ready a moment later. Lena lifted herself from car to chair, released the hand brake, and rolled forward. Kim saw beads of perspiration on her forehead.

As she approached the front entrance, Lena's face bore a look of entitlement. It said she belonged here. It was as though she were striding in that morning on two strong legs. The wheelchair was that inconsequential.

The desk sergeant was the same man Kim had seen on her previous visit. Whatever his first reaction on seeing his former colleague, he concealed it. "Hey, Lena, good to see you."

"Hey, Rich, how's it going?"

He shrugged. "Busy, as usual. Who are you looking for?"

"Is Stankowicz in? Or Moss?"

"Both, I think. You want to wait here or come on back?"

She chose to wait. A moment later, Stankowicz came through the double doors.

"Hey, Lena, Kim," he greeted.

"I need to see a file," Lena said. "It's something I worked on way back."

"Okay. And it has to do with—what?"

"I don't know yet. I'll tell you when I know."

He crossed his arms over his chest. He hesitated a fraction of a second too long. By then, Kim knew he was debating some question, probably one having to do with policy and Lena's questionable status in the department. "Which file?" he said.

"Jane Barton. She went missing fourteen or fifteen years ago."

His eyes and brow crinkled in puzzlement. "You have any ideas about her?"

"Not really."

Her nonchalance should have served as a warning. When Stankowicz hesitated a second time, heat rose in her voice. "Jesus, Mark. What's the big deal? I just want to look at a damn file. Clock me. Give me five lousy minutes."

He scowled. "I'll give you however long you want." He held the door open and allowed her to pass through. Kim followed. "Make yourself comfortable in the conference room. I'll get the file."

Kim felt every pair of eyes in the room following her and Lena across the floor. Lena nodded at one person, then another, perceptibly quickening her pace until they entered the room.

"Goddamned freak show," she muttered.

Kim sat down at the round table. Lena withdrew to the far wall. Stankowicz joined them a moment later and slid a folder onto the desk. "Take your time," he said. He closed the door when he left.

Lena approached the table and opened the folder.

Without having been told as much, Kim knew her role was to sit and wait. There was nothing for her and Lena to discuss. There was nothing for her to do.

It wasn't what she ought to have been thinking about, but an image born slowly in her mind grew vivid. She thought about a different folder in a different police station. For the first time, she wondered whether a missing person file existed for her.

She was sure the answer was yes.

Her thoughts drifted back to the day she left Chicago. Betsy, her assistant, would have been the first to know she was gone. Betsy would have expected her back at the office immediately after her doctor's appointment, which would have been right after lunch. Betsy might have texted before then and been puzzled by the lack of reply. Within two hours, her assistant would have discovered that she had canceled her doctor's appointment minutes before she was due to arrive.

The sensational news that she was missing would have spread rapidly at Blackwell Industries. It would have taken longer for the report to reach her closest living relative. Thad, her brother, wouldn't have given a damn. He would have shrugged and gone back to doing whatever he was doing before the interruption. Julia, his wife, would have eventually persuaded him to go to the police.

Kim could easily picture how *that* interview had gone: *How long has it been since you've seen your sister?* a low-ranking officer would have asked.

One year.

Kim pulled herself out of the reverie. She glanced at the sheaf of pages spread in a half-moon in front of Lena. Her file would be less robust than Jane Barton's. Maybe only one sheet: name, address, date of birth, place of last employment, surviving family members. What else could anyone say about her? The truth would be helpful—that she had been duped by a man who had committed heinous crimes and painted a trail of evidence leading directly to her.

She stopped short of releasing a sigh. She looked at Lena. A sudden urge to tell Lena everything welled up. Kim understood something she ought to have grasped long before now: Lena would help her. Michael Leeds had died not because of anything she had done but perhaps because of something she had left undone. She needed Lena to know the truth. She had to put the only faith she had left in a damaged woman whose passion for justice still reigned strong.

Lena looked over. Wholly absorbed in her reading, she didn't see the story in Kim's eyes. "What?" she said.

Kim blinked. "Nothing." She noticed the edge of a photo protruding from the stack of pages. "What's that?" She pointed at the grainy black-and-white image.

"Jane Barton. Her picture was in the paper for a solid week." She pushed the photo across the table.

Kim took it. At first glance, she was puzzled by something familiar about her. "How long ago did she disappear?"

"Fourteen years."

Lena continued reading. Kim studied the photo. Eventually she decided this woman, with her long hair and warm, shining eyes, bore no resemblance to anyone she had ever known. Jane Barton looked like a contemporary hippie. She lacked the polish and guile of the professional women Kim had once rubbed shoulders with.

"Seen her lately?" Lena said facetiously.

"No. Although she does look familiar. I don't know why."

"She looks like a lot of women. What I mean is, there was nothing particularly distinctive about her appearance. That went against us, and her, back when she disappeared."

Kim took another look at the picture, then pushed it across the table.

"You mind returning the file to Stankowicz? His desk is in the center of the room, toward the back."

"Sure."

"I'll wait here."

Kim knew exactly where the detective's desk was located from her previous visit to the station. As she made her way to the spot, she felt herself being watched. She fought the impulse to lower her head and walk faster. Instead, she checked out the desk of the young patrolman she had noticed last time. She wasn't looking for him. She was looking for Jaye Dewey. The instant she recalled Jaye, she knew. The woman in the photo resembled Jaye Dewey.

Sheila Moss was with Stankowicz at his desk. Both officers stood up when Kim approached. Stankowicz reached for the case file.

"Is Lena still in the conference room?" Sheila said.

"Yes."

"I'll walk out with you."

Stankowicz nodded goodbye. Sheila accompanied Kim to the conference room.

Lena's exit from the building wasn't as simple an affair as her entrance. It was as though a signal had been sent, alerting every officer and staff member on the premises to her imminent departure. The crowd gravitated toward the corridor along which she had to pass. Initially, Kim and Sheila flanked her chair. Both women quickly yielded to the others.

It became an impromptu honor processional. Lena spoke to every man and woman who stood waiting for the chance to pay homage to her. Kim withdrew to an alcove near the door. She was still there, lost in thought, when Lena said, "Are you ready to go?"

Kim jumped. "Yes."

"You look like you've seen a ghost," Lena said as they left the building.

"I'm always seeing ghosts."

Neither spoke again until they were inside the car. "Whose ghost?" Lena said.

Kim laughed. If Lena had turned that look on her fifteen minutes earlier, she would have folded. Given it all up. Begged for help. But too much had happened since then. "No ghosts. It was a joke." She put the car in gear and pulled onto the street. "What did you find?"

"Everything. Nothing. I'm not sure. Listen, you need to get to work, and I need to think. Let's leave all of this until later."

Kim grudgingly agreed. "I'm driving to work today. Do you want me to pick up anything at the store on my way home?"

"No. We can make do with whatever's in the refrigerator. Just come home as soon as you can."

Kim nodded. She averted her glance, unwilling to let Lena see the emotion filling her eyes.

CHAPTER 30

"I had it wrong," Lena said late that afternoon. "Kennerly wasn't Jane Barton's boss. He was her landlord. She lived in a cabin on his property. I believe it was a renovated cowboy bunkhouse. The Kennerly family used to run cattle on that land. Cows and acreage," she said dryly. "Those were two subjects I heard plenty about when I was with Paul."

Branches swayed in the afternoon breeze. Brilliant sunlight filtered through the leaves. Kim held her grip on a glass of ice water while trying to mentally shrug off a day spent tracking numbers. She had no sooner walked in the door than Lena had ushered her onto the patio to talk about Kennerly.

"Paul was never considered a suspect in Jane Barton's disappearance. The fact is we never had a solid suspect, period. Problem was, we never had clear evidence of a crime. Besides, Paul had an alibi. He left town early on the day Jane disappeared. He drove to Salt Lake City."

"How did you know Jane Barton didn't leave town for reasons of her own?" Kim said, with effort keeping her voice composed. The question cut too close to home.

Lena frowned. Just as quickly, her features softened. "Oh. I guess I didn't mention. Jane Barton had a daughter. A little girl, eight years old. The kid lived with her father out of state and had arrived that day for a summer visit."

"A daughter," Kim said. Her heart thudded. A wave washed over her, of fear and uncertainty. She was afraid she was out of her depth.

"Yeah. Do you mind if I tell this story my way?"

Lena proceeded to report what she had learned from the case file. The best information about the twenty-eight-year-old woman came from Jane's friends. According to them, Jane wasn't dating anyone at the time of her disappearance. She was working two jobs, trying to save money. She wanted to regain custody of her daughter, who was living in LA with her father and stepmother. She couldn't do that until she could prove she could make a decent life for them both.

"There's not a lot more to tell. The point is, had Jane been dating anyone, her two girlfriends swore they would have known. They said they were always teasing her about letting the best years of her life pass by. They also said that, besides wanting her daughter back, the one other thing Jane was nuts about was her home. It was more of a cabin than a finished house, and again, according to the friends, there were problems with the place. The oven hardly ever worked, the toilet leaked, and she didn't always have hot water, but she loved living with a view of the San Juan Mountains."

Kim didn't have to try to work out a theory. One appeared of its own accord. "Any chance she paid her rent with something besides money?"

"If she did, we'll never know."

"I suppose if Jane had been known to have a sexual relationship with Kennerly, he might have been looked at more closely."

"Are you kidding? He would have become the prime suspect!"

The silence absorbed the heat in Lena's voice. After a moment, Kim said, "What was known about the last day anyone saw her?"

"Jane worked that morning. Picked up her daughter at the airport at noon. They went to lunch. Went swimming at Trimble Hot Springs. Then they went home. The next morning, they were supposed to leave for Glenwood Springs."

"Where's that?"

"North. Small town on I-70. It's famous for a huge hot springs pool. Apparently the kid loved to swim. Friends saw her and the girl during the day, but the last report is from her daughter who said her mother went out that night and never came back. Wherever she went, she didn't take her car. It was still at the cabin."

"You met the daughter?"

"Yeah. I was there that morning. An adorable little girl."

Lena spent the next minute sunk in silence. She drifted away as surely as if she had climbed aboard a skiff and pushed off from shore. In the interlude, Kim tried imagining having a job where you had to comfort little girls who had just lost their mothers.

With renewed vigor, Lena picked up the story. "The kid spent the night alone in the cabin. At daylight, she called her father in LA. He went ballistic. He called the station and, from what I heard later, screamed bloody murder at every single person he spoke to until, finally, he got his message through: his little girl was alone in some cabin. I got a call before six. I was in uniform and at the station ten minutes later. A goddamned fleet drove out of town."

She stopped there. Her face moved with memories she chose not to share.

"What happened?" Kim said when the silence grew long.

"We found the cabin. The kid had locked the door. We called to her, but she wouldn't open. About one second before some jerk was ready to kick down the flimsy door, we find a key under a flowerpot."

"Who found the key?"

Lena eyed her flatly. "I did."

"Okay, so you got in."

"Yeah, we got in. And find this ramshackle cabin. I swear, not a single doorframe in the place hung straight. Everything was made of wood. The whole place could have gone up in flames in a heartbeat. Anyway, back in a bedroom, we find the kid. God, she was tiny. And beautiful."

"You talked to her?"

Lena nodded. "Yeah, I talked to her. I was an idiot. I promised her we would find her mother. I never should have said that."

In the same detached voice, Lena described the girl's account of the previous day. She said it had been like pulling teeth to get the eight-year-old to talk. Eventually she did say that at some point in the evening, her mom said she had to go out. That was it. The kid never saw her again.

"What was her name?" Kim asked, wondering why it had taken so long to ask.

"Jesse."

"And the father's name?"

"Michael Barton. Why?"

"No reason."

Kim warned herself to move slowly. This was too much information to take in all at once. More than anything, she needed not to jump to unwarranted conclusions. "If Michael Barton was in Los Angeles, presumably he couldn't have been responsible for his ex-wife's disappearance."

"Well, that's where you're wrong. Yes, he was a suspect. We knew right away he wasn't directly involved with Jane's disappearance. It's too hard to get from Durango to Los Angeles in the time period we're talking about. But he sure as hell could have paid someone to take her."

"His motive?"

"The kid, of course."

Kim tried to picture it. A father who has custody of his little girl and wants to keep it. A man who wants to sever all ties between his daughter and ex-wife, contriving to do so in a manner that will persuade the little girl her mom is really and truly gone. As schemes went, it worked.

"What?" Lena said.

"Nothing. I was just thinking how hard it had to be for the kid. I mean, how do you get over something like that?"

"You don't."

"What happened to the girl?"

"I presume she grew up and went on with her life."

Maybe, Kim thought. *And maybe not.*

"Remind me when all this happened."

"Fourteen years ago."

Kim drew a deep breath. "Let's stack the deck against Kennerly," she said, wrestling her way through a fog. "Let's say he did have some other relationship with Jane Barton."

"Call it sexual. Let's not mince words."

"Okay. I assume someone provided an alibi for him."

Lena's mouth curled in a frown. "Like I said, he was never a suspect." Angrily, she said, "He claimed he met his girlfriend in Salt Lake. She was at a conference. They drove on to spend time in Park City. He said he arrived on Saturday. No one checked. The girlfriend was never interviewed."

The air grew heavy with the knowledge that a mistake had been made. Kim tried to look beyond it. "Let's play with this idea for a minute. So Kennerly does drive to Salt Lake that day, but maybe he doesn't get out of town as early as he claimed to."

Between them, they worked out a scenario. The day he's supposed to leave town, Kennerly wants a quickie with his tenant. But something goes wrong. Jane says no. He gets miffed.

Lena laughed harshly. "Miffed, my foot. He would have been enraged." She sobered instantly. "My God." Emotion drained from her expression. A look of horror emerged on her features. It was as if everything up to now had been a parlor game, a chessboard on which they moved pieces to different squares without consequence. "I went out with that man."

"Tell me about him," Kim said, anxious to keep her talking.

Lena shook her head, not refusing. Rather, it was as if she was searching for words. "I don't expect you to know how it was," she said in a strange, quiet voice. "I had a good life before Paul came along. All the drama I ever saw was on the job, and there was less of that than you might think. But then—" She stopped. "I never dreamed someone like Paul could want someone like me. The first time he came on to me, I thought he was drunk, or confused. Or leading me on. When he called, then when we met for coffee—by then, everything in my head had gone haywire."

"How often did you see him? And what did you do together?"

"I saw him a couple of times a week. We had dinner, sometimes drinks."

"Sounds like you spent a lot of time talking."

"Yeah. We talked. About our town and the way it had changed since we were kids. We both loved Durango."

"But you never had sex?"

Lena's eyes flashed darkly. "That's none of your damn business."

Kim thought it was—or that it was someone's business. It was part of this story.

"Before you started dating Kennerly, did he have a girlfriend?"

"Yes. Same one he met up with in Salt Lake City. He had been with her for years. He told me they broke up."

"And after you stopped seeing him?"

Lena made an angry sound. "He went back to her. That's assuming he ever left her."

She fell quiet. Kim ran out of questions. There was nowhere else to go.

The problem was the timeline. It made no sense. If Kennerly was involved in Jane Barton's disappearance and, perhaps, murder, he had gotten away with it for nearly fifteen years. That case hadn't been reopened. Kennerly had no reason to embark on a secret pursuit of privileged information through a romantic conquest of Lena. Jane Barton's missing person case was buried deep in police department files and would have stayed there.

Kim wondered what she and Lena had wrong.

CHAPTER 31

Jeannette Winchester wanted her job back. Not in two weeks, per the terms of Kim's contract at Legrand Construction. She wanted to come back now. She felt terrific. She had her doctor's permission. Would Kim mind stepping aside early? Legrand Construction had several critical deadlines approaching. Jeannette thought it in everyone's best interests if she were there to handle them.

Kim did mind. After fielding her second phone call in as many days from the absent manager, she spoke to Skip. "What do you want to do?" he said after she explained the situation.

The photo of the handsome Legrand family hung on the wall behind his desk, near the portrait of Skip's gorgeous wife with her fair features and upturned wave of blond hair. His cowboy hat was perched on a desk corner, as usual. He kept one finger on the page in front of him, marking his reading place. "I want to stay. As long as you'll have me," she said.

He laughed. "Wish I could keep you on indefinitely. But I don't have the work for three gals."

It wasn't the scenario Kim had in mind. She wanted him to say he'd boot Jeannette and keep her.

"If Jeannette makes too much of a pest of herself, have her call me," he said with some reluctance. "We'll stick to the terms everyone agreed to."

Leaving the office, Kim caught Trina's glance. The receptionist obviously had been listening in. Her thoughts were inscrutable behind two overly made-up eyes.

Kim fidgeted while trying to settle back to work. From the window, she watched several large white clouds knit into one another. A cold front to the north was bringing early snow to the Rockies. In Durango, the morning had dawned unseasonably cool, though no precipitation was forecast.

She reread a job ad in the paper. A national oil company was looking for a corporate accountant. The company wanted someone who possessed the skills to track leases and monitor inventories. Someone who knew how to depreciate assets and write off liabilities. It was her kind of work.

In the last day, she had reached a decision. She meant to stay in Durango. It would mean finding another job once she finished at Legrand. She hadn't yet decided about enrolling at Fort Lewis College. The price of tuition stopped her. It seemed ludicrous to pay for courses she could have taught. Still, she had to do something to pad her meager résumé.

There was more to it. She had decided to tell Lena the truth about her past. Not soon. Not until the case against Paul Kennerly was made. Lena was far too distracted to listen to her story now. But she would listen when the time came. More than that, she would know what to do.

Kim exhaled quietly. For the first time, she dared to look ahead to a future where she didn't have to lie about who she was. It wouldn't be easy—none of it. Not coming clean to Lena. And not doing whatever would have to be done after that. But once everything was behind her, she would be free again. She could pursue any accounting job she wanted. She could live wherever she wanted. Even in Chicago.

The thought left her feeling strangely empty.

At five o'clock, she shut down her computer. She filed a couple of documents, turned off the light, and left the office. Cycling in the fresh air, she shook off the mental cobwebs of the day. She left the bike path at her usual spot and wound her way home through late-afternoon traffic. She was within a few blocks of the house when a contrary impulse led her to the police station. Once there, she circled adjacent blocks, checking cars parked on both sides of the street.

She was playing a hunch.

It didn't pan out.

Disappointed, she headed for home. Just across Third Avenue, she found the car she was looking for. It was a gray Honda Civic with Arizona license plates, a car she last saw parked at a gun club. The car, she believed, belonged to Jaye Dewey.

Kim leaned her bike against a tree and walked toward the police station. She had no intention of going there. She didn't know whether Jaye was in the building, though her car parked nearby suggested she was.

All she wanted was another good look at the young woman.

Since yesterday, she had clung to her suspicion that Jaye resembled Jane Barton, the missing woman. She knew the likelihood that she was wrong was high—enormously high. One clear look was all she wanted.

If Jaye was Jane's daughter, Kim thought a host of people would have many questions for her, including why she'd taken pains to conceal her identity.

She checked her watch and decided to wait ten minutes.

Fifteen minutes later, she was still there. She paced, ignoring her own best advice to go home. With the hour drawing close to six, she opted to wait until a few minutes past the hour on the chance that Jaye's shift at the station was nearing an end.

The time came and went. Kim retrieved her bike and pushed it to the far corner. She gave one look back and caught sight of a blond head tucking inside the car, accompanied by the sweep of the driver's side door closing. An instant later, the engine roared to life. She had missed Jaye by less than two minutes. The car pulled out of its parking spot. Kim spun the bicycle around and followed.

Jaye drove fast. She rolled through two stop signs before coming to a full stop at College Street. Along the straight avenue, it was easy to keep her in sight. But when Jaye wheeled left without setting her turn signal, Kim had no choice but to brake to a hard stop and wait for a truck to pass. Back in motion, she sprinted after the car, which grew discouragingly smaller as it receded in the distance. The last Kim saw of the Honda, it turned right on Eighth Avenue. Less than half a minute later, she made the same turn. Jaye was nowhere in sight.

Several hundred yards ahead, three cars, none a gray Honda, wove around a curve. Kim scanned both sides of the road between here and there, looking for anything promising. Seeing nothing, she pedaled on.

Eighth Avenue was a busy thruway that connected downtown Durango to homes and businesses on the east side of the Animas River. Kim assumed Jaye had gone around that bend. If she had, she was too far ahead to be caught. Kim gave up the chase before she reached the curve. There was no point in rounding that bend.

She pedaled slowly through the adjacent neighborhood, checking cars parked in driveways and on the street. She consoled herself with the thought that she could execute the same plan tomorrow and be more vigilant. Halfway down the block, she made an abrupt U-turn.

At Eighth, she waited for a break in traffic. Passing by the first time, she'd glimpsed a dark shingled building at the end of a lane on the opposite side of the street. Belatedly, she recognized the structure as an apartment complex. Cycling toward it, she passed a couple of houses fronting the quiet street. Where the lane dead-ended, she entered a parking lot. The gray Honda with the Arizona plates was there.

Its owner was nowhere in sight.

Kim studied the two-story structure meant to resemble a ski chateau. Behind it, trees grew thickly on the hillside, framing it in a swath of green. Crumbling asphalt in the parking lot, a loose gutter, and chipped paint gave the place an aura of shabbiness. But a couple of Jeeps of recent vintage and one BMW suggested these tenants were not down on their luck.

A breezeway divided the building. Kim saw a few bicycles chained to upstairs balconies. Brightly colored toys were near the door of a downstairs unit. She didn't see a directory.

She walked the length of the building, counting eight apartments. She was beginning to feel uncomfortable lingering on the premises even though she'd seen no one. That changed when a downstairs door opened.

Jaye Dewey walked out. Surprise and recognition dawned simultaneously when she saw Kim. "What are you doing here?" she demanded.

Kim seized the opportunity to peer at Jaye. Jaye's features were drawn tightly. She shared none of Jane Barton's smiling warmth. There was nothing the least carefree in her demeanor. But in a split second, Kim knew she was right. By the curve of her face and the set of her eyes, she knew she was looking at Jane Barton's daughter. "I need to talk to you," she said.

"Look, if it's about a police department internship, I already told you to talk to someone at the station."

"I know who your mother is."

A terrible stillness eclipsed Jaye's former brash swagger. One cheek muscle twitched. Her eyes shrank in a tremulous squint. "I don't have a clue what you're talking about."

"Your mother was Jane Barton."

"Jane who?" Jaye backed up a step. "Listen, I don't mean to be rude, but I have to go."

Kim saw what she hadn't until then. Jaye was dressed for a night out. She wore a short skirt, a close-fitting sleeveless blouse, and heels. She carried a jacket and a leather bag. All of the clothes were well made, and expensive. She looked good in them.

A roaring sound filled Kim's ears. "You should talk to Lena," she said, shouting at the young woman who had already turned and walked away.

"Why the hell would I want to talk to Lena Fallon?" Jaye shouted back. She got in her car and peeled out of the parking lot.

Purely reflexively, Kim jumped on her bike and followed. Jaye's tires squealed as she made the turn onto Eighth. When Kim reached the same corner, she glimpsed the Honda turning at the next street. Because she couldn't do anything else, she pedaled madly after it. She kept the car in sight for two blocks until it turned again. By the time she made the same turn, the vehicle had disappeared in the dusky-gray twilight.

CHAPTER 32

Lights were on in the living room where Lena, atypically, sat reading. "You're late," she said when Kim entered the room from the kitchen.

"I'm sorry. The bakery—dinner—have you eaten yet?"

"Yes." Lena started to wheel away. "Did you eat?"

"No. I was working," Kim lied, perpetuating the tale begun hours ago, when she had phoned to tell Lena she had been called into work at the bakery. She hadn't gone there. Instead, she'd spent the time sitting on a bench, knees curled to her chest, arms clasped around her legs in a feeble effort to ward off the night's chill. While the bustle of cars, bicycles, and foot traffic slowly ebbed, she replayed every moment of the disastrous encounter with Jaye Dewey.

"There's pasta left. Some salad," Lena said. As she spoke, she moved toward her suite. Before she got there, almost as an afterthought, she said, "By the way, the gun matched."

The words shook Kim out of her stupor. Lena obviously had been waiting for hours to deliver the news. "Lena, wait. My head's a mess. Can you please tell me what happened?"

Lena paused. She swiveled around. "You need to eat," she said, giving an order. She motioned for them to go to the kitchen. "Why is your head a mess?" she said while food warmed in the microwave.

Kim lied for the second time that night. "It's stuff at work. The bakery is having cash flow problems again. A supplier is threatening to cut Dennis off. Plus, the woman I've been filling in for at Legrand wants her job back. She's been calling every day, harassing me about it."

The timer on the microwave beeped. Kim took the plate and sat down. "The gun. Please tell me about the gun."

By degrees, Lena told her story. All three rifles had reached the police station that morning. Tests confirmed bullets from the Reno gun matched the bullets removed from Lena seventeen months ago. "So that's that," she said. "There's little doubt now. Chase was the shooter, although that may never conclusively be proven."

"Any word about his manner of death?"

"No. Five days into it, and no one can prove it was a homicide. That tells me it's going to go as undetermined. The hell of it is, these last few days, everyone's been looking so hard at Chase, no one's been looking anywhere else."

"Like at Kennerly."

Lena shrugged.

Kim struggled to wrap her head around the information. She could only imagine the elation running through the police station. Lena's case was solved. The fact that no one there had solved it—or that only two of the big three puzzle pieces were filled in, means and opportunity—mattered little. The case was solved. The shooter had been identified, and in a roundabout way, justice, with Chase's death, had been served.

Only Chase's motive was left flapping in the wind. Kim didn't doubt someone would pursue an investigation into it. But how hard would anyone look? And how quickly might the investigation fizzle if it crossed paths with a prominent, wealthy, seemingly upstanding citizen?

She sympathized with Lena's uneasiness.

It was a bad night for sleeping. Kim tossed and turned into the wee hours of the morning. Chills racked her body. She shivered beneath a blanket pulled close to her chin. Behind closed eyes, she saw Jaye Dewey's face—her haughty expression giving way to a complete absence of affect. She wondered what fourteen years spent living in the shadow of her mother's loss had done to her. How did a kid get over something like that? She didn't, Lena had said.

By morning, Kim had slept no more than two hours.

At breakfast, she begged off from answering Lena's questions. She insisted she felt well enough to go to work. At Legrand, the day passed uneventfully. Even her flu-like symptoms disappeared. Late in the afternoon, she returned home to prepare dinner.

The menu was a simple dish of grilled chicken over salad greens. Without waiting for an invitation, she set two places on the patio table. She warmed multigrain rolls and had drinks poured when Lena joined her.

"Stankowicz stopped by today," Lena said. "He didn't have a lot to say for himself, although he did happen to mention Kennerly."

Kim held her breath.

"He found the money Kennerly gave Chase. When he didn't seem inclined to think much of it, I jumped all over him. Reminded him what a lousy cheapskate Paul's always been. He asked if this was something personal." Lena studied her hand. "I told him it wasn't. I also told him he should go back to the Barton file. And then I threw him out."

Kim would have laughed at the image of Lena tossing Stankowicz out of the house if she hadn't been so relieved. That was it, then. The detective would see the photo. Maybe by now, he'd already seen it and had discovered Jane Barton's resemblance to Jaye Dewey. The ball was in his court. He had exactly as much information as she'd had twenty-four hours ago, before she had made her terrible mistake.

"What?" Lena said.

"Nothing. I'm happy. It's going to be okay."

"Don't get your hopes up. Stankowicz agreed to look into it, but I have to tell you, he was skeptical. Anyway, it doesn't matter. Either there'll be an evidence trail and he'll follow it, or there won't be. Right now, it's about being patient and letting the guys in the department do their jobs."

"And the girls."

"Whatever."

Kim didn't know why Lena was pretending to be so calm about the development. Maybe because there wasn't another thing she could do. The moment passed too quickly. When thirty seconds of silence elapsed, Kim felt jittery all over again.

She stood up and cleared plates. On her second trip to the patio, she mentioned she was going to work at the bakery again that night. She dodged Lena's suspicious glance and left with a promise that she wouldn't be late.

CHAPTER 33

"Whoa, Tiger. Take it easy. It's six o'clock in the morning."

Jaye Dewey glared at her trainer. Strands of damp hair clung to her forehead. Her jaw was clenched in iron determination. "Let's do this," she said, despising the man's puerile belief that the hour of the day factored into how it should be spent.

"You're the boss," the easygoing man with long hair said.

He held the punching bag while Jaye pummeled it with gloved hands. Leading with her left, she followed with her right, dancing on the balls of her feet, never lunging, and never striking the target without bringing the whole of her body into the thrust. She executed the combinations, ignoring the trickle of sweat that ran into her eye, indifferent to her own soft gasps of breath.

"You're winded," the trainer said. "Take a break. Clear your head. Don't fight stupid."

She backed away from the long leather bag still swaying after her last assault. She didn't mean to glance at the shaggy blond man who was her first and only coach, but she did and saw respect glinting in his eyes.

A swell of noise from the gym reached her ears. The place had been dead quiet when she arrived. Now she heard a clang of barbells being returned to racks, an undercurrent of conversation, and the omnipresent buzz of white noise, dominated by fans pushing air through ventilation ducts.

Jaye blocked out all distractions and resumed her workout.

Two hours later, showered and dressed in fresh clothes, she was home, sitting at the butcher-block table in the kitchen. A pad of white paper and a black pen lay in front of her. For the moment, she stared at the pad, thinking. Preparation and intelligence were key to the success of any mission. Emotion had to be eliminated. Never mind that she had been laying the groundwork for this mission for years, only to reach this moment and see it compromised by—of all people—the Jackson woman.

"Your mom loves you, that's what you need to remember," her dad had told her long ago, when she was still young enough to believe her relationship with him was special. That was before she realized the bastard had taken away all the mementos she'd ever had of her mother. The cards and gifts had disappeared from her room one by one until there was nothing left. *She* was ashamed of herself for letting him—and Chloe—strip her of her memories. They got her a puppy. Then her first little brother came along. Then her second. She was kept busy in sports and with music lessons, and if life with her stepmother wasn't always harmonious, it wasn't because she was mourning her real mother.

She had found the letter from Jane, her mom, stuck between pages in a book, buried in a box she was sorting through in preparation for the big move three years ago. Her father and Chloe had bought a fabulous new house in the Hollywood Hills. It pissed her off that her brothers got the best rooms. ("You're already in college. You'll always have a room here, but you'll be on your own before long!" Chloe had said in an excited voice, as if she couldn't wait.)

The envelope had her mother's return address on it. It gave her a place to start.

Her dad and Chloe were totally oblivious to the fact that she spent her summers in Durango. They thought she was in Flagstaff. She visited them once at the end of the academic year and once before the new term began in the fall. That was enough family time for everyone. Two years ago, she had been thrilled at the opportunity to intern at the Durango police department. Her excitement had faded fast. After only a few weeks on the job, she knew the bitter truth. No one on the force gave a damn about finding her mother's body or identifying her killer. Not even Lena Fallon.

Finding Paul Kennerly had been ridiculously easy. Real estate records had led her from her mother's address to him. Almost immediately, Jaye had zeroed in on him as the man her mother most likely had left the house with on the night she disappeared. The more she learned about Kennerly, the more convinced she became that he'd killed her mother. Her first plan had been to try and provoke him with letters meant to coincide with the anniversary of her mother's disappearance. Jaye could have laughed at how nervous she'd felt, dropping that first anonymous letter in a mailbox, except it wasn't funny. If nothing else, she'd wanted him to know there was someone out there who knew *exactly* what he'd done. Except nothing had come of that letter, and not from any of the others that followed. He hadn't panicked and made a mistake, exposing himself. The asshole stayed smugly in his nest and kept bringing women to it.

Now it was up to Jaye to get justice for her mother.

This summer, she came to town with a new plan. She needed to end this chapter of her life by ending his life. It was time to move on.

Jaye stared across the breakfast nook, but it was his room she saw. She was standing in it, holding a gun and phone, the call already made to police. She meant to shoot him before the cops arrived. She meant to claim self-defense. The abundance of tapes of women forced to do his bidding in this room would support her version of events.

Before then, she meant to stop the camera and start a different tape running. One on which she captured his confession for the kidnap and murder of Jane Barton, complete with the location of her body. A copy of that recording would eventually find its way to the police department. By then, Jaye Dewey would be long gone. As if she had never existed. Because she didn't.

That was plan A. It was the one she preferred.

Plan B was inordinately simpler: sneak into the bastard's house and shoot him in his bed. Leave the house locked and his murder a mystery never to be solved.

The Jackson woman's interference ruined both plans. Jaye seethed with fury, knowing she could never kill Kennerly now and escape becoming a suspect in his murder.

But there was another way.

Plan C was taking shape. Its execution would yield a deeper satisfaction. But its success depended on factors outside her control.

She needed more intelligence.

CHAPTER 34

Late in the evening, Kim left the bakery. She trudged home in the dark, weighed down by a heaviness that had clung to her since her confrontation with Jaye Dewey twenty-four hours earlier. Her only solace came from the hope that Jaye's identity was common knowledge by now. Lena had told Mark Stankowicz to read the Barton file. Assuming he had, the detective now had the same information she'd had after a glimpse of Jane Barton's photo in the case file. It was up to him to connect the dots. He needed to make the link to Jaye Dewey.

And if he didn't, Kim knew she had no choice but to confess what she'd done and suffer Lena's wrath.

The closer she drew to home, the more she dragged her feet. She doubted Lena would be waiting up tonight. Even so, she resisted the tug leading to the house. Cars passed by sporadically, their headlights sending narrow beams into the distance until the vehicle turned and the blackness of night again prevailed. Kim dallied crossing the last street. Lena's house was second in from the corner.

She meant to slip around and enter through the back door. She never got that far.

There was a sound of twigs cracking, and a subtle shift in the air around her. Too late, she realized someone was there. She turned. Something hit her square on the side of the head. Howling began in her ears, a high-pitched keening sound. She tripped and fell facedown in the dirt.

A vicious kick landed along her side. The next followed, and another, battering her ribs. She tried to curl into a ball, but the kicks came too fast. Through blurred vision, she glimpsed a figure in black looming above her. The last kick caught her chin. Her neck lurched. She tasted blood in her mouth and knew nothing except she was at the mercy of an assailant who, inexplicably, ran off.

She lost track of time. Ringing blared in her ears. Finally, her brain fired the order to move. She rolled onto her stomach, pulled her knees beneath her, and pushed up. She stood, surprised to find she could balance. Hunched over, she limped toward Lena's front door.

She was still digging in her pocket for the key when the door opened.

"I thought I heard you," Lena said. "Kim, what happened?"

Kim stumbled inside.

"Jesus Christ, Kim! You've been beaten to a bloody pulp." Lena wheeled into her bedroom. She grabbed a phone and dialed 911. She was still on the line, reporting the attack to a dispatcher, when she returned to the living room.

Kim tried to say she wished she hadn't done that.

"Lie down on the sofa," Lena insisted. "Or on the floor, if you can't walk that far. Jesus Christ, I hate this bloody chair!" She slammed her palms against the chair's arms. The ferocity of her emotion was enough to persuade Kim to walk the short distance. Once there, she collapsed on the sofa.

"Who did this, Kim? Where did it happen?"

"Next door." She tried to point.

Already, sirens were audible. Swirls of red light filled the blackness beyond the window. Kim closed her eyes. "Really, Lena. I'm all right. I'll be all right. Please don't—"

"Please don't what?"

"No hospital."

"We'll see."

Lena opened the door to two uniformed patrolmen, who were followed by a pair of paramedics. Kim answered their questions as best she could. More police officers arrived and were sent to search the neighborhood. As if her attacker might be anywhere nearby. He wouldn't be. Kim knew that. Maybe someone in the area had seen something, she heard Lena or someone say.

There was no question of not taking her to the hospital. "I'll be there, Kim," Lena promised. "I'll see you in a few minutes."

CHAPTER 35

It was past midnight before Kim was released from the ER. Her summary diagnosis included badly bruised ribs and lower back, facial lacerations, mild concussion, and shock. Given the viciousness of the attack, it was a comparatively minor assortment of injuries. Sheila Moss gave her and Lena, who'd caught a ride to the hospital with one of the responding patrol officers, a ride home.

"I want you to stay downstairs tonight," Lena said after Sheila left. "You can sleep on the sofa in my room."

Lacking the will to argue, Kim acquiesced. Lena provided a sheet, pillow, and blanket. Kim slipped off her jeans. Still wearing the clean T-shirt Sheila had provided at the hospital, she lay down on the makeshift bed. All she wanted was to close her eyes and sleep.

In the morning, she awoke to see Lena sitting nearby. Lena had been up long enough to dress for the day. Her soft flannel shirt curiously seemed to match the softness around her eyes. At that observation, Kim had to wonder about her concussion.

When she started to move, Lena spoke. "Take it easy. As soon as you move, you're going to feel like everything inside shatters into a million rough cuts of glass. And every time afterward, you're going to feel like you're bumping up against one of those shards of glass."

Kim relaxed. "I guess I'll take my time."

They continued to look at each other without speaking.

"I don't repulse you, do I?" Lena said.

It was the last thing Kim expected to hear. "Of course you don't."

After a minute, Lena said, "No need to bring a shrink in to tell me I repulse myself. Have you ever seen a shrink?"

Kim was having trouble keeping up. Nevertheless, she knew the answer to that question. "Yes."

"Did he help?"

"She. And no, not much." She glanced down the length of her body. This conversation was too strange.

For Lena, too, apparently. "How do you feel?" she said.

"I don't know." More to the point, she thought she didn't want to know. "I need to use the bathroom."

The instant she sat up, Lena's warning rang true. Pain blistered through her, from the tip of her head to her toes. It knocked her flat against the pillow. "Easy," Lena repeated.

"Easy for you to say," Kim muttered. The next time, better prepared, she gritted her teeth and sat up. Lena wheeled away to give her space.

"Careful when you stand. You may be dizzy."

Kim managed to walk from the sitting room through Lena's bedroom to the bathroom. A minute later, she walked back.

"Lie down. I'll get you some orange juice."

As the fog in her brain began to clear, Kim became acutely aware of her battered body. She felt puzzled by her impression that the separate events of last night—the attack, getting home, being rushed to the ER—had rolled into a single collage. Everyone wanted her to dissect the image. Everyone wanted to know about the assault. It wasn't what she wanted. She believed she could move past it if permitted to leave it intact, a nightmare dissolving with the passage of time.

"More juice?"

"No, thanks."

"There's a pitcher of ice water on the table behind you. Let me know when you want some. What about food, could you eat a piece of toast?"

Her stomach heaved at the suggestion. She shook her head. She lay down, feeling more unnerved with each passing second.

She had cause. Lena wheeled closer. She positioned the chair parallel to the sofa. From there, it was an easy reach to where Kim reclined on the cushions. With extreme gentleness, Lena touched her face, nudging Kim to look at her. "Do you have a headache?"

"Everything hurts," Kim said. The significance of the question registered. She remembered a doctor's concern about a concussion. "I don't think I have a headache, specifically. It's more like a full-body ache."

"Tell me if that changes. May I?" She reached for the T-shirt.

The simple gesture threatened far too great an intimacy. Kim tried to shrink from the touch, except there was nowhere to go. Lena took her nonresponse as consent. She lifted the shirt gingerly, then exclaimed, "Good effing God. It's a wonder he didn't crack every rib."

Kim closed her eyes and pressed her head against the pillow. "It feels like he did." Tears sprang to her eyes.

Lena replaced the shirt. "We may have to get a doctor to tape you up. They took x-rays last night; you may not remember. Nothing's broken. Taping your ribs would stabilize them. Kim, look at me, please."

Kim squeezed her eyes shut. Tears leaked from beneath the lids and streaked her cheeks. In a reversal of roles, Lena had become the caretaker. "The man who did this to you, was it the man you've been afraid of?"

Kim answered with a short shake of her head.

"How can you be so sure?"

"Because he would have killed me."

Fiercely urgent, Lena demanded, "Who is he? Tell me his name."

Dizziness obliterated every other sensation. Kim pitched backward into blackness, catapulting into a chasm that opened without warning. She couldn't have saved herself if she had tried.

Eventually she heard Lena's voice. "Kim, wake up."

Something cold and damp pressed against her forehead. "What?" she said. Her eyes jolted open. She started to sit up. A spasm of pain stopped her.

"Stay where you are," Lena said. She continued to press the cold cloth to Kim's forehead. "You fainted. That's it. I'm calling the paramedics. You belong in the hospital."

"No, Lena." Fresh tears filled Kim's eyes. "I'll tell you everything. I promise. I need your help. But not yet. Not while we're dealing with Kennerly."

Lena fixed her with a long stare. "If I see another sign— of anything—you're going to the hospital. And believe me, I intend to hold you to that promise."

Kim pressed her palms to her eyes, staunching the flow of tears.

When the doorbell rang an hour later, Kim was dressed in a pair of shorts and a long-sleeve cotton shirt of Lena's. She was propped on pillows on the sofa in the living room.

"Hey," Sheila said. "You're looking better this morning."

Kim grunted. "I'll take your word for that."

"You just strung a complete sentence together," Stankowicz said, coming in behind the other officer. "That's an improvement."

Kim looked at him, perplexed. She had no memory of seeing the detective last night.

They went through the details of the attack again. Kim told them what she remembered: some guy jumped her when she passed the house next door.

"Tell us everything you can. Concentrate on body type. Short, tall, heavy build, thin—anything come to mind?" Sheila said.

"Tall. Not heavy. I never got a good look at him. I was on the ground before I knew what was happening, and after that, well . . . I was just trying to make myself as small a target as possible."

"Did he say anything?"

"No."

While Lena and the officers talked about the neighborhood canvas, which had netted little information, Kim explored her memory. There was something about the attack that didn't make sense. She wanted to say the guy was good, whoever he was. He could have hurt her a lot worse than he had. That was the part that didn't make sense.

"Kim, are you listening?" Lena said.

"What?"

"Residents one block over reported hearing gunshots. Did you hear anything like that?"

"No."

"Could have been a car backfiring," Mark Stankowicz said.

"Yeah, ever notice how often we say that? When was the last time you actually heard a car backfire?" Lena said.

"There are lots of older, beat-up cars in Durango, Lena. You know that," Stankowicz said.

Kim watched Lena grill the two police officers with questions about similar attacks around town. She wanted to know whether there had been any reports of suspicious activity in the neighborhood in recent weeks. Her face was animated. It shone with passion, and incongruously, Kim thought, *She's beautiful.*

"You didn't hear anything at all last night?" Stankowicz said, seizing the opportunity to turn the question back on Lena.

"I had the damn TV on."

The police officers left without learning anything new. The attack could have been random; everyone conceded as much. No one believed it.

By noon, Kim had moved from the living room to the patio. The pain hadn't gone away, but at least all of her limbs worked. She had one black eye, bruised and swollen, blurring her vision slightly. Her jaw hurt too much to attempt chewing. She ate a small bowl of soup while Lena ate a sandwich for lunch. The day seemed to stretch interminably.

Lena spoke without preamble. "So, you've seen a shrink. You've been to college," she said idly, sitting in a patch of sun near where Kim lay on the chaise longue. "I don't know whether you finished college. But hell, why not? You've had money in your life. None of those things happen without money. Have you lied to me about anything, Kim?" she said, seeming to think nothing of the oddity of this opening.

Kim shook her head. "I don't think so." The words were no sooner out than she remembered she *had* lied. About living in Minneapolis.

"So it's a sin of omission, then."

"What?"

"It's what you haven't told me."

Cold dread stopped Kim from denying the accusation. Her mind raced, but her thoughts couldn't outstrip the terrible feeling seeping from behind her battered ribs. "When Mark and Sheila were here, did either one say anything about Kennerly, or the Jane Barton case?"

"Do you do this on purpose?" Lena said in a forced neutral voice. "Do you actually think I don't notice every blessed time you change the subject to avoid talking about yourself?"

Kim postponed the inevitable as long as she dared. "There is something I haven't told you." She fought a sense of impending doom. "It's not about me. It's about the case."

"What is it?"

Stankowicz hadn't found Jaye. Time had passed, and he hadn't found her. He couldn't possibly have known and not told Lena.

"Do you know Jaye Dewey? She's a summer intern at the station."

"Of course I know her."

"Does she remind you of anyone?"

"Sorry, I don't go in much for the pink-hair crowd. What the hell are you talking about?"

"What are you talking about?" Kim said, flustered.

Lena sighed angrily. "That dyed-hair shit. Jaye's pink hair and nasty black glasses. She might be a nice-looking girl except she makes herself out to look like a freak."

"When was the last time you saw her?"

Kim regretted asking the moment the words were out. The answer was obvious. Lena hadn't seen Jaye for two years. Not since the last time they both had jobs at the police station.

"Just tell me what you're getting at."

Kim couldn't process the rush of information—namely, that Jaye had taken pains to disguise her appearance at some point during her tenure as a summer intern.

"I think Jaye is Jane Barton's daughter."

Lena's eyes grew rigid in disbelief. "Why do you think this?"

"I recognized her. After I saw Jane's picture in the case file."

Lena's mouth twisted furiously. She seemed unable to speak.

"I spoke to her," Kim said.

"You what?"

She fought to say the words. "I told her I knew who she was."

"And?"

"She denied it. But she was lying."

Lena didn't wait to hear another word. She wheeled inside to the phone located on the kitchen wall, made a call, then withdrew behind the closed door of her suite.

CHAPTER 36

"Tell me exactly what happened," Mark Stankowicz said in a voice as angry as Kim had ever heard him use.

In vain, she tried to ignore her violent heart palpitations. Harder to ignore was the woman sitting at the kitchen table who hadn't spoken a word since making the call to Stankowicz fifteen minutes ago.

Kim described the two occasions when she'd seen Jaye Dewey, prior to seeing Jane Barton's photo in the case file. Her first reaction to the photo was that Jane Barton reminded her of someone, though she couldn't think who. As she was leaving the police station—the place where she'd first seen Jaye— she had made the connection. It was Jaye and Jane who bore a resemblance.

"Tell me why it would have been too much trouble to mention this that day," Stankowicz said.

Kim blushed and averted her eyes. "I didn't know Jane Barton had a daughter then."

"What happened next?"

Kim told the rest. About discovering Jaye's car parked near the police station two nights ago, waiting for her but leaving two minutes too soon. Her face grew hot as she recounted her pursuit of the Honda Civic through the neighborhood, losing Jaye, then unexpectedly finding the car in an apartment complex off of Eighth Avenue. "I was only there a few minutes. I had no idea which apartment was hers. I wasn't intending to go knocking on doors looking for her. But then she came out and saw me. We talked. I knew this was my chance, so I took a long, hard look at her, and I knew. The resemblance was too strong."

She struggled to breathe. Her ribs ached. She did not want to say the next part.

"I blurted out words I wish I hadn't. I told her I knew who her mother was. She denied it. But she was lying. Then she got in her car and drove away. That was it."

Stankowicz didn't say anything. Kim had the uneasy feeling that he was doing preliminary damage control. Just as Lena had been doing since the moment she had learned about Jaye. Eventually Stankowicz asked why she hadn't informed anyone about Jaye's identity earlier. Kim admitted that was a mistake. She told him she had assumed he would see Jane Barton's photo when he read the case file and make the same leap she had.

"Did you?" Lena said.

"Did I what?" Stankowicz retorted.

"See the photo."

"I read the reports. I thumbed through the pictures. Obviously I'm no good at my damn job, Lena. Why don't you just tell me what the hell you think is going on here?"

Lena ignored his baiting tone. "Jane Barton was living in a cabin on Kennerly's property when she disappeared. Her daughter was with her that night. I interviewed the kid the next morning. She wouldn't tell me or anyone else anything. Now I'm thinking the daughter knew something. Somewhere there's a link between Jaye Dewey and Paul Kennerly. Someone needs to find it. And yeah, while you're at it, I'm convinced there's a link between Paul Kennerly and Brad Chase."

She proceeded to lay out her view of the connection between the two men.

Chase, everyone agreed, had lain in wait that night in Wildcat Canyon. Bobby Hill had done his job—he had lured Lena to the spot. After Chase shot her, he shot and killed Bobby Hill. Paul Kennerly had engineered the plan. He paid Chase through the community fund to do it. Speaking acerbically, Lena suggested Stankowicz wouldn't have to dig too deeply to find some connection between Bobby Hill and Kennerly. After all, it was Hill's carefully choreographed actions that night that had set the scene in motion.

The detective shook his head. "We're still short on any reason why Kennerly would have targeted you."

"For Christ's sake, Mark. I'd just finished working the Aaron Booth cold case when Paul came on to me. For a solid week, there were write-ups in the paper about other cold cases in our files. One of the reporters was trumpeting the breakthroughs in DNA technology. The guy wanted more cold cases reopened, including Jane Barton's, which he mentioned specifically. I kept the damn news clippings!" A moment passed. "Who knows? Back then, Paul might have thought I was getting close to something."

"Or could have gotten close to something," Kim said. Instantly she was sorry she had said a word. Lena shot her a venomous look.

"Listen, I really can't say what we have here," Stankowicz said. "I've already put in a call to have Jaye picked up. I want to hear what she has to say." He threw his hands in the air. "The hell of it is, she was, what? Eight years old when this happened? Do you have any idea why she came back to Durango?" he asked Lena.

"She wants to solve her mother's case. That has to be the reason."

"But if she knew something, she would have told us, right? There wouldn't have been any reason to hide her identity."

"You'll have to ask her about that when you find her."

"Got that right." He stood up. "I'm personally going to talk to Jaye. And before that, I'm going to work on Kennerly. When I know a single goddamned thing," he said, wearily shooting off a look at Lena, "I'll be back."

Kim escorted the police detective to the door. When she turned around, Lena's dark eyes were fixed on her. For once, Kim had no energy to try to disassemble the mask. "I'm going upstairs," she said.

It took an eternity to climb the stairs. When she got to her room, she collapsed on the bed. Tears rolled down her cheeks, creating a sticky blotch on the fabric beneath her face. She sobbed until she fell asleep.

Much later, she heard someone calling her name. She awoke to broad daylight and a room grown stuffy in the afternoon heat.

"Kim! Can you come down here?"

Kim limped to the head of the stairs. From there, she saw Lena perched at the foot of the staircase, looking up. Kim dropped onto the top step, looking back.

"Are you okay?" Lena said.

The question was too complicated. Kim punted. "I fell asleep."

"I assumed you must have. I've been calling you every fifteen minutes for the last hour. Will you come down?"

Kim made the return trip downstairs, wincing at every step. Perversely, she welcomed the pain. "I'm sorry, Lena," she said when she reached the first floor. "I'm so sorry I didn't tell you."

"Stop with the apologies. Come on. You must need something to eat and drink."

Lena had apparently recovered from the shock of the morning's revelations. Kim had not come close to recovering. Still, she let herself be coaxed into eating part of a sandwich.

"I reverted to being a cop," Lena said when they were on the patio. "It was personal too. Don't get me wrong. Withholding evidence, obstruction of justice—those things used to piss the hell out of me when I was working. It's not as if a cop's job isn't hard enough without someone on the sidelines holding out. Anyway, forget it."

Kim looked at her over the rim of a glass of iced tea.

"If any of it could have changed this"—she slapped the top of her legs—"then it would have mattered. But that was never the issue. When I remembered that, I figured, what the hell."

"I was wrong," Kim said softly.

"Some calls are easy to make. Some are tough. This was an easy one. But you didn't know that. How are you feeling? Physically?"

Kim started to lie, then didn't. "Pretty awful. The stairs nearly killed me. What day is it? Friday? I was supposed to go to work."

"I called your office this morning and told some woman you wouldn't be in. Is there anyone else I need to call?"

She shook her head.

"Damian is driving up tomorrow. We're planning to go to the cabin, at least for one night. I want you to come with us."

"Lena, no. You and Damian get so little time together as it is."

"It's just one night. I don't want you staying here alone."

Lena was determined to have the final word. Kim couldn't muster the energy to argue. As patterns went, it was one she decidedly did not want to get into. She would worry about that later.

Apparently satisfied, Lena reached for a pen to make a note about something to ask Stankowicz. Her brown eyes tracked the letters woven across the page. Her brow furrowed in concentration.

Which do I love her more for, Kim wondered, startled by the feeling. *Her strength? Her courage? Or the compassion she keeps secret in her soul?*

Her gaze moved from Lena's hand holding the pen to the invisible thought reflected in her eyes to the equally invisible breath Lena inhaled, fueling her warrior's spirit.

But that she loved her, Kim didn't question.

CHAPTER 37

Jaye Dewey had disappeared. Mark Stankowicz relayed the disturbing news in a brief phone call late in the afternoon. She hadn't reported for work at her job at the Iron Horse Hotel the last two mornings. Neither had she been at the police department. Her car was gone. She was gone. No one had reason to suspect foul play.

"Jaye withdrew several hundred dollars from an ATM yesterday," Lena said, repeating what she'd learned from Stankowicz. "Since then, there's been no further activity on that card, nor on any of her credit cards. Background check confirmed her identity. Her birth name was Jesse Jane Barton. Apparently she's gone by the name 'J. J.' for the past few years."

Kim listened while Lena continued.

"She was more of a loner than anyone realized. She was a waitress at the Iron Horse restaurant, but no one there knew much about her. She worked the early shift. The manager offered her the dinner shift, when she would make more money, but she declined. She spent two afternoons a week and Saturday mornings at the station. She was friendly with a couple of the patrol officers. One guy wanted to date her, but she refused. Stankowicz hasn't found a soul in town who knows how she spent her free time."

Kim was less surprised by the report than by Lena's casual tone. She seemed nonplussed by Jaye's disappearance. When asked why, Lena said, "We will find Jaye Dewey, no question. Her version of events is critical to this investigation. As soon as we locate her, someone will be on a plane to wherever she is. In the meantime, there's plenty that can be done. What should we have for dinner?"

Kim barely registered the abrupt change of subject. "I don't know. I'll have to go to the store."

"You're not going anywhere. Let's order a pizza."

It was an hour before the pizza was delivered. Kim started to set the table inside only to have Lena argue for eating outdoors. "I want the fresh air. Grab a sweatshirt from the bottom drawer of my dresser. If your legs are cold, you can throw a blanket over them."

Kim was still dressed in the shorts and long-sleeved T-shirt she had put on that morning.

"How cold is it going to get around here this winter?" she asked when they sat down to eat.

"Plenty cold. We should get half a dozen major snowstorms, if we're lucky."

"Lucky?"

"Snowpack. Water. Haven't you lived in the West long enough to know how critical water issues are?"

Kim shrugged. Yes and no. She had read stories in the paper, but they hadn't made a big impression.

Lena finished her first slice of pizza. She reached into the box for a second. Before taking a bite, she said, "Kim, you must know I could have answered all of my questions about you long before today."

Kim stopped chewing. "I'm sure that's right."

"With your social security number and date of birth, I could have pulled any number of records, beginning with criminal history, former addresses, and places of employment." She paused. "Actually, that's not quite right. I could have ordered a background check, just like the one Stankowicz ran today on Jaye. I won't say the thought of doing so never occurred to me."

Kim waited.

Lena gave a soft laugh. "On a perfectly ordinary summer day, you show up at my house, a lost look on your face and obviously scared to death of the bitch of a woman in a wheelchair. You're young and attractive, and I had the gall to assume that, because you ended up here, you had to be a loser. Look at me, Kim. Please."

Reluctantly, she did so.

"I've never run a background check on you and I never will. Would you like to know why?"

Kim shrugged.

"Because the second I do, you'll leave. And I don't want you to leave. It won't matter what I've learned. You'll be gone."

A dull thud of warning pounded inside Kim's head.

Lena hadn't finished. "Besides, with your financial expertise, there's going to be something else I need from you. Eventually I'm going to get a settlement from the department. I have no idea how much that will be, or when I'll get it. Best case, I'll get a lot and have some leeway in deciding how I want to supplement my income down the road. Worst case, I'm going to get screwed and will have to scramble like hell to figure out how to make money. I don't expect that to happen, but you never know. My problem is, I don't know anything about investing. I'm sure as hell not comfortable with the idea of turning my money over to someone else to manage. Damian's persuaded me I'm going to have to do something, invest in mutual funds at least. I thought you might be some help when it comes to that."

"I'm no expert in financial planning, Lena."

"I know. Your field is corporate accounting." The look she gave Kim was without accusation. It only held a question. "I want to ask you something. Why do you take such low-paying jobs? With your background, whatever your background is, why don't you aim for something higher?"

Kim fought back tears. She knew it had never occurred to Lena that she wasn't who she said she was. The realization cut deeply. "I never thought I'd be staying in one place long enough. When I found the right place, maybe then I'd look for something better."

"You're not planning on leaving here, are you?"

"No, I'm not."

After dinner, Kim loaded the few dishes into the dishwasher. She put away what was left of the pizza. Later, she and Lena spent a quiet evening watching TV. Kim reclined on the sofa where she had slept the night before. Lena's plan was for her to sleep there again that night. Kim hadn't decided.

At ten o'clock, when the movie ended, they settled on a compromise. Kim would sleep on the sofa in the living room. Lena would have her own space. They would both have privacy. With a borrowed pillow, sheet, and blanket, Kim made her bed in the outer room. She turned on a radio and tuned in to a jazz station. Bright light shone in from the street. The DJ cooed softly between the jazz pieces, reminding Kim of another place, somewhere more soulful than the arid atmosphere of Durango. She drifted off, then was awakened by sharp sounds from the street—voices, she realized. They were followed by the piercing sound of breaking glass.

The latter sounded too close. Groggily, she sat up. She made herself go to the window. Outside, she saw a group of kids turn the corner and walk down the next block. Watching the group move on, she assumed one of them had tossed a bottle.

A light shone beneath Lena's door. Kim tapped lightly.

"Kim? Is everything all right?"

Kim opened the door. Lena was sitting in bed. She had a book in her hands. A blanket pulled to her waist covered her legs. For one instant, she appeared physically whole. She looked exactly like what she was: a woman sitting in bed, reading. "I heard some kids on the street. I think they were smashing beer bottles. It spooked me."

"Do you want to come in?"

"No. I got up to check on the noise and saw your light. I'm going back to sleep. Good night."

She turned the radio up a fraction louder and settled beneath the light blanket. She listened closely to the music, lulled by the long riff of a bass guitar. The piano joined in. It was a sweet selection. She wondered who was playing.

Next thing she knew, glass shattered, somewhere in the house this time.

Lena screamed.

CHAPTER 38

Jaye Dewey was sick of the laughter. Most of it was high-pitched and giddy, louder in the lounge than in the adjacent dining room. The Mining Company was more crowded than usual, not surprising for a Friday night. Tonight, Jaye sat at the bar, back turned to the door, nursing a club soda and actively ignoring every man who slipped alongside, anxious to make her acquaintance. The bartender offered only a sympathetic shrug to the gents she scorned. He knew who she was waiting for.

She was beginning to doubt whether Kennerly would show up.

They'd had drinks together twice in the last week without Kennerly hinting that he wanted something more. In an odd twist, he had been content to talk, rambling on about his family and the land they had owned for generations. There was something wistful in his voice. Jaye had the unwelcome impression he was falling in love with her. It was a complication. It would slow down his timetable. She needed to speed this show up.

"Hello," a young guy said, taking the seat next to her, recently vacated. "Can I buy you another?" He pointed at her glass.

"Thank you, no."

"What a day," the guy said, laughing at some private recollection. "I came this close to busting my knee coming down the trail." He showed a slender distance between his thumb and forefinger. "Damn, I was lucky."

The words hung in the air.

The guy finished his drink in one swallow and kept talking. "It was the asshole guide who was lucky. I said I was on a mountain bike, right? I'd have sued that idiot's ass if I'd crashed."

The bartender answered the man's call for a refill, pouring a brand of Scotch Jaye recognized as expensive. She glanced at her watch.

"I didn't catch your name," the man said.

Jaye heard the challenge in his voice. This one wasn't going to be as easy to get rid of as the others.

It was late. Kennerly wasn't coming. She needed to shift her operational plan, starting with getting out of here. She swiveled on the barstool, propelling herself off as though it were a slingshot. Kennerly, who was two steps away from joining her, caught her by the elbow.

His face lit in a smile.

"I thought you weren't coming," she said.

He misread her flushed face and the flustered air about her. "I'm here now," he said, as if that would fix everything. He led her to a table for two in the corner, signaling for their drinks along the way.

They sat down. They commiserated about the crowd and noisy atmosphere. Their drinks arrived. She took a sip of hers, no more than moistening her lips on the Jack and Coke. It was strong. She put it down.

Kennerly took a hefty swallow from his glass, exhaling in satisfaction. He glanced around the room. In a voice she registered as familiar, he began lamenting how Durango had changed. When he broke off long enough to reach for his drink, she touched his arm. "Paul, there's something I need to tell you."

She told him she was leaving Durango. It was why she had come here tonight, to tell him. They hadn't known each other long, it was true. Still, she wanted to say goodbye in person.

"Leaving when?" he said.

"This weekend."

She talked about the graduate school she had decided to attend. She hadn't known whether she would go, but had decided it was for the best, even though it meant leaving old friends, and new. Watching him, she was rewarded by a shift in his demeanor. All traces of warmth cooled. Gruffly, he cupped his glass and finished it in one swallow. She reached for her leather bag, as if she meant to stand up and leave.

"It's too late to do any packing tonight, isn't it?" he said. "What do you say we go somewhere else?"

She pretended to take her time considering the invitation. Then her smile softened. "I'd like that."

He led her to his truck. He said he had a special place he wanted to take her. It was a little ways out of town, but he promised to bring her home later.

"Can we make a quick stop first?" she said.

She directed him through side streets to an alley in the nearby neighborhood, to a house set one in from the corner. When she told him to park in front of the garage, he objected.

"This is Lena Fallon's house. What the hell are we doing here?"

By then, she had her gun out. "Give me the keys, Paul."

He laughed. The sound came out as an ugly, dirty laugh. "Are you working for her? You're out of your mind."

She kept the gun trained on him with her right hand. With her left, she pressed a Taser against his leg and squeezed the trigger. He yelped. His body went rigid from pain, but he didn't make another sound. She reached over, turned off the truck, and took the keys. A moment later, she was out of the car and at his door.

A full minute passed before he was able to speak. By then, she had persuaded him to get out of the truck and enter Fallon's yard. Along the way, she picked up the bottled liquid she had left as a present for herself earlier.

"I don't know what the hell you think you're doing," he said thickly.

"Don't worry, Paul. I know exactly what I'm doing."

There was a flash in the night of a cigarette lighter's small flame. It spawned a larger flame on the fabric protruding from the bottle top. With a pitcher's deadly accuracy, Jaye hurled the object. The flaming arc penetrated the house with a crash of glass in what Jaye knew was Lena Fallon's bedroom.

CHAPTER 39

"Kim!" Lena screamed a second time.

Kim opened the bedroom door to the sight of flames. Pockets of fire near the broken window cast a garish glow in the otherwise dark room. She smelled kerosene.

Lena was still in bed.

For a fraction of a second, Kim debated trying to extinguish the spreading flames. Instead, she sprinted to the bed and threw off the covers. Between tugging and coaxing, she managed to get Lena into the wheelchair. She pushed it toward the door, the sole exit out of the room.

"Close it," Lena said in a thready voice.

"What?"

"Close the door. Trap the fire. For a while."

Kim did so. She looked around the darkened living room for anything of value she might grab on her way out. But all of that was upstairs. Though she had no intention of going there, she looked at the stairs. Framed in her view was the entryway to the kitchen where, impossibly, the shadowy outlines of two figures appeared.

Crazy thoughts quelled her terror at seeing two people where none should be standing. Neighbors came to help, she thought a split second before she recognized Jaye Dewey. Jaye held a gun on a man Kim recognized as Paul Kennerly.

Jaye's arm swung in an easy, practiced motion. As if she had done it a hundred times before, she took aim and fired. Searing white-hot pain ripped through Kim's arm and into her back. She stumbled against the wall. A second shot rang out. Lena crumpled forward in the chair.

"Now that I've got your attention, it's time we all had a talk," Jaye said.

Kim fought pain and a tidal wave of dizziness that threatened to pull her under. She forced herself away from the wall. She stood next to the wheelchair, one hand on Lena's shoulder.

"Sit. Down," Jaye said to Kennerly. She pushed him toward the sofa where minutes ago Kim had been drifting off to sleep.

"What the hell's going on?" Kennerly said to her. "You're never going to get away with this." He looked at Lena. "Did you put her up to this?"

"Tell me why you killed her," Jaye said to him in a voice of infinite patience.

"Killed who? I've never killed anyone."

Jaye shot Kennerly in the knee. He slammed backward, howling in pain.

"I suggest you answer the young woman's question, Paul," Lena said.

"You bitch!" Kennerly screamed. "You're all insane!"

"'I know who you are. I know what you did,'" Jaye said in a taunting lilt to Kennerly. "Do those words mean anything to you? Jane Barton was my mother, you bastard, and you killed her! Tell me why!"

In a room poorly lit by a streetlight's distant bulb, Kim saw disbelief eclipse the pain etched on Kennerly's face. In a strange voice, he said, "You're her daughter."

"Ding, ding! Score one for the asshole! Damn straight, I'm her daughter, and I want to know why you killed her. Was it because she wouldn't dance your dance? Did she refuse to strip for you? Is that why you did it?"

Something worse than disbelief overtook Kennerly's lined features. It was horror commingled with incomprehension.

Jaye wasn't finished. Pointing at Lena, she said, "She wouldn't dance either, and she's not dead. What made her different?"

"How the hell do you know—" Kennerly said, unable to finish. It didn't matter. He'd said too much. His words were his confession.

Kim glanced at Lena, trying to understand.

Kennerly recovered his bravado. "Oh, look at her. She's different, all right. She paid!" he yelled.

A terrible silence descended on the room. It thickened like a fog, linking three people in some darkly held secret. Above it, Kim heard the steady roar of oxygen being consumed behind the door, punctuated by the crackle of objects burning.

"You shot her? You did this?" Jaye said. She looked from Kennerly to Lena while she tried to absorb something Kim couldn't understand. Too many pieces were missing. Her hope for a de-escalation of the violence shattered when Jaye shouted, "No! We're not going there! You called my mother. You came for her in your truck. She was afraid of you, but who's afraid now!"

Kennerly, Kim, and Lena all stared at her.

Lena broke the deadlock. "Why didn't you tell me?" she said in a voice that sounded hollow, full of regret.

Jaye took aim at Lena.

Kim sensed what was about to happen and knew she had to stop it. She began shouting, making up the story as she went along. "Your mother chose to go with him! Don't you get that? Your mother made the decision to leave you!" She would have gone on shouting, saying anything to keep Jaye's attention on her, but her ploy worked.

Maintaining the same easy rhythm, as though she had all the time in the world, as though no fire burned behind the wall, ready to explode in its insatiable need for oxygen, Jaye pointed the gun at Kim. Exactly then, Kim knew what she ought to have known long before now. This was an endgame. Everyone, except for Jaye, was meant to die in this house.

A shot rang out.

Kim choked for breath.

Jaye fell.

Out of the cacophony of the inferno raging, Kim saw the gun in Lena's hand.

Ignoring Lena's screams, Kim pushed the wheelchair to the door, opened it, and carried Lena out of the burning house.

CHAPTER 40

The world was a noisy place. Kim registered the fact while lying in a hospital bed. Hours passed, then a day. Medical machines hissed and pulsed. Electrical systems reverberated in low monotones. Unfamiliar voices jarred her already battered state, whether a doctor or nurse was speaking directly to her or the voices floated in from the hallway along with louder, stranger sounds that she made no effort to identify. No less disturbing were the familiar voices, namely two, one belonging to Sheila Moss and the other to Mark Stankowicz. Yet even if the world had gone utterly still, Kim would have felt deafened by the noise inside her skull, the shrieking, wailing, explosive sounds that never quit.

The audio chaos did not absolve her from the need to add her own voice to the mix when pressed to answer the police officers' questions.

Neither did her bandaged left upper arm where Jaye Dewey's bullet had penetrated her flesh and exited her back. Both wounds had since been surgically repaired.

Jaye Dewey was dead. She had died from a single gunshot wound to the chest. Her body was pulled from the house when firefighters arrived on the scene.

Paul Kennerly was alive. He had been rescued from the blaze and, like Kim, was recovering from surgery in Durango Medical Center.

Lena was not a coresident of the facility. She had been airlifted to Denver where doctors were trying to save her leg. Shot by Jaye in her lower extremity, Lena's compromised circulation system was failing to deliver enough blood to heal the new wound. So far, she had refused to give her doctors permission to amputate.

"Hey, Kim, are you still with us?" Sheila said.

Kim surfaced from the shadows in her mind.

Sheila asked a question about Lena's gun. She and Mark were trying to establish the precise sequence of events of two nights ago. The trail of evidence told most of the tale. Jaye Dewey had abducted Paul Kennerly at gunpoint, firebombed Lena's house, and entered it with the likely intention of killing Kennerly, Lena, and Kim. Kim had no idea what version of events Kennerly had reported. She was adamant on one point: Lena had shot Jaye in self-defense.

"I know it must sound stupid, but I didn't know Lena had a gun," she said dully, refusing to meet Sheila's eyes.

"So she didn't show it right away?" Mark said.

"She didn't have a chance. Jaye shot us both the instant she and Kennerly walked into the living room."

Kim explained what she had before, that Jaye had wanted to know why Kennerly had killed her mother. Failing to get an answer, she grew enraged and lost control of the situation. "She was on the verge of shooting Lena. I yelled something. Next thing I know, Jaye's pointing the gun at me. That's when Lena shot her. Lena didn't have a choice. Jaye would have killed me."

Sheila said something. Kim missed it in the buzzing that swelled in her mind each time she came to this part, her unarticulated sense that the other three—Kennerly, Jaye, and Lena—had been bound by some secret knowledge.

Kim looked at the female police officer. Sheila shrugged and said, "Never mind. It's not important."

Stankowicz spoke. Kim cut him off. "Jaye was behind everything, wasn't she?"

"What do you mean?" he said.

The strange words Jaye had said to Kennerly popped into Kim's mind. She repeated them now. "'I know who you are. I know what you did.'" When she looked at Stankowicz, he was watching her intently. "That's what Jaye said to Kennerly, right before she told him she was Jane Barton's daughter. She expected him to know what she meant. Do you know what she meant?"

"That's a part of the case we're still working on," he said in a tone that didn't brook further discussion.

Sheila said, "Kim, could Jaye have been the person who jumped you a couple of nights ago?"

"Maybe. I assumed it was a man, but I never got a good look at him. Or her."

The police officers spent another few minutes asking questions, all of which Kim had previously answered. By the time they left, she realized the point of the visit. They were checking to see if her version of events remained consistent. It would. She could have told them as much and saved them the trouble of future trips.

Jeremy came to see her that night.

"I guess I should have brought something," he said, noticing the flowers on her bedside table, sent by Dennis Royal of the bakery.

"I'm just glad to see you."

He tried to smile. "How's Lena? Have you talked to her?"

"No. I've talked to Damian. She's with Lena."

Kim fingered the edge of the bedsheet, tortured by the memory of that conversation.

"Lena's in a bad place, Kim," Damian had said. "She's paralyzed emotionally now, as well as physically. It's the guilt."

"Guilt for what?" Kim had asked.

"For killing Jaye."

Damian had sobbed when she said Lena had told her their relationship was over, and that she should leave.

"What are you going to do?" Kim had asked.

"I don't know," Damian had answered.

"How's Zeke?" Kim asked Jeremy.

"He's great. Worried about you. I, ah, didn't tell him I was coming. I figured maybe another time."

Kim tried to laugh. "Hopefully there won't be another time. I'm supposed to be released tomorrow."

Kim asked Jeremy whether he had seen the house. He had. He said it was still standing. From what he could tell, Lena's suite was destroyed. There was a cop guarding the place night and day.

"What about the garage?" she said.

"It's fine. I'm sure your bike's fine. Oh, and your car too," he added, teasing, and eliciting a smile from her.

Earlier, Sheila had said that some of Kim's possessions had been recovered from the second floor. She didn't have a complete inventory but promised everything would be returned to her.

"How's work? Is the store still open?" Kim said, belatedly remembering the reason why it might not be.

"It's okay. Maggie White—Brad's girlfriend—is running it. He left everything to her and his kid in his will. We've had a few bumps, but I think she'll be all right as a boss."

They talked about Zeke. They talked a little more about the events that had played out at Lena's house. Only the surface details had been reported in the paper. Kim sensed Jeremy's curiosity to know more but resisted telling what she knew, even the uncensored parts. Too much was at stake in the need to make a criminal case against Paul Kennerly. Beyond that, it felt too soon to talk about what had happened to anyone besides Sheila and Mark.

Kim soaked in all the comfort she could muster from Jeremy's presence. Still, she wasn't sorry when he said he had to get going.

CHAPTER 41

Sheila Moss arrived the next morning with clothes for Kim to wear home from the hospital. In light of the extensive damage done to Lena's house, arrangements had been made for Kim to move into a studio apartment owned by the mother of a police officer.

"These are going to be big on you," Sheila said, holding up a pair of sweatpants. "The T-shirt should fit."

A nurse's aide helped Kim dress. She was settled in a wheelchair and pushed to a side entrance where Sheila waited in a patrol car. The process of getting in and out of the car, then walking into the apartment attached to the large, attractive home located on the north end of town, proved exhausting. She sank onto a sofa situated in front of a TV, then wondered whether she ought to have gone straight to bed.

"Here's your stuff," Sheila said.

Kim frowned when she saw the smallish box.

"I bought you a new toothbrush," Sheila said. "Actually, I didn't buy it. It was a freebie from my last appointment."

Kim smiled. She pulled the box close, heart pounding in fear. Inside the box, she found an assortment of toiletries, a comb and other incidentals. There was a second, smaller box, and inside it, she found what she was looking for: her wallet and two key rings. One ring held her car key, the key to Lena's house, and a third to the Royal Baking Company. The other ring held the keys to her life. The heaviest wasn't a key at all but rather a fob inscribed with the distinctive *L* of the Lexus car company. Kim palmed it. Of the three keys on the ring, the tiniest opened the padlock on the Montrose self-storage unit. The other two were flat keys that unlocked safe-deposit boxes, one in Durango, the other in Chicago.

Sheila said, "I didn't have the heart to tell you, but your clothes, well, they smell of smoke. They're packed in boxes. Beautiful suits, Kim, really, they are. Anyway, they'll need to be dry-cleaned."

Sheila didn't say what she might have: *You have a weird collection of shit, Kim Jackson. Everything you own reeks of secrets.*

At the moment, Sheila clearly had other things on her mind.

"Was anything of Lena's salvageable?" Kim said.

Sheila shook her head. "Listen, I hate to leave so soon, but I need to get going. Stankowicz should have the warrant by now. The search of Kennerly's property is expected to start this afternoon. I'll let you know what I can, when I can," Sheila said, speaking a cop's familiar language. On the way out the door, she said, "It's starting to piss me off that you don't have a cell phone. Hell of a lot easier to get in touch with you if you did."

"Me too," Kim said.

She meant to stand up and walk through her new quarters once the door closed behind Sheila. Instead, she leaned her head against the sofa cushion and exhaled an emotion she couldn't identify. It wasn't relief at being reunited with the key ring, still in her hand. It wasn't fear or anger, or even pain, which she'd had plenty of lately. It was a feeling of being suspended in a strange new world. Worse, of being lost there. And the only person on the planet she wanted to talk to lay in a Denver hospital bed, refusing to take her calls.

Sheila stopped by that evening. She said the judge had signed the warrant and the search for Jane Barton's body was underway. Fourteen years ago, Kennerly's ranch had spanned five hundred acres. Since then, half had been sold off for development. The problem searchers faced was daunting. If Jane Barton's body was there, it could be anywhere.

Two excruciating days passed without result. On the third day, frustration gave way to elation when searchers found skeletal remains of an adult female. They dug the bones up from beneath concrete poured for a new portable outbuilding erected, curiously, fourteen summers earlier. No one doubted the remains were Jane Barton's. The police expected dental records to confirm her identity within twenty-four hours.

"The lousy son of a bitch," Sheila said when she gave Kim the update that night. "He's nothing but a cocky, arrogant son of a bitch."

"What are you worried about?" Kim said, sensing an undercurrent of tension.

"I don't know. He's gotten away with murder all these years. He's the kind of asshole that gets away with everything. I just want a lock. You never get a lock. Lena was always telling me that."

They might not have a lock, but Kim knew investigators had two new pieces of evidence against Kennerly. One was the phone record of a call made from his house to Jane Barton's cabin the afternoon she disappeared. The other was Kennerly's lack of an alibi. When interviewed, his girlfriend said she had no idea what time Paul had arrived in Salt Lake City on that long-ago Saturday night. He had insisted he'd arrived at seven. She had been out to dinner with friends, came back to the hotel late, and hadn't seen him until the next morning.

"That detail wouldn't have amounted to much, even if we'd had it on record back then. But you already know. Kennerly was never a suspect. In a circumstantial case like this, it's going to be about putting the puzzle pieces together and counting on a jury reaching the same conclusion as the rest of us," Sheila said.

"Jaye Dewey would have made a powerful witness against him."

"Yes, she would have."

Kim heard something in the other woman's voice, which compelled her to add, "The three of us never would have gotten out of that house if Lena hadn't done what she did."

"I'm not disagreeing."

Sheila struggled with something. Kim watched her mouth curl in displeasure and braced against hearing something she didn't want to hear. Something about Lena. But that wasn't the source of Sheila's agitation.

"Jaye called it plan C," she said abruptly. "We found her car. I already told you that. What I didn't tell you was what we found in it. A couple of notebooks. And keys, my lord, the keys we found." Sheila shook her head.

"What?" Kim said.

"I keep thinking about how much I liked that kid. How much I told her, what I thought I was teaching her. And it's not just me. Other guys at the station feel the same way. Betrayed, for sure."

Kim waited for Sheila to work out whatever she needed to. "You were telling me about plan C," she said, finally prompting her.

"Right. I have to be careful. There's some stuff I definitely can't tell you, at least not yet. First thing you need to know is that even though Kennerly had a regular girlfriend, that didn't stop him from stepping out with other women. He had a pattern about it. Jaye figured out his pattern. Looks like she was trying to become his next pickup."

Kim opened her mouth.

"What?"

"I wonder if she was going to meet him the night I saw her dressed up."

"Could be. She definitely hooked up with him at the Mining Company on Friday night. They were seen leaving together. She had a plan, and it came damn close to working. She had a Taser plus a couple of guns—her own and one she stole from Kennerly. She meant to shoot you and Lena with Kennerly's gun, then shoot him with hers and later claim she followed Kennerly to Lena's house, suspicious about what he was up to, but arrived too late to save the two of you. The fire would have obscured anything awkward, such as the absence of gunshot residue on Kennerly."

"So, what? Lena and I were just collateral damage in her plan?"

Sheila shrugged. "Seems that way."

"It might have worked," Kim said, speaking slowly while she worked out the scenario. "She could have shot and killed Lena and me when she had the chance. But she wanted us to know what was happening. She waited too long."

"Yeah, well, it might not have worked ultimately, regardless. But she would have been alive to try and squirm out of the mess, and the three of you wouldn't have been here to dispute her story."

Sheila said Jaye had keys to Kennerly's house, property access gate, and to cabinets in his house. "She was one scary woman. The best damn stalker I've ever heard of. If she'd only wanted to kill Kennerly, she could have done that. Easily. But she wanted more, including exposing Kennerly for the bastard he was."

Kim hesitated before asking the next question. She wasn't sure she wanted to know the answer. "Any idea how things would have gone had Jaye taken a different approach and told someone in the department who she was and what she remembered from the night her mother disappeared?"

"No idea. Obviously that was a risk Jaye felt she couldn't afford to take."

Kim nodded. She was surprised to feel a flicker of sympathy for Jaye. If you were only ever going to get one shot at telling the truth about the darkest moment of your life, you would want to make damn sure you got the result you wanted.

CHAPTER 42

Two weeks later, the *Durango Herald* reported the startling news that Paul Kennerly had accepted a deal in exchange for pleading guilty in the death of Jane Barton. Kim read the article while at work at the bakery, the only job she still had. She reached for the phone on her desk. "Why didn't you tell me?" she said when Sheila Moss took the call.

"I couldn't. Don't think I'm happy about it."

They made plans to meet that night. Kim arrived at the bar early. She was sipping a soda when Sheila joined her, carrying two glasses of beer.

"Involuntary manslaughter?" Kim said in disbelief before Sheila sat down. "You've got to be kidding."

Sheila's expression was grim. "Kennerly will serve the max. That's part of the deal."

"Sure. And that's written in stone somewhere?"

"It's supposed to be."

Sheila told what she knew. Kennerly claimed Jane Barton's death was an accident. They were having sex. For kicks, she tied something around her neck. She stopped breathing. By the time he realized it, she was dead. He panicked. He hid her body, and later, when he realized he had waited too long to come clean about the circumstances of her death, he buried her body beneath the new building. He had made a terrible mistake, he was very sorry for keeping the truth from her family all these years, but by no means had he committed murder.

Kim didn't buy the story. "If he's so sure it was an accident, why did he take the deal?"

"There were other pieces of evidence he didn't want coming to light."

Kim mulled over what she had heard. "So what do you think—he strangled her?"

"He's not saying that. The forensics are inconclusive. All the coroner had to look at was bones. No flesh to tell the story about bruising or how it happened to get there." Sheila took a long pull from her beer.

Kim fingered the moist edge of her glass. "It's not good enough."

Sheila's voice rose heatedly. "If you think any of the rest of us are happy about it, you're wrong. It was the DA's decision. Take what you can get was her attitude. In the meantime, we'll work the hell out of the other cases pending against Kennerly."

"Chase's murder and conspiracy to inflict bodily harm against Lena," Kim said flatly.

Sheila nodded. "Oh. I forgot to tell you. We talked to Bobby Hill's mother again. Kennerly and Bobby did know each other. Bobby did landscaping work for Kennerly a couple of summers ago."

"Still no trace of a payment from Kennerly to Hill?"

"No." Sheila was quiet for a moment. "Sometimes a case gets built by adding up all the little pieces."

Neither said what they both knew. A telling piece of evidence might yet turn up linking Kennerly to Brad Chase's death. But there was virtually no chance now, short of a confession, to tie Kennerly to Lena's shooting.

"Lena's not going to like this," Kim said.

Sheila threw her head back and laughed. "Stankowicz said she went ballistic when the captain told her about the deal. Only damn thing that's gotten a rise out of her so far. She said she was obviously going to need to come back and teach a lot of people around here how to do their jobs. The captain said he would like nothing better." Sheila's expression tightened. "That's when Lena told him she wasn't coming back."

"What?" Kim had trouble taking the next breath.

Sheila shrugged.

"She couldn't possibly have meant it," Kim said. When Sheila still didn't respond, she pressed on. "She was just pissed as hell when she said it, don't you think?"

"I wouldn't know, Kim. She's not taking my calls either."

There wasn't a lot more to talk about. They finished their drinks and went their separate ways into the night.

Over the next few days, Kim tried to find a silver lining in the Kennerly deal. There wouldn't be a trial. He was going to spend five years in prison, possibly the rest of his life, if Sheila kept her promise and was able to nail the bastard for the murder of Brad Chase. By no means did Kim dismiss Sheila's vow. The evidence existed. Someone just had to find it.

As the days flowed one into the other, Kim tried to fill her hours with something besides an obsession with the case. She was waiting for Lena; she made no effort to conceal that truth from herself. Deep in her heart, she believed Lena would come back to Durango once she recovered. Her leg had begun healing. This town was her home, despite what had happened to her house.

Kim hadn't yet seen the burned-out house. She had avoided going anywhere near it on the two occasions when she had been in the neighborhood to visit Jeremy and Zeke. They had plans, when her arm and back healed, to get out on their bikes. The aspens, Jeremy said, were glorious this time of year.

One morning, having sworn not to let another beautiful autumn day slip away, Kim left her apartment and drove to the edge of town. She walked the length of Main Avenue, alternately chilled and warmed depending on prevailing sun or clouds. She went to her favorite coffee shop. As she handed over a ten-dollar bill for the beverage, she thought about the job at the national oil company that was still open, according to the ad in the *Herald*.

When the latte was ready, she turned to go outside. On the way to the door, she met a man coming in. He wore an oxford, shirtsleeves rolled back, and smart-looking khaki slacks. His face shone with youthful energy, yet on reflection, Kim doubted he was as young as he looked. They exchanged a smile. The instant her hand touched the door handle, she felt something chilling. He was familiar. Not him, personally. He had the look of a type she recognized. In his eyes and in his clothes, he reminded her of the men she had passed daily in Chicago. Belatedly, she realized the intensity of his scrutiny, belied by a friendly smile.

Her heart was beating wildly before her foot hit the sidewalk. She forced herself to walk casually past the coffee shop window. Two doors down, she darted across the street. She ducked inside a bustling diner, trusting no one would pay her a bit of attention. The drill here was seat yourself or starve.

From there, she watched the man exit the coffee shop and stride in the direction she had gone. She saw him searching both sides of the street, looking for something. Rather, for someone. When he crossed the street to the next block, she made her move.

She tossed the latte in a trash can and sprinted across the street. Defying her rattled nerves, she casually approached the counter and said, "Can you believe it? I forgot to buy a muffin when I was here a second ago." She dug in her pocket for a couple of bills. With effort, she made eye contact with the woman who had waited on her not three minutes earlier. In an engaging voice, Kim said, "That guy who came in after me, was he gorgeous, or what?"

"He was kind of cute. For a button-down type," the woman said. "I think you caught his eye too."

"Really? Why?"

"He wanted to know if I knew you. I told him I'd seen you in here lots of times but I didn't know your name."

"Oh, my name's Jill," Kim said.

"Nice to meet you, Jill."

Kim clenched the bag holding the muffin. "See you next time."

"Right."

On leaving the coffee shop, Kim gave one long look down the street where she last saw the man. He was nowhere in sight. She turned right and sprinted to her car. She drove to the apartment, packed her bags, and left Durango.

ACKNOWLEDGMENTS

With thanks to:

Faith Black Ross, Rachel Marek, Michelle Hope Anderson, Carrie Olschner, Tiffany Taing, Georgie Hockett, Katherine Richards, Marilyn Hutchinson, Carmel Lenski, Tom Kane, and the Lewises: Diann, Pam, Jim, and Sharon.

THE LAST
TEMPTATION

PROLOGUE

It was decided. They were going back to France.

Yesterday's startling announcement rattled around in Laurie Beltran's mind as she ran up the side of the mountain. Two years living in Santa Fe had done nothing to improve her parents' marriage. At least in Nice, or wherever they would settle this time on the French Riviera, Peter and Marilyn Beltran would be free to pursue their separate agendas.

Their separate affairs, their eldest daughter amended bitterly.

Beads of sweat glistened on her forehead as she sprinted up the Atalaya Mountain Trail. When a rare trickle of perspiration tracked toward her eye, she backhanded her wrist across her face to catch it. At seven thousand feet above sea level, the air in Santa Fe was thin and dry. It was completely different from the air along the Mediterranean coast. Laurie reached back in her memory to when her family had last lived in Nice. She recalled the gentle sea breezes blowing in from offshore and, more strongly than that, the stunningly clear blue of the Mediterranean Sea.

It hardly mattered to her what her parents did or didn't do. Three months from now, she would be in college in Santa Barbara.

She smiled at a different thought.

"Just do it with Brent, Laurie," Melanie, her best friend, had said in something akin to a frenzy last night. "You're out of your mind if you don't! You're leaving for the summer anyway, what's there to lose?"

Laurie's smile spread. Her breathing grew more ragged, possibly from the incline, more likely from the turn of her thoughts.

Brent was the senior class president and state track star. She'd had a crush on him for months. Last week, he broke up with his longtime girlfriend. Two days ago, he asked her out. Tonight they were taking his Jack Russell to the dog park and, later, going to a classmate's graduation party.

"I don't even know if he wants to do it with me," she had exclaimed to Melanie.

"Trust me. He does."

She wouldn't. She knew that. Not the first time they went out together. Not even when she felt herself going crazy, wanting to.

"Yeah, and what if he never asks you out again?" Melanie said, getting in the final word as always.

Laurie tore into a sprint. She survived fifty steep yards before the terrain got the better of her. Hands on her hips, she swallowed great gulps of air while she gazed at the view of treetops cascading down the mountain. Below, the city built on a broad plain spread into the distance beneath a cloudless crystalline-blue sky.

The kids in her class couldn't wait to get out of Santa Fe. Talk about being stuck in the middle of the desert, they complained, lamenting there was nothing to do here and no decent places to hang out. She supposed that was why Brent had invited her to go to the dog park. "He's taking you to the *dog park*?" her sister, Natalie, had exclaimed when she'd heard. On Natalie's last date, she'd insisted on going to Geronimo's for dinner.

Laurie was perfectly happy with Brent's invitation. She couldn't imagine what they'd find to talk about seated across from one another in a fancy restaurant.

She resumed her run. Halfway down the long hill, she left the street for the maze of roads that wound in serpentine fashion into the hills. Her family lived a mile east of the historic Santa Fe Plaza, opposite St. John's College, in one of the most prestigious neighborhoods in a city that prided itself on such things. It wasn't, strictly speaking, their house. Her grandparents owned it, a detail that troubled no one. Laurie loved the house for its sunset views and its proximity to the mountain trails, not to mention it was near enough to Santa Fe Prep for her and her brother and sister to walk to school. Not that Natalie ever did. Laurie didn't think her younger sister had walked once in the past two years.

She rounded the last curve. As she did, the house came into view. Her new BMW was parked outside.

"I assumed you wouldn't mind if I washed it. *Her*," Ricardo said, smiling, standing alongside the dark-blue car, a soft cloth in his hand.

"Of course not. Thank you, Ricardo."

Laurie lightly fingered the buff-dried trunk as she walked past. Even the feel of the gleaming steel seemed to reverberate with excellence. She glanced inside the driver's side window as if to reassure herself the interior was exactly as she remembered.

"Will you be taking her out soon?" Ricardo asked. "Or should I return her to the garage?"

"The garage is fine. I need to shower."

She entered the breezeway outside the kitchen. The spicy aroma of tomatoes and chilies wafted from an open window. "Hello, Anna," she called to the woman inside the house who was stirring something in a tall pot.

"Hello, Laurie," Anna called back.

The BMW was a surprise graduation gift from her grandparents. It had shown up yesterday morning before she left for school. A waste of a day, really. Classes and tests were over. Graduation itself wasn't until next week. She'd had to wait all day to get behind the wheel, crank up the music, and test the car out on the road up to the ski basin. It hadn't disappointed.

The BMW was her grandparents' second gift to her in the last month. A few weeks ago, after she'd turned eighteen and it was clear she was going to graduate from high school, her grandmother and grandfather had given her the first disbursement of her trust fund—a stock portfolio valued at several hundred thousand dollars. There was more to come. Under the terms of the trust, she would get the second disbursement when she graduated from college, and the remainder when she turned twenty-five. She didn't know exactly how much was in the trust. Plenty, her father had said once when Natalie pestered him about it. Identical trusts existed for Natalie and Danny, but they wouldn't get theirs for years.

For the first time, Laurie felt like the chosen one in their family. She harbored no doubt that Natalie truly was her parents' favorite. Just this once, it felt great to be singled out and rewarded. She grinned. And just this once, Natalie was being punished for screwing up. Natalie had failed two courses this year. Natalie wasn't going to France. She was staying in Santa Fe to attend summer school.

Laurie entered the house through the mudroom. At the end of a long hallway, she jogged up the steps leading to the great room. She turned the corner and bounded up the staircase to the second floor. Passing Danny's room, she heard the blare of a TV and a single woof from Hutch, their black lab.

Though she'd meant to go straight to the shower once she got to her room, the sweat she'd worked up on her run had already evaporated. She grabbed her phone and flopped into a chair, slipping in earbuds. She turned up the music in the hope of breaking down her inhibitions.

Melanie had said it didn't matter if Laurie had sex with Brent. There was no possible downside to seriously making out with a guy. Anyway, he would have a condom. Melanie said the first time was kind of a waste anyway. It took a while to get a feel for doing it.

Laurie tried to let her imagination run free. It wasn't as if she never fantasized about making out. She wasn't a prude. She just wasn't sure Brent was the right guy. Or tonight was the right night. She held her breath and pretended she could feel him reaching for her. She imagined his fingertips on her skin. She released her breath, and she knew. Melanie was right. It would be okay if she didn't overthink it.

A loud bang sounded from somewhere in the house.

Jarred, Laurie opened her eyes, unable to tell if a door had been slammed shut or something large had been dropped. She listened, and when no other sound followed, she closed her eyes and tried to slip back to where she'd just been.

She and Brent were only going to the dog park. And later, to a party. It was casual. They were two friends wanting to hang out together. No big deal.

A second loud bang sounded. This time, it came from somewhere closer. Laurie opened her eyes to the sight of her bedroom door flying open. Natalie was there.

Instantly enraged, Laurie leapt from her chair. "You're not allowed in here!" she yelled.

Natalie took two steps into the room.

"Get out of here!" Laurie screamed.

Natalie ignored the order and drew closer. Natalie, two years younger, bore down upon her with a determination Laurie had never witnessed in all the years of living with a very determined sister. Too late, Laurie saw the knife in her hand.

She retreated, falling back into the chair as a rush of terror flooded her.

A moment later, Natalie raised the knife and, without hesitation, plunged it into her sister's chest.

Laurie's fear fled with the first bolt of pain.

Blood spurted from the wound. Laurie gasped for breath, unable to comprehend the sight of her sister looming above her. Natalie raised the knife a second time, bringing it down harder, plunging it deeper. Laurie choked on her own blood. She fought for a clear swallow of air and found none. Natalie raised the bloodied knife a third time. Knowing she was about to die, Laurie searched for the reason in her sister's eyes. All she saw was a rock-hard intensity. It was as if she were possessed. Yet Laurie knew she had never seen her sister more alive than she was at this moment.

The words sprang to her lips out of nowhere. "The Lord is my shepherd," Laurie prayed.

CHAPTER 1

The overhead light was too bright. The acoustics were sharp and brittle. Despite the room's shortcomings, the woman's voice carried through the cavernous space with melodious authority, sounding more like a spoken song than a sermon.

Kim Jackson leaned her head against the wall and closed her eyes. She didn't attend Sunday-morning services in the basement of the town hall in Creede, Colorado, seeking spiritual edification. She came for the pleasure of hearing Laurie Beltran speak.

"It is springtime, the season of rebirth," Laurie said. "The first tiny buds are showing on trees and shrubs. Lying just behind the protective fold of pale-green leaves, blossoms await their moment to explode in an array of vibrant colors. Nature brings itself forth, without intervention. So, too, can we bring forth from within ourselves what is natural to each of us and is, in its own way, as vivid and beautiful as the flowers we will soon see bursting into bloom."

Laurie continued in the same vein. Kim tracked the young woman's voice as it rose and fell, seeming to burrow deeper toward some promised treasure. Occasionally a word or a phrase caught Kim's ear, and for reasons she couldn't explain, she smiled. For a few blissful moments, she was released from both the past and the future.

Too soon, the sermon wound to a close. Laurie announced the final scripture reading, something from Luke, Kim thought, recalling the verses posted on the chalkboard she'd read when she arrived.

"Forgive me," Laurie said. "Instead of reading from Luke, I'd like to read one of my favorite passages. The twenty-third Psalm."

There followed the sound of pages shuffling and a faint undercurrent of grumbling among those who had marked the reading and now had to backtrack to the book of Psalms. Kim glanced at the rows of parishioners seated in folding chairs in front of her and saw what she always did: one pair of eyes after another riveted to the sight of the woman standing at a lectern draped with a cloth, a simple cross woven into the fabric.

Laurie wore a long-sleeved navy-blue dress. Its shapeless form hung loosely on her slender frame. A hairband held back her straight, dark hair. It took no effort to imagine Laurie Beltran wearing the triangular-shaped dark-blue headpiece of a Catholic novitiate, the attire she was recently rumored to have worn. It required a massive leap to picture her in the black and white of a nun's habit, the garb the same rumor mill reported as her destiny.

"'The Lord is my shepherd; I shall not want. He maketh me to lie down in green pastures: he leadeth me beside the still waters.'"

Kim warmed to the sound of the Psalm, familiar even though she'd never been a regular churchgoer at any time in her life. She resumed her former posture, head against the wall. But a verse or two later, her reverie was disturbed. Laurie's normally fluid speech grew stilted. Puzzled, Kim straightened up. Laurie was standing stock-still. Though she continued to speak, Laurie's gaze was fixed on a point on the rear wall. Kim glanced that way and saw nothing. The Bible lay open in the young woman's hands. She wasn't reading from it.

"'I will fear no evil,'" Laurie said tersely. She soldiered on. "'And I shall dwell in the house of the Lord forever.'"

The words sounded like a prison sentence.

Strumming guitar strings sent haunting notes through the air. Several people coughed or cleared their throats. With a decisive modulation, the guitarist lit into a chord pattern that became the opening of a favorite hymn. The congregation rose. All traces of Laurie's torturous recitation of the psalm disappeared with the joyful song.

The service ended with a prayer.

Afterward, Kim observed the predictable swelling of the crowd around Laurie. Voices rippled throughout the room. It took a moment for the resumption of normal life to displace the hour of quiet. For the fourth time in as many weeks, Kim was surprised to find herself at the conclusion of a religious service in Creede's town hall basement. But she was long past the point where she relied on logic to account for the shape of her life.

She picked up her jacket and threaded her way through the row of chairs toward the stairs.

"Kim—wait, please."

Laurie had succeeded in separating herself from the throng and had a bead on Kim, who, at a distance in the rear of the room, was not an easy target to reach. When she drew close, Laurie lowered her voice. "There's something I was hoping to discuss with you. It's a small matter, really."

The dismissive tone of her words was belied by the urgency in her eyes. Kim smiled at the incongruity. Laurie mistook her reaction for something else.

"Oh, you don't ordinarily stay for the group talk. Maybe we could arrange to meet another time."

"It's fine, Laurie. I'll stay today."

"Thank you. I promise I won't take up much of your time. You could join us," she said, pointing at the circle of folding chairs presently being drawn together. A plate of cookies sat on a side table along with two pitchers, one of ice water, the other fruit punch.

Kim eyed the emerging formation dubiously. "I don't know. I don't think I have anything to contribute."

"There's no requirement to participate. Besides"—Laurie paused to smile wryly—"even if you wanted to, there's little chance you could get a word in edgewise."

Kim poured a glass of water and took a vacant chair, nodding casually to the woman next to her.

Laurie had no sooner tucked the fold of her dress beneath her and sat down than a woman named Valerie Crane spoke peremptorily. "I don't have a clue what the point of your message was today. With Easter only a few weeks away, you go off half-cocked on some bizarre notion about the merits of self-sufficiency? Would you please explain to me what that has to do with the death and resurrection of Jesus Christ?"

Valerie was a broad-shouldered woman with dark hair and an imposing presence. Neither tall nor overweight, she possessed a striking force that found expression, at least at the moment, through her shrill voice.

Laurie smiled disarmingly. "I had thought to talk about that," she said, faintly sardonically. "Yesterday, as I was preparing my thoughts for this morning, I found myself humbled by the beauty of the day and of the season it so perfectly represented. To my surprise, I found I was forcing my thoughts around the subject you've named. It seemed a travesty to force anything when all around me new life was simply springing into being. I thought of the wonder of that. Then I thought of the wonder of who each of us is as a unique individual and how poorly we sometimes appreciate that in ourselves and in each other."

It wasn't clear that Laurie had finished. Valerie gave her no chance to go on. She launched a second assault, more vitriolic than the first. Others in the group chimed in, some agreeing, others not. Laurie took the part of referee until the allotted time had passed, and with a sigh of relief, Kim realized the session was over.

"Honestly, I should have known better," Laurie said when she and Kim reached the top step outside the building. Kim had expected their meeting would take place in the basement hall. Laurie had a different idea. After turning off the lights, lowering the thermostat, and locking the door, she invited Kim to her home, a five-minute walk from the town center, she promised. The proximity hardly merited distinction. As Kim had learned in her brief sojourn in the former mining camp, nearly everything in Creede, Colorado, was a five-minute walk from the center of town.

They passed tourist shops, most still closed. This early in April, the town snared few vacationers, though Kim was always surprised by at least one car with an out-of-state license plate parked on the street. Creede's natural beauty never went out of season. Today the mountains were dwarfed by low-hanging clouds. Yesterday the sun had shone, lighting the rock in a golden glow beneath a brilliant-blue sky.

Laurie turned left at the next street. When they reached the section of road spanning the creek, Kim's eyes were drawn to the rushing water, still weeks away from the height of spring runoff, according to John Carlos, her boss. A thunderous roar accompanied the muddy froth on its downstream surge. This was a different breed of water than she had ever encountered before. The novelty of seeing and hearing it hadn't worn thin.

Midway down the block, Laurie said, "This is it." She opened a picket-fence gate and led the way around the main house to a small wooden house at the rear of the property. With a twist of the doorknob, she entered.

"You don't lock up when you leave?" Kim said.

"No. The lock broke. I latch it from inside when I'm here. Well, at night, anyway."

Having entered, Kim inspected the locking apparatus. The broken lock was of the flimsy, push-button-on-the-doorknob variety. The latch was even less substantial. It was a simple slender hook that slipped into an eyelet on the opposite wall. "You have to be kidding," she said.

"About what?"

"Your home security. This is terrible."

"Oh well. It's fine." Laurie pointed toward a chair. "Make yourself at home. I'm going to change clothes."

Still frowning, Kim turned from inspecting the shabby lock to acquaint herself with her surroundings. She stood in what passed for the living room. The smallish space had a congested feel, furnished with two chairs, a coffee table, an end table, a lamp, and a bookcase. Laurie had disappeared behind a closed door to the adjacent room, presumably her bedroom. The kitchen was to the left. Kim took two steps and saw a small refrigerator and stove, a porcelain sink, and a plastic dish rack on the countertop with a single bowl and cup set out to dry. A narrow table with two high-backed chairs occupied the space against the wall.

Bright light filtered in from the window above the sink. By contrast, the living room was dark. The one window was adorned with a lowered blind and curtains. There were no photos or framed pictures hanging on the walls. No TV, no music system. However compact and sparsely outfitted, the cottage's interior was cleaned and scrubbed thoroughly.

Prior to today, Kim had exchanged introductions with Laurie only once. It felt odd to be standing inside her home.

"Was today's discussion group fairly typical?" she called through the closed bedroom door.

"Are you really asking whether Valerie is always so belligerent?" Laurie called back.

"Yes, I guess I am."

The door opened. Dressed in blue jeans and a wool sweater, and with her hair hanging loose, Laurie's appearance was completely transformed. No longer a prim, religious devotee, she looked like a young coed. The change went deeper. Laurie was a beautiful twentysomething woman. Kim checked her surprise at the transformation.

"To answer your question, no, Valerie isn't always so angry. She and I have had our disagreements, but she's never lashed out in public before. I think I set her off today."

Kim was about to say she had enjoyed the day's message before realizing she hadn't paid enough attention to be sure what it was. More to the point, she had no desire to share any opinion.

Laurie indicated the chairs in the living room. "Please, have a seat."

Nearly an hour had passed since Laurie had begged a few minutes of her time. Kim was no closer to knowing what the woman wanted than she had been when she agreed to the meeting. For no clear reason, she began to suspect Laurie Beltran had a hidden agenda, a prospect that both intrigued and irritated her. "What was it you wanted to talk about?" she said.

"You're an accountant, right?"

Kim flinched. The words sent an arrow-like bolt through her scar-toughened flesh. "Not an accountant, exactly," she lied. "I've been working with the local tax guy, helping him process tax returns. 'Tis the season," she added, angling for a light tone.

"John Carlos," Laurie said, and she laughed.

"What?"

"From what I've heard, you're a welcome addition to his office."

Kim refrained from commenting. It was nothing to her what kind of business John Carlos ran. She had been hired a few weeks ago to help with the crush of tax returns that needed to be filed before April 15. In that time, she had seen plenty of evidence that her boss had failed to get his customers their full due from the government in years past. She also knew she had earned the gratitude of many townspeople for her efforts on their behalf. But the fact remained that she would leave and he would stay, and life would go on as it always had for John Carlos and his clientele.

"You wanted to talk about a tax problem?" she said.

It was Laurie's turn to flinch. "No. I wanted to ask whether you know anything about nonprofit organizations. We do have a problem. The church, that is. If you can call it a church."

"What kind of problem?"

"Several months ago, shortly after I came here, I joined a prayer group that met weekly. It was a large group, even before I joined. Several people asked whether I would be willing to lead a Sunday service. It seems to have worked out. The problem is, we have no official status as a nonprofit, and I'm afraid we may need to do something about that."

"Why?"

"Because of the money."

"What money?"

"It's the money we take up from collection. Our expenses are few, but we have them. We have a secretary who has been keeping the money. Or, I should say, had. When it got to be too much, she wasn't comfortable having it in her house. So she brought it here."

"How much money?"

"It's a bit over five hundred dollars. I haven't added in today's collection."

"Why would you keep any money in an unlocked house?" Kim said incredulously.

"No one except me and our secretary knows it's here. Besides, no one could find it even if they did."

Kim doubted that. "What exactly do you want from me?"

"We need a safe place to keep the money. But I've been told we can't open a bank account in the church's name without first establishing ourselves as a nonprofit. I don't know that any of us want to go to that trouble. If we have to, I thought maybe you could help."

"I know very little about nonprofit organizations." Kim flashed to the few occasions the subject had been mentioned in lectures taken while she was earning her MBA. "I suspect it's a matter of filing certain papers with the IRS, establishing a board of directors, submitting tax forms annually. That may be all there is to it."

"That's all?" Laurie said sarcastically.

Beyond the curtained window, Kim glimpsed a patch of blue sky breaking through a thick band of clouds. Her heart leapt at the hope for another springlike day. Oppressed by the dankness of the room and by the curious fusion of Laurie's simplicity and willfulness, she stood up, finished with this conversation.

"It's probably less complicated than it sounds. Even John Carlos could walk you through it." She added in the mean dig before realizing her esteemed boss would no doubt charge in fees nearly the whole amount the group had in reserve. Another thought occurred to her. "If all you're worried about is keeping your cash safe, you could get a safe-deposit box at a bank."

"How does that work, exactly?"

"You just rent a metal box that's kept locked in the bank's vault. You would have a key to it. Anytime you wanted access, you would have to sign in and present your key. But you could have a couple of names on the account. No record is kept anywhere of what's inside. Your money would be safe." She took a step and reached for the broken knob of the front door.

"Kim—wait."

Laurie's eyes were white with fear. Kim glanced from them down to the other woman's hand, grasping her forearm.

"I do have a tax problem. I need your help."

ABOUT THE AUTHOR

Amy O. Lewis lives in New Mexico. Her debut novel, *A Mountain of Evidence*, is the first book in the Colorado Skies mystery series and was released in 2021.

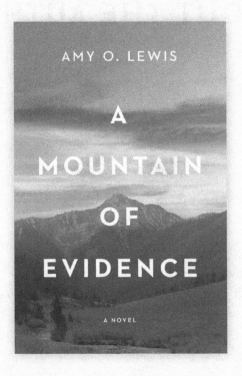

CPSIA information can be obtained
at www.ICGtesting.com
Printed in the USA
LVHW052041050422
715338LV00005B/614

9 781737 297727